THE MARIGOLD GANG

The Marigold Gang

THE MYSTERY OF THE
FOUR BODIES IN THE FREEZER

GREGORY C. RANDALL
BONNIE RANDALL

WINDSOR HILL
PUBLISHING

This novel is dedicated to those fellows who were a part of Greg's Gang when he was a young man growing up in the southern suburbs of Chicago.

"All happy families are alike; each unhappy family is unhappy in its own way."

Leo Tolstoy – *Anna Karenina*

INTRODUCTION

The initial assault was the overpowering odor of lilies, not the white flowery funereal kind, but the stench manufactured by car deodorizers, like those pine tree–shaped cardboard ones found at car washes. Second, taller than the top of my head, were the unsteady stacks of newspapers. The initial pile, about three feet inside the door, was the first of three equally high piles leaning precariously against the right wall of the narrow entry hallway. All looked to be *Chicago Tribunes*, most likely in chronological order, bottom to top. The air fresheners were blue and all shaped like a squashed lily. The first dangled on a nail on the inside screen door of the entry; we eventually found thirty of the little stinkers before we finished. Not to be outdone, the rest of the house proved worse; it was a toxic nightmare of debris, trash, wealth, and loss.

Barbara Fisher Nesmith, Allen's only daughter, and executor of what could generously be called his estate, asked me to clean out Allen Fisher's house. I enlisted the other guys in our gang for moral support and physical logistics. Barbara lives in San Jose, California, and could not leave her job at Microsoft for the two weeks she believed it would take to clear out Allen's house and settle his affairs. After asking for my assistance and apologizing profusely, she said she understood what we would go through and would cover our expenses (including refreshments). "No worries," I'd said. "I'll keep all the invoices and send them on when we are through." My worry grew when I saw the stacks of newspapers. Later we concluded it would have been better to bulldoze the house, or as Larry said prophetically, "We should volunteer the house for fire department practice."

We knew Allen was a hoarder. Well, he was not just your casual hoarder; he was a serious accumulator (or collector, as he called himself) of everything that he bought, borrowed, or seemingly touched during his seventy-seven years on God's earth. Psychologists refer to it as the fear of parting with possessions. I've come to believe it was a fear of parting with a chunk of yourself, maybe in Allen's case, his troubled soul. And to add to his overall state, his house, 9 Marigold Court, was the only home that Allen had known since his folks moved there in 1956. We also discovered that hoarding was not only Allen's problem; it was his parents' problem as well. They both passed away on the same day in this house, under horrific circumstances, thirty years ago.

Growing up, I lived two doors up the court from Allen; the rest of us in the gang were spread around Marigold Court's twelve other ranch houses. Allen was an integral part of our gang. Back in 1959, we were all, give or take a few months, twelve years old. We rode hand-painted bitch'en iron-framed and wide rubber-tired bikes, wore white tough-guy tee shirts with our sleeves rolled up like James Dean in *Rebel Without a Cause*, smoked unfiltered cigarettes when we could find them, and harassed and arm-punched each other like blood brothers. We called ourselves the Marigold Gang, and for the past sixty-five or so years (we survivors still debate the exact time frame), we've supported each other through some of the best and worst times of our collective lives. We knew that Allen had this hoarding problem; it was the scale of it that shocked us.

2

The Marigold Gang

Over the last half century, I'd attended, by my count, at least twenty-five Marigold Gang–related happy weddings of children and grandkids and unhappy funerals of wives and even children. We fished and hunted for an untold number of days, hiked uncounted miles, and sat bedside through surgeries that ran from knees to hearts. You know us; we are that company of silver-haired older men who gather every Wednesday morning at Bell's Coffee Shop on Highway 30—the famous Lincoln Highway—halfway between Chicago Heights and Lincolnville. Every village and town from Cape Cod to Balboa Island has a coffee shop like Bell's, and every Wednesday morning at seven, gangs like ours get together to tell the same stories, the same lies, plot the same adventures, and show the same family photos. As Mike would say, it's the support we crave, the camaraderie, the backup to the backup. We were the official reserve unit when you needed an excuse or alibi.

There were initially nine in the Marigold Gang back in the late 1950s. On the fringe, one kid was the new guy on the court (and I don't remember his name), another was too independent, so he dropped away early that summer, and the last, Robby Peterson, left when his family moved to Tulsa. Why I remember his name, I don't know. We never heard from Robby after he left.

Back then, during the two post–World War decades of the fifties and the sixties, Marigold Court and the surrounding neighborhoods were constructed, all bright and shiny-like, in the brand-new village of Lincolnville. Populated with married men and women, mostly under forty years old, filling this new town. All had survived World War II in some impressive way. Some fought in the Pacific and others in Europe, some stoked the war industry's home fires, and some stayed home and raised the first crop of Baby Boomers. Others grew food, and others canned it. One-half of American adults—of the 130 million

Americans then—labored and fought to rid the world of fascism. After the war, hundreds of new towns and villages, like Lincolnville, sprang up like fields of corn across America from New York to Los Angeles. Some, like our beloved Lincolnville thirty miles south of Chicago, sprang from nothing more than fallow farmland, while others sprouted along the fringes and edges of the larger American cities. This era began the infamous post-war suburbs, a cultural phenomenon still with us and still debated today. To us kids, it was heaven.

By the end of the school year that June 1959, a solid half dozen of us cul-de-sacers made up the gang. God's honest truth, we held a meeting deep in the Sauk Trail Woods, took a vote, and under a blood oath, declared ourselves the Marigold Gang. Our moniker came from the dozens of gangster movies produced in the fifties. We were aficionados of the genre. Half of us went to St. Jude Catholic Elementary School, and the others to Dogwood Grade School, a fine public grade school. Frankly, the odds of us becoming tough guy delinquents like James Cagney or Edward G. Robinson—even in our white tee shirts and cigarettes—were remote. Mike Jasicki envisioned himself as Charles Bronson, mostly because of the many Polish roles Bronson played. Allen Fisher (our hoarder) was a fan of Marlon Brando, and seeing how Brando turned out, it may have been a prescient choice. He even owned a Harley (we found it buried under tarps in the garage), though we seldom saw him ride it. Larry Martini was a fan of the big fellow Italian Aldo Ray and the movie *Battle Cry*. Larry is still a big man and would spend thirty years as a cop in Chicago, eventually becoming the chief of police for Lincolnville. Tommy Ellis was the brains of the outfit and a comic book collector. Batman, the Dark Knight, was, and still is, his hero. Sidenote here: Tommy sold one of his pristine comic books in a Sotheby's auction for over a half million dollars. His graphic designer father, James, worked in the Loop; Jimbo, his moniker, began collecting comic books in the 1930s. Now, seventy years later, Tommy's occasional comic book sales funded his kids' and grandkids' college educations. Cool, right? He, Larry, and I attended St. Jude's.

Garry Hughes was the athlete, handyman, and now semi-retired real estate developer. His family arrived from Iowa and were farmers. During his college days at the University of Illinois, the kid worked for a housing contractor during the summer and, after graduation, settled down with Angela in Flossmoor.

Me, I'm Craig Martin. More about me later.

For the late 1950s, our gang was as ethnically diverse as America, at least that part living on the right and white side of the proverbial tracks. Irish, English, German, Italian, and Polish; Catholic and Protestant (and later, I learned a couple were serious agnostics. We even had one atheist). We became Republicans and Democrats and remained civil—what's not to love?

More remarkably, unlike many of our other school chums, we stayed in the area—the much-maligned Southside of Chicago. We've debated this many times during the past fifty years; why we stayed when opportunities abounded throughout the United States. Texas and California called, so did New York, and even the expanding Northside of Chicago around O'Hare Airport. Tommy spent a few years in LA doing graphic design and a couple of years in the Disney studio; he returned in the mid-1980s, saying that it would have ruined his marriage if they stayed there in all that sun and fun. We never questioned his decision.

The Southside of Chicago was great until it wasn't. The villages and cities continued to grow and stretch out in frantic post-war fashion along the Illinois Central Railroad and other rail commuter lines like the limbs of a growing tree. The tonier villages, like Flossmoor and Olympia Fields, had the draw of their mansions, country clubs, and leafy green streets. The sixties and even the seventies still projected magic, then, mysteriously, it all began to slip away. Maybe it was the interstate highways that carved up the region into isolated islands of wealth and poverty. Maybe it was the unstoppable growth around Chicago to the west and north, facilitated by these new expressways. Maybe it was the change in the racial structure: the Blacks could finally escape the cities, the whites fleeing this latest urban out-migration. Maybe it was a change in state politics from diverse to monolithic; maybe it was the young packing up and going to places like California, Texas, and New York. Maybe it was like our street, a cultural cul-de-sac with no way out. Nonetheless, today—sixty-one years after that fateful year 1963—we Wednesday breakfast survivors count our pills and scars and wonder about the why of it all.

CHAPTER 1

June 2024

One of my earliest memories was when they found Mr. Jasicki dead asleep on his newly sprouted bluegrass front lawn. I did not witness it personally; I overheard my parents talking about it. He lay halfway between his shiny 1957 blue and white Ford Fairlane Skyliner (parked at a strange angle on the driveway, the left front tire leaving a dent in the new lawn) and his front door. A mostly empty bottle of Canadian Club in his hand, its cap secured. Mr. Jimmy Peal, the milkman making his Tuesday morning rounds, discovered Mr. Jasicki. Jimmy wasn't sure if Mr. Jasicki had collapsed from overwork, was drunk, or was dead. He poked him with a shoe, expecting a stiff response. He received a guttural, "Leave me the hell alone." Jimmy politely knocked on the Jasicki front door. Mrs. Jasicki answered, and according to Mr. Peal, her only words, after taking her usual four quarts of homogenized and enriched Grade A milk and two quarts of chocolate milk, were, "Leave the son of a bitch there to rot for all I care. I'll send Mike out to collect the loser in an hour." Hell hath no fury like the wife of a newly unemployed spouse.

My close friend Tommy Ellis reported this to me. Tommy lived three doors down from me (and next door to Allen Fisher) and directly across the street from our fellow gang member Mike Jasicki, eldest son of the aforementioned drunk. I can attest that Mr. Jasicki was probably drunk because, during the three years my family lived on Marigold Court, it was—after returning from work—Mr. Jasicki's evening habit. He would pull into the driveway, collect his briefcase from the rear seat, take off his suitcoat, go into the house, and then, after dinner, sit on the front porch with his cocktail and pack of Chesterfields and wave to the neighbors that strolled the cul-de-sac. However, this was the first time he'd spent the evening (and night) asleep on the bluegrass lawn. Mike did go out and collect his father with the help of his younger brother, Ed. Their sister, Jean, stood on the stoop with Mrs. Jasicki; they just shook their blond heads and hoped that the street understood. Within this close-knit community, any embarrassment from one neighbor's actions had long passed. Most were barely out of the Army or college; it was more like a fraternity. Bad and good habits were hard to hide.

I was informed about the Jasicki family drama when I returned from our two-week vacation at my grandparents' farm in central Michigan. We left three days after school closed for the summer and returned the day before the Fourth of July (we did not want to miss the fireworks). The day of Mr. Jasicki's great lawn nap (as it was later titled to reduce Mike's embarrassment) was the Tuesday the week before. I also learned that Mr. Jasicki was fired from the Armour Meat Company the previous Monday. A job in sales that he held since returning from three horrendous years fighting the Japs in the Pacific (two Purple Hearts and a Silver Star). Fourteen loyal meat company years and then a boot in the pants, the bastards. I learned later that Mr. Jasicki was an alcoholic. That, and the stress of his WWII PTSD, would eventually lead to the heart attack that killed him three weeks before his sixtieth birthday. Drinking

was a condition not unusual in the neighborhood and an affliction of the wives as well. Most likely, by the mid-1950s, a good
percentage of the residents had issues with liquor. Most of our
parents had been born during Prohibition; the battle with the
bottle was not a foreign war. After returning from Vietnam,
Mike Jasicki fought the same demon in his post-war twenties.
We all agree that Lucy, his wife, saved Mike's life. She heroically
fought the demons and manned the battlements with Mike;
she eventually saved her husband—and was there when he,
too, like his father, suffered a heart attack at fifty-nine. His father's heart attack was fatal and took the veteran at sixty. Mike's
doing great now.

As previously noted, my name is Craig Martin; that summer
of 1959, I was twelve. My eight-year-old brother was Charles,
and my three-year-old sister, Constance. My mother, it appears,
eternally tagged us with names that began with the letter *C* and
middle names that began with *W*. I could live with that. If I
had a dog, I'd have named him Cap. To other adults, Dad was
called Christopher Martin, and Mom, believe it or not, was
Cathy. Later I told people it was to cut down on monogram
issues.

Dad and Mom were from the small village of Berrien
Springs, east of Benton Harbor, Michigan, which back then,
before the freeways, was about a three-hour drive from our
village. During the summer and until air-conditioning arrived,
the drive seemed like a tour of hell. Dad fought in North Af-
rica and Sicily; he earned a Purple Heart and returned to marry Mom in 1946. I wrecked their happy and modest lives in
July 1947. Dad was a journalist and copy editor and worked
in Chicago. He took the Illinois Central commuter train into
the Loop every workday. His first job was marketing copy for
an industrial magazine. He later built a manufacturing plant
from scratch and became a producer of automobile parts. At

the height of the post-war industrialization, he employed fifty people. Mom had enough to do managing us delinquents, as she called us. I had assumed for years that it was in jest. Fifty years earlier, she was certain all my cul-de-sac friends would turn me into a juvenile delinquent. She didn't trust any of them, especially Allen Fisher.

Dad was a confirmed Oldsmobile man (he supplied their radio grilles and glove box chrome bits for thirty years). He drove an Olds Ninety-eight, and later a Cutlass, until a month before he passed away in 2006. I had a hell of a time selling that Cutlass; no one wanted to touch an Oldsmobile in 2006. Mom was two years younger; we lost her in 2009. They were part of the Greatest Generation, the killers of fascism, Mussolini, and Hitler. My siblings and I are proud Baby Boomers and will be until the very end, mostly because we had the coolest cars, the greatest music, and most of the money by the time we reached our seventies. All my buddies (except for Allen, we later learned) can attest that if you save and live long enough, you can take your wife on that cruise she always wanted—maybe twice. Such is the American dream.

On Marigold Court, there were twelve houses (and surprisingly still are, Allen Fisher's disaster and suggested immolation notwithstanding). All were built and sold by Allied Builders Corporation in the summer of 1957. Our bulb was one of three cul-de-sacs in a neighborhood of 275 homes. Most homes were situated on 65' x 100' lots and were pre-planned three-bedroom houses of about 1,200 square feet set about twenty feet from the sidewalk. They were built with no garage, only a carport. A green strip of lawn between the curb and sidewalk was there for the snow. Dad built a two-car garage on the side of our house (he was an optimist); in my opinion, it appeared like a carbuncle on the face of the *Mona Lisa*. I loved that house. By the summer of 1959, two houses on the court had sold twice, and the one on the corner at Lakewood Boulevard was vacant. The Han Lees would move into that house that fall; they were from China. Later I learned they were refugees and were on lists, if caught, to be executed by Mao's communist regime. Due to the current economic slowdown, Dad said it would take some time to sell. My buddies and I didn't know what an economic slowdown was. Garry Hughes said his dad talked about cutbacks at Gary Steel and said they were now on a budget. Only Tommy Ellis was flush; his old man was a pediatrician, and his mom a nurse. Dr. Ellis said that the baby boom was a godsend for someone in his racket, whatever that meant. He was also the first with a color television. His house became our headquarters, and we made sure we never got on Tommy's wrong side. I saw *The Magical World of Disney* in color for the first time on that TV.

* * *

I slid into the last seat at the end of the long table in the back of Bell's Coffee Shop. I was late and the last to join the guys. There were, including me, four this morning. Two empty chairs sat at the far end.

"Where's Tommy?" I asked.

Larry looked at Garry and sighed. "He'd forget his hat if his head wasn't attached."

"You never get them right," I said. "If you're going to sound smart at least get the aphorism right."

"You know what I mean," Larry said with a smile. "Tommy is on that cruise to Alaska with Heather."

We all paused and thought impure thoughts of the goddess, Heather. Mike was the first to call her the goddess, tall, with long legs, a beautiful face, blonde, Claudia Schiffer–like. Tommy hit it out of the park (to use the correct phrasing) with

Heather. He found her a few years after Ellen passed away. We all loved Ellen; she was the earth mother we remember from our faux hippy days. Tommy was a heartbroken man for a long time; we were concerned. He discovered Heather at an industrial design conference in New York; she was modeling the latest product designs from Black and Decker (I kid you not), drills, power saws, and sanders. He offered to buy her a drink, then found out she had gone to the Rhode Island School of Design and couldn't land a job at an industrial design studio. Tommy joked that it was because she was too pretty; she was a threat to the females in the office and the wives. She smiled, gently slapped his face, and said something about his anti-feminist behavior. He said au contraire and explained the reality of his life: widower, two children—thirteen and nine—at home, and his growing design business. He was the complete package, all or nothing. She said she was doing a gig in Chicago at the McCormick Center in a couple of weeks and offered to buy *him* dinner. He agreed, and a year later, they married. She became the chief designer in his expanding shop and his bride. The kids loved her, all sweet wine and roses stuff. Yes, the guys like Heather—a lot.

"That's the third cruise in two years," Garry said.

"You are down to counting cruises? Jesus, Garry, you should go on one—you'd like it. Spend some of that dough and give Angela a treat. You sure as hell can afford one," I said.

"They are nothing but steel test tubes full of COVID and other fatal diseases. I will take my place in Vail, thank you very much. And Angela gets seasick and has shown no desire to cruise."

"I'll bet that's not true. He's afraid to ask," Mike said, pointing at Garry. "She may turn him down."

Garry continued, "Locked up on a massive boat full of old people trying to get their last kicks in before dying—that does not sound like fun to me. Do you know they even have a morgue somewhere inside the ships?"

"Sounds like Vail's emergency room," I said.

"Ha ha. I only had to wear that boot as a precaution, and nothing was broken."

"I want to see the X-rays," Larry said. "You were in that thing a long time. You still walk with a limp, Chester."

"Tommy sent pictures of the glaciers; did you see them on Facebook?" Garry said, changing the subject.

"That was a hell of a halibut, damn near as big as him. It has been years since we were up in Alaska. We need to do it again," I said. "Penny loves it up there."

"Long way to go to get away. I'll take Upper Michigan, thank you very much," Larry added. "In six hours, I'm as far away as I want. And the fishing's not bad. Fly fishing the Escanaba."

". . . and neither is the hunting," Mike added.

"See, there is absolutely no reason to go halfway around the world to sit in a tin box and watch the world drift by," Garry said.

"Sounds good to me," I said.

"Aren't we a cranky lot this morning," Mike said. "I need my protein." He looked up. The waitress, Karen, after listening to our whining, took up her order book. She had primed the pump by filling coffee cups fifteen minutes before I arrived.

"You guys done? Can I get to work? The usual?" she asked.

Everyone said yes.

Karen Quist had served our crew since her first day in 1998. Twenty-six years is longer than most marriages. She was not only our waitress but the co-owner of Bell's. Garry Hughes, two seats over, was the quasi-secret owner. He'd bought the coffee shop in 1997 when Joan Bell retired after thirty years, and, believe it or not, went on an around-the-world cruise.

Garry hated losing the restaurant to a condominium or fast-food operation, so he bought it. After seven years, Garry decided Karen would be the ideal manager. He gave her a 25 percent stake. When we were there, we were the only table she serviced (as a group, we only came in on Wednesdays, so I can't totally verify that). So, as a result, we all paid into Garry's retirement annuity.

"Now, down to business," I said. "You all agreed to help. No backing out. Friday morning at ten we start. We get the lay of the land, make assessments, and plan our attack. The dumpster will arrive at noon."

"Will one be enough?" Garry asked.

"God, I hope so," Larry said. "Good thing I have a box of leftover COVID masks. I'll bring them; we'll need them. I also suggest heavy gloves, clothes you never want to see again, and beer."

"This is work, not a party," Mike said. "But I say it will take at least four days. It will be like an archeological dig."

"No weekends. Friday, ten o'clock, work until two, then reconvene Monday," Garry said.

"You will not miss your Saturday tee time," I said. "But yes, beer. A case of Goose Island? I'm buying." There were no objections.

CHAPTER 2

The Marigold Gang formed during Eisenhower's last years, and now, thirteen presidents, five wars, and eight marriages later, we still had enough tolerance for each other to sit and break bread once a week. Sixty-five years fly by, at least from the perspective of longingly looking back over your shoulder. We had been lucky. Allen was the first of the group to move on, the first to die, and force all of us to reassess our place in this world. Our regrets filled a book, we listed our mistakes alphabetically, our triumphs (such as they were) were the chapter headers, and we were well into the grandkids phase of life. Allen's death forced a couple of us into a short bout of survivor's guilt; the rest offered a hand and held them. Our roles changed, yet our friendship never wavered; we celebrated every success and failure together.

We stood on the cracked concrete driveway to Allen Fisher's house Friday morning, assessing the task ahead of us. All we could do was shake our heads. The house desperately needed a paint job, and God knows what else was inside needing fixing. We grew up on this court. Tommy, who was enjoying Alaska, his cruise, and Heather, was missing out. His old house was next door. Fifty years and a poor remodel had not been kind. Mike Jasicki's house, still one story, sat directly across the street; it appeared well-kept, newly painted, flowers along the driveway. Larry, Garry, and I lived at the end of the court. All the houses on Marigold Court were originally one-story ranch homes. A couple were renovated by adding a second floor. As an architect, I shuddered at the results. However, originally designed in the mid-fifties, these were the height of domestic modernity. Now they were sad reminders of a past when, to move up, you had to move out. That's what all our families did then, all except Allen Fisher.

"They cut down the elms; that's when it all started to go wrong," Garry said. "This was a beautiful cul-de-sac then, large American elms thirty feet tall. They gave shade and style. The street was like the interior of a cathedral with the elms' straight trunks and arching branches. Then the blight came, and they cut them down—it was a damn shame."

"They were small and lacked bedrooms, and after the third kid, there was no room. I remember when your dad converted the garage into your family room," Larry said to me. "After that, you had to park out on the driveway. That really sucked in winter."

"Yes, it was first a one-car garage, then a family room," I said. "Winters? Climbing into a car when it was twenty below was not fun. Dad talked about adding a master bedroom and two bedrooms over the house like the Thompsons and the Scotts did. It didn't pencil out; that's how he put it. That's when we moved to the Heights."

"Yeah, but the real reason was the change—who was moving in," Mike said.

"We had no control over that. Besides, that's the way it should be," Garry said. "People have rights. It is only proper."

"It sure didn't mean people accepted it—many didn't. They voted with their feet," I said. "Besides, we were twelve years old. How were we supposed to know? Lincolnville was a good town."

"Kind of still is," Larry said. "Yeah, but now, with taxes that will choke a horse, houses so cheap you can buy them by the dozen, a town center that once was great and cool—the place is now an economic wasteland—nobody wants this. They bulldozed the Heights."

"Tough times," Mike added.

"And greed," Larry said.

"And piss-poor management," said Garry.

"And white flight," I said.

"Maybe that's what it has going for it now, affordability," Larry said as he walked toward the garage door. "I watched it all: our weekly staff meetings, changes in the social structure, and people relearning to be civil. But the slow decline, decay, and drug problems all cut into my heart. The state's money moved on; it chased the interstate west and south. That state and federal money went into new homes, new utilities, new roads, new shopping centers, and new voters. They got the mine; we got the shaft. And it's not proper to say, but troubles followed."

"Craig, remember when that Black family moved in on Lakewood?" Garry said. "Weren't your parents involved with all that? The protests?"

"Yes, I stood with my folks on the front lawn of that family's house, along with a dozen other Lincolnville parents and their kids. When cars full of bigots drove by looking for trouble, and they saw two dozen white faces standing there, it changed their minds."

"Wasn't that just after a Little League game?" Mike asked, knowing the answer.

"Yes, Dad said we should bring our bats with us just in case we wanted to shag some fly balls out in the street," I added with a laugh.

"It still had an impact," Larry said. "Sometimes change is

hard."

"Not sometimes. I remember Allen getting into it with a kid at school. One of the new Black kids, he was from up around Chicago somewhere. His folks had just moved in and it was his first day. A couple of white kids were giving the fellow a tough time. Then Allen walked up and put his arm around the kid—you remember that? Allen was the biggest kid in eighth grade, and he sat with the fellow at lunch; nobody did anything after that. Probably called patronizing now, but back then the times were a-changing."

From across the street, a garage door opened, and a tall Black man walked out. Next to him was an equally tall teenage boy. They made a beeline directly to us.

"Can I help you fellows?" he said when he was about forty feet away. He stopped and reached into his pocket and put on his glasses. "Holy Christ, it's you guys. My eyes have gotten so bad I thought you were some gang coming to rip off Allen's place, not that there's much to steal. Hi, Craig, Garry, Larry, and Mike. Hershel, say hello to the only real gang here in Lincolnville. They call themselves the Marigold Gang, after the street here."

"I know them, Dad. They are legends," Hershel said. He greeted us; we all shook hands.

"We are not old enough to be legends," Garry said with a smile.

Delmar Johnson had owned the Thompson house for about fifteen years. He moved in about the time Hershel was born. I remember that distinctly because Delmar Johnson was, and still is, a reserve Army officer, a captain. He grew up in Lincolnville, was a star athlete, and got a full ride to Notre Dame for either basketball or football, his choice. Then came 9/11, he joined the Army; he felt it was his duty. He was in logistics, became a captain, and is now a senior manager with

United Intercontinental Moving. These days a moving company in Illinois is busy, too busy; the outgoing far more than the incoming. Do not ever get into a game of horse with this man. All of us have lost more than our pride on Delmar's driveway.

The roar of a diesel motor echoed up the cul-de-sac, and a flatbed carrier turned into the court. A beat-up yellow box sat on its back. Ten minutes later, it sat on the driveway.

"Enough reminiscing," I said. "I'm sure there will be more memories to unearth before this day is over than I care to think about. I'm guessing ghosts and mysteries."

"We are off to practice," Delmar said, taking the basketball from Hershel.

"Is that true, Hershel?" Mike asked. "Seems a little early for the season."

"Yes, sir, practice. Never can have enough practice," he said, a little too coached.

"Look, guys," Delmar said. "I liked Allen, he was a good guy, but there is no chance in hell that I'm going down that rabbit hole with you." He pointed at the house. "He was your buddy, and that's what buddies do. We wish you well, and don't forget to wear your masks—and don't forget to say your prayers."

* * *

Late Spring 1959
The gang walked single file along the old Indian trail that paralleled the lake nestled in the middle of Sauk Trail Forest Preserve. Allen led the way; I pulled up the rear. Allen was always point during our adventures in the forest. Seven years later, leading another platoon of men, Allen would take two rounds to his right leg on another narrow trail in another forest half a world away.

This portion of the trail, the village librarian and local historian told us, was one of the sections of the ancient Sauk Indian Trail that began east of Detroit up in what is now Canada and wound its way south and west across Michigan and then circumnavigated the southern end of Lake Michigan. The trail was far enough inland to avoid the low swamps that filled the southern post-glacial antediluvian basin of the lake. It was one of the interregional trails that tied the Native American tribes together and enabled their trade. Last summer, we'd set out on a two-day hike led by Tommy's dad that followed the old trail in a northeasterly direction. It wasn't too challenging. Tommy's father speculated that Sauk Trail could be more than five thousand years old—how about that, Interstate 80? There were locations in Michigan, deep in the woods, where the trail was eight feet wide and two and three feet deep from wear. Over the years, all of us had found at least a dozen Indian points (arrowheads), and even an axe head. As Tenderfoot Boy Scouts, these arrowheads added to the Indian-based mystique of scouting. By the summer of 1959, we were all working toward our Second- and First-Class ranks.

Today was a day hike, and we were reconnoitering for a longer hike we would take with the troop late in the summer. That hike was to be led again by Tommy's dad and mine, and it would be a three-day, twenty-mile march. Our scoutmaster was Jim Ellis, Tommy's dad. The hike would be with the other patrols in our Troop 305, about thirty fellows from ages eleven to sixteen. Today it was just the six of us: the brave, the heroic, and never-equaled Eagle Patrol. We carried rucksacks, canteens, sandwiches, hundred-foot coils of rope, and the usual assortment of knives, compasses, and first aid kits. *Be Prepared* is more than just a scout motto.

Don't judge me on my allegiance to the Boy Scouts; the scouts have been through a lot of crap over the last sixty-five years, many self-inflicted, the latest issues of molestations and pedophilia notwithstanding. These problems and solutions were sadly and poorly managed. But in the 1950s and 1960s, all that pain was in the future. The Vietnam anti-war movement was also having an impact on scouting. Boy Scouts were now lumped together with the Army and anything military (primarily because of the uniforms, the whiteness, and the homespun discipline and character the scouts professed—no one wants to be embarrassed by a fourteen-year-old saluting the flag). However, for us boys, hiking through the primeval Illinois forest along an ancient Indian trail was as cool as it could get.

When we took a break at the overlook (the lake resulted from an earth dam constructed to bridge a narrow canyon for a purpose we didn't know), Mike pulled out his pack of Pall Mall cigarettes and passed them around. We all unquestioningly lit up (and don't start with all of today's too-young-to-smoke mumbo jumbo; then, it was—the trail, arrowheads, and smoking—all cool). The humid air and the lack of any breeze permitted the cigarette haze to hang like smoke from a campfire.

I must say here that those halcyon days come up often when we have breakfast, not so much as "those were the good old days." It is more like "what the kids today are missing." Those woods are still there, that lake is still there, and those great oaks, beech, and hickories are still there. The air still buzzes with cicadas, and their billions still sing their "choruses." Flints, arrowheads, and stone axe heads still appear after the rains. However, you will never find them if you don't go searching.

"Don't get much better than this," Garry said. "A fag, best buds, and no girls."

"There you go with that no-girls thing. Did you see Barbara Lasky the other day? I think she's wearing one," Tommy said.

"One what?" I asked.

"You know, one of those."

"Come on, Tom, it's called a brassiere. Can't you say brassiere?" Garry quipped.

"I can say it. I just don't want to."

"You are missing Tommy's point, Gare—Barbara Lasky is wearing one," I said with a smile. We all stopped to consider the image.

"You guys ever think we will see a man in space?" Tommy said, changing the subject—one of his classic non sequiturs. "How cool would that be?"

We all nodded; Tommy was our resident space nut. He had a poster of the first seven astronauts announced that April pinned to his bedroom wall. He even knew what NASA meant, the National Aeronautics and Space Administration. On overnight hikes, he would sit outside his tent and trace the various constellations in the clear night.

"Learn how to find the North Star," he told us. "Once you got that, you will never be lost."

I couldn't argue with that. More than once, when foolishly confused, I stepped out of the car and scanned the skies for Ursa Minor and Polaris. Now you look at the car's dashboard, talk to the inanimate object, announce your destination—and magic is lost (and often you included). When John Glenn died, Tommy was demonstrably upset. He spent an entire Wednesday morning breakfast reminding us of his World War II fighter pilot record, test flight pilot, space flights, and senator's record. They don't make them like that anymore, he reminded us. Tommy is one of the Democrats in the gang, and he is tight about John Glenn.

"What the hell?" Garry said, turning out to face the lake. "Quiet, all of ya. Did you hear that? Listen!"

Garry's hearing was always better than ours; and was, hormonally speaking, ahead of us—he was growing a half-inch a month. None of us, including him, knew he would become one of the best tight ends that the University of Illinois would ever have at six-foot-four and two hundred and forty pounds.

"Listen."

Then all of us heard it. It was a scream, a series of sharp, penetrating, scared-out-of-your-mind screams. They came from below our overlook, along the shore of the lake.

"Grab your gear," I yelled. "Something's not right."

We stumbled down the trail, and the screams grew louder with each step. Reaching the lake's edge, we confronted a Black kid who couldn't have been nine years old. None of us knew him. He was screaming and crying and yelling and pointing. A small yellow dog, covered in muck, ran back and forth along the lake's muddy edge, yipping and yapping.

"Jesus Christ," Allen said as he pointed. "A kid is holding onto a raft out there. Holy crap. What the hell?"

The kid kept whining and jumping up and down. "Micky, you gotta save Micky." He kept pointing. The raft looked more like a floating mess of debris held together with twine and strips of canvas.

"What's your name?" I asked.

"Billy," was the answer.

Allen had already stripped to his skivvies. Next to him, so had Larry. Garry and Tommy were pulling rope bundles from their bags; I did the same from mine. We tied one end of a rope around Larry's waist and then another around Allen.

"They should be long enough," Allen said. "If not, add another length from my bag."

Both Allen and Larry were strong swimmers. Last year, I'd seen them race to a floating platform at scout camp, which was more than twice this distance. The issue here was Micky—they had never rescued a panicked kid desperately holding onto a sinking raft. Then they each calmly tied another length of rope to the one already around them. Tommy and I grabbed the shore end of the ropes tied to our friends. Nobody took their eyes off Micky.

They waded out into the gray-brown water. The bottom was mud and clay, the natural land around these parts.

"Be damn careful," Mike said. "The bottom is soft; don't get stuck."

I'd never heard Mike swear, ever.

"Slowly," Allen said. "Gentle-like—it's gooey and sticky. Keep moving; don't let your feet get stuck. When we are deep enough, we will breaststroke out to the raft. There's no current, just the breeze pushing him out. When we get there, you tie your rope onto the raft, keep it from going further. I'll work my way around to the kid."

"Roger that," Larry answered.

The kid on the shore had stopped screaming but was still huffing and puffing. He was, like the four of us, transfixed on the rescuers. The dog still barked.

"Whose idea was this, kid?" I said, slowly paying out line and keeping both eyes on our swim team.

"We made a raft," Billy said. "We was going to play Tom Sawyer and Huckleberry Finn. It were in a book we was reading at school. We collected the wood, and Micky wanted to see if it floated. We tied it all together, climbed aboard, and started paddling with flat sticks, and it slowly floated away. I jumped off and got back here. Then Micky lost his paddle; it just floated away. Then Micky started to yell and used his hands to try and paddle back. That's when he fell off."

"How old are you?" Tommy asked. The boys were just ten feet from the raft.

"I am eight years old," Bill said.

"Figures. And Micky, how old?" Tommy said.

"He's ten, and my brother."

24

"If those boys don't get to him, you'll be an only child," Garry added.

"What?"

"Stop that," I said. "Not useful."

The raft was a hundred feet from the shore, and the lake was deep and cold. It wouldn't warm until July. Allen and Larry quickly breaststroked to the raft.

"The water's numbing, Larry. The kid's most likely getting chilled. How long has he been out here?" Allen yelled back to us.

"How long has Micky been in the water?" I asked.

"I don't know, a while, don't got a watch. A while."

"Allen, hurry," Tommy yelled. "The sooner, the better."

"Roger that," Larry yelled.

They both reached the raft at the same time. Larry untied one of the ropes and threw a loop around the end of one of the makeshift raft's frames. He secured it with a bowline knot. Allen worked his way around the edge to Micky. He'd cut his hand; blood covered the wood. The kid had managed to wedge his hand between two lengths of wood. It likely saved him from drowning.

"They used a couple of f'en wood pallets, the kind they use for freight, then some damn cardboard. Jesus Christ," Allen said.

We cleaned up our conversation for later adult consumption.

"I've got Micky," Allen said. "The rope's around him. Pull us both in at the same time. I'll keep his head above water."

"Don't forget me!" Larry yelled.

Five minutes later we had Micky on the dry bank. The raft, such as it was, was now secured to an old willow. We wrapped our jackets around Micky. He shook all to pieces from the cold, and his teeth chattered to where I thought he would bite his tongue off.

"I'll get a fire going that will warm him and our heroes," Garry said.

"I'm going to the road and get help," Tommy said.

The afternoon went quickly. By the time the fire department and a half dozen policemen arrived, Micky was warm and dry and had eaten two sandwiches. Billy learned a lesson about nautical safety and building a raft. The gang's first official photo was posted in the local newspaper (the first of many over the next ten years). Being celebrities was cool; our parents were impressed by our resourcefulness; we were heroes. Mrs. Dubois, the boys' mom, was in tears and said God had a hand in our being there. Privately, a few days later, we went into post-rescue depression and clinical review—which is never a good idea.

"What if we hadn't been there?" Allen said.

"We were going to do this hike the next day," I said.

"What if we went around the other side of the lake?" Larry said.

"For Christ's sake, listen to you guys," Tommy said. "We were there. We knew how to save the kid, and we did it. All of us can swim. Nobody died. It's us, the gang, all for one. Right? Don't be such pessimists."

Tommy was and still is the most optimistic of all of us, and he's married to Heather.

CHAPTER 3

My first thought as we unlocked Allen's front door was Tutankhamun. Is this how Howard Carter felt as he rolled away the last stones before squeezing into the young Egyptian king's tomb? Inside we found stacks of newspapers filling the hallway, a hundred pieces of mail under the door slot, the overpowering smell of lilies, and a light switch that failed to work.

"The man probably didn't pay his electric bill," Garry suggested. He reached around the corner for the switch for the living room. The lights clicked on.

"First thing, replace the hallway bulb," I said. "Second, open the windows and doors, get some air moving. It smells like a funeral home. If you find a fan, set it up in this hallway and blow it out the door."

"Roger that, I'll steal a bulb from a back bedroom," Larry said. He turned sideways to embrace the wall as he slid down the hall.

"We need an assessment before we start," I announced. "Having a plan is a good idea."

"That's my boy," Mike said. "Everybody take ten minutes to look around. Then we'll all meet back on the driveway to pow-wow—Craig will make a plan."

"I didn't say I was going to make—" I began.

"Hey, Larry. Craig's going to make a plan," Mike yelled.

"Craig's going to make a plan, cool," Garry said. They were laughing.

Ten minutes later, we stood on the concrete drive. Larry doused himself with his inhaler. Thirty years a cop had had an impact on his lungs. The dust and God-knows-what-else in that house had me coughing and blowing my nose. Larry passed around COVID masks.

"We've worn masks for the last four years, and I'm still not used to it. Nonetheless, no strange hoarder's disease will take me down," Larry said.

"Okay, what did you see? Larry, you start," I said.

"In the back bedrooms, there are a dozen boxes of clothing. The beds have been broken down and leaned against the walls to provide more room. There are a couple of big dressers, but you can barely open the drawers. They are full. Debris, clothes, and garbage are everywhere. One of the bedroom doors is locked. We'll have to force it."

"The living room is the same," Garry said. "Cardboard boxes, piles of magazines, shelves on stacks of bricks. On the shelves are clear plastic containers like those from the Container Store. Lord knows what's inside them—but it looks like more clothes."

"In the kitchen," I said, "are half-full cereal boxes, empty soup, and vegetable cans. The refrigerator door is stuck, probably the seal. Dirty dishes are in piles, and rat and mice shit everywhere. Also, used frozen dinner aluminum pans are stuck together in stacks, empty Coca-Cola cans in plastic bags, and garbage sacks in the utility room."

"Rats, great," Mike said. "Why does it have to be rats?"

"You sound like Indiana Jones in that *Crusade* movie," Larry chirped.

"I liked that movie, but I still hate rats," Mike confirmed. "The garage, I could barely get around the only car. It looks like a 1963 Studebaker Lark. There's a light blue color under the thick dust."

"No way," Garry said, "a Studebaker? I don't remember a Studebaker."

"Yes, tires are flat. There's an inch of dust on it, but it looks in good shape. You remember his old Harley—he drove it that summer maybe twenty years ago? It's parked between the car and the garage door. There are more plastic bags, tools on the shelves, and cardboard boxes in the back. And yes, Garry, I don't remember Allen's dad driving that car. Ron was his name, right?"

"Yes, Ron, Ronald Fisher. Wife's name was Lois," Garry said. "Didn't he drive a blue Grand Prix? Would park it in the driveway."

"There's also a couple of dozen license plates nailed to the studs," Mike added. "I remember doing that as a kid. Then they started sending those sticky tabs. I like the old ways."

"Don't we all," Garry added.

"The door to the basement is blocked," Larry added. "I don't want to think about what's down there—Dante's rings of hell come to mind. It's always in the basement where the greatest evil lurks. We need to clear the hallway first."

"Thank you, Stephen King," I said. With my boss-voice, I announced, "Here's today's plan. I don't know what is valuable or what's not. We will clear the front living room first. If there's anything worth more than a buck, we will store it there—temporarily. Everything else goes in the dumpster. We will then split up into pairs and attack the remaining rooms on Monday. Today is the living room. Think of this as the site of a nuclear accident—Chernobyl comes to mind. We can only stay for short periods before the radiation kills us. Take a breather—often." I checked my watch. "It's ten to noon, and we are out of here at two thirty. That work?"

"You da boss," Garry said. "Cocktails are on me at the club at five."

"Can't—grandkids at five," Mike said. "I will be here at ten, Monday."

Mike held the current record for grandkids at nine. Seven were boys, all played baseball, and ranged from six years old to nineteen. The two girls were both high school athletes. They played basketball. The man was bust a button proud of his kids and grandkids.

I told Garry I'd shower first, then drop by the club. It was Friday, and tonight was Penny's mah-jongg club; I was free. Larry would join us for one beer, then go home. His wife's father was living with them, and he needed to give Teresa a break. Terry's father was in the early stages of dementia and, at ninety-three, had had a good run; his words, not mine. She usually joined Penny's mah-jongg foursome.

We turned, took deep breaths, re-secured our leftover COVID masks, and dove in.

We'd heard about hoarders, but to a man, we stayed away from any detailed study of the condition. It freaked the hell out of us. We knew about Allen but didn't understand his affliction or the cause. The theories are many, and the results are painful. There is even a television series on the Discovery Channel; those shows were scarier than a horror movie. I tried to find out what drove Allen to end up this way. Maybe searching through the debris of his life will give us a clue. Allen came back from Vietnam broken. It took us ten years to help set him straighter, and he never was whole. He'd been wounded and earned a Purple Heart, even a few commendations and a Silver Star, yet the heroics weren't enough to cover the pain he faced at home. We knew both of his parents were nuts, certifiable. They should have been in some institution. Allen decided he'd take care of them, just as he'd cared for his men in Vietnam.

30

And he did, especially as emphysema and cancer took hold of them both. He called me the night he found his parents.

"Craig, buddy, I need your help," Allen said over the phone. We'd had breakfast a few days earlier, and he was in good spirits then.

"What's up?" I asked.

"I found Mom and Dad dead this afternoon; they are in their bedroom. I don't know what to do. I need help."

Standing in the hall, holding the phone, I was more than stunned; I was speechless.

"They are dead? Both of them? Ron and Lois, they are dead?"

"Yes, it looks like Dad shot Mom, then turned the gun on himself. Can you make some calls, then come over? I really need some help."

I called Larry. He wasn't Lincolnville police chief then— that wouldn't be for a few more years. He was still a Chicago cop. I told him what Allen had told me. Then I called Mike. I couldn't reach Garry or Tommy. Mike and I arrived twenty minutes later to find four police cars, an ambulance, and what seemed like a million questions. Allen was cleared of having any part in their deaths. What had happened was painfully obvious.

As we continued through the house, one bedroom was locked. It was the scene of the tragedy. We forced it open and found a dust-free museum dedicated to his parents. Family photos on the dressers, pictures on the walls, a made-up bed, and his folks' clothes neatly placed in the dresser drawers and hung in an orderly fashion in the closet. It was the only room in the entire house that was habitable. From the moment of their deaths, Allen built a wall around himself, never threw out anything (or that's what it looked like), and survived on frozen dinners and Coca-Cola. There were thousands of cans in the house.

Up to that point, we believed that Allen had been left financially comfortable by his parents. He never asked for money. He was funny and up to date on the state of the world, the markets, and politics. After seeing this mess, we understood that Allen was of two worlds, one outside and one inside this prison. He had a sister, Brenda, and a brother, Dennis, both younger. We remembered them. Both were aloof and cold, even as children—Larry thought them weird, broken. They came to the parents' funerals, and that was the last time we saw them, more than thirty years ago. When asked, Allen said he wasn't in touch with them. We never asked again.

All of us had large extended families through our kids or the relatives of our spouses. As far as we knew, Allen had his two siblings, and that was all. He never mentioned in-laws or nieces and nephews. Of course, he had two kids, Barbara and Steve, and, at that time, an ex-wife, Bess.

Allen married soon after he returned from 'Nam. She was a cute thing, as we said back then. Elizabeth Tomes was bright, had a wonderful sense of humor, saw no fault in anyone, and went to Lincolnville High School with us. She was in our class; we called her Bess. She moved into the Fisher house with Allen. Soon after the wedding, Ron and Lois rented an apartment in Lincolnville. There was a détente between the newlyweds and his folks for about five years. Later, they moved back in with Allen when their infirmities took hold—a big mistake.

Barbara assigned me the cleanup job and told me she had no contact with her aunt and uncle. None of the gang had the siblings' addresses or phone numbers. They took off after the parents' funerals. Barbara and Steve flew in and attended Allen's funeral. They looked well and prosperous. Both were married and had three children between them (I don't remember which were whose). They both left the day after the funeral. They did not stay in the house. If they even breached the door, I'm not aware of it. But somehow, Barbara knew what was there, the stinker.

The Fisher family chaos began when Allen had his parents move back into the house—he told us it was to save money and provide care. That was around 1981, six people in a tiny three-bedroom house. Bess left Allen soon after Steve was born. Allen was up front with all of us.

"She said it was either put my folks in a home, or I'm leaving with the kids," he'd said. "I couldn't just warehouse them. Bess left, took Barbara and the baby, and went to live with her folks in Franklin. I saw them as much as I could, but my heart had been struck with an axe. No one should have to make those kinds of decisions."

Ron and Lois lived with Allen for another ten years; they died in the messiest and most hurtful way. Vietnam caused a wound to Allen's soul that festered, and for the past thirty-three years, he slowly melted. The murder-suicide destroyed what was left. We did what we could.

"I can't believe this shit," Larry said as he wheeled a stack of boxes out to the dumpster. "And there's a dozen more."

"What's in them?" I asked.

"Old videotapes, eight-track tapes, cassettes, old stereos, there's even a couple of record players, you know, the kind that played 45s. They might be worth something."

"If you want to deal with them, go right ahead. What's your time worth?"

"I get it—to the dumpster," Larry said as he passed Mike in the hallway.

We agreed that if it was something that you wanted to take responsibility for, go for it. If not, it goes to the dump. I'd hate to think about doing this with Allen alive and his kids helping. There would be theatrics over every item. Barbara and I agreed on a few rules or guidelines: If we find money, keep it separate. We decide what to do if anything looks valuable. If there is jewelry, put it in a box and mail it to her. If his medals, or those of her grandfather, are found, send them as well. Pull any photos from the frames and send those too. Save the photo albums. She'd figure out what to do with those after she talked with her aunt and uncle.

At two thirty, I yelled, "Time!" We had cleared one room, the living room. The dumpster was full; I ordered another for Monday. Spread out in the living room were some decent pieces of furniture, a dozen old paintings, a few boxes of books in reasonably good condition, and a mahogany box of real solid silver silverware. I'd check its value over the weekend. I took photos of the hallmarks and the label inside the case. It might be something that Barbara might want. Three oriental carpets looked valuable. Even Garry thought so. It was the paintings and ceramics that caught my eye.

Again, out on the driveway, I stood waiting for the guys, a suitcase at my feet.

"I always had the impression that the Fishers had money," Larry said. "And after going through this initial cleanup, I see nice furniture, and the artwork is collectible, the silverware, even the carpets. There's general filthiness to it all, but there's quality underneath."

"Yeah, same thought," Mike added. "Then again, my idea of class is Worchester on my steak, not A-1. I'm a butter on my baked potato guy, not chives and sour cream."

"You have been boring the whole time I've known you," Larry added. "And it's Worcestershire."

"Which no one can pronounce," Mike said.

"I've got something interesting to show you," I said. "I found this under the bed in the locked bedroom."

I placed the suitcase on the folding table we'd set up next

to the dumpster, then opened it. There was a collective gasp.

Larry, eyes wide, said, "Is that real? If so, holy shit."

Stacked inside, in neat bank paper–wrapped bundles, were what had to be thousands of dollars. Some bank wrapper–strapped bundles were one-hundred-dollar bills; others were fifties and twenties. Next to the bills was a plastic box filled with gold coins. The topmost coins had dates from the 1950s and 1960s.

"Any idea how much is here?" Mike asked.

"No idea. There are tens of thousands of dollars in cash, the gold coins are worth $1,900 each, and there are hundreds of them," I said. "These belong to Barbara and Steve. I suggest putting them in a safe deposit box for now. Any objections?"

That much money in one place could make any man's head spin—larceny was just an excuse away.

"We could all just retire to my place, open that thirty-year-old scotch, and split it equally," Larry said with a laugh. "No one the wiser."

"And then what, Officer Martini?" Garry said. "Not declare it, spend the rest of our years in a federal penitentiary for tax evasion, leave the rest of our money to the wives so they can step out while we rot in jail?" Garry placed his hand on the topmost bundle of cash and smiled. "It's tempting, though."

"All right, enough fantasizing," I said. "Garry, can you come with me to Lincolnville Federal? We'll get a safety deposit box. Who knows, there might be something else in this house that we need to save for the family."

We all sighed collectively, thought good thoughts, and headed home. Garry and I went to the bank.

CHAPTER 4

Bright and early Monday morning, we all gathered again on the driveway; an empty yellow dumpster replaced the full one from Friday afternoon.

"How'd you all sleep?" Tommy Ellis said, joining us. "Nothing like a cruise to set your mind and attitude right. We had a great time, thanks for asking."

I looked at our quintet standing on the fractured concrete. Four of us looked like we hadn't slept for three days. I know I hadn't. When I told Penny, my wife, about our find, she was stunned. She liked Allen but never had a clue about what was happening in his home or in his head.

"Did you count the money?" she asked.

"Garry and I used one of the bank's cash counters," I said. "Garry sits on the bank's board, and they set it up for us. While he went through the paper, I counted the coins. There was $145,340 in cash and 195 one-ounce gold coins, or $370,500 at the current value, more than half a million dollars. Certainly enough to tempt someone if they knew that Allen Fisher was also a cash hoarder. I called Larry and Mike. Both were stunned. Most of the bills were twenty-, fifty-, and one-hundred-dollar denominations, and dated from 1952 through 1962."

"Are they worth more?"

"No. Their face value is all they are worth. A buck's a buck, though."

Tommy called me Sunday afternoon after he returned from Vancouver. I emailed him Friday night that we were cleaning Allen's house on Monday. He volunteered to be there. I also told him what we found.

"I commend you, Tommy Ellis," Mike said, sipping his coffee. "After a week of good times and probably more sex than a human your age could endure, you had the nerve to face us. I'm sure there are tales to be told."

Tommy smiled.

"Now, you layabouts, back to work," I said.

"Just a minute. I have a little bit more to add to that suitcase full of money," Larry said. "Most of you know me as a sophisticated guy, champagne over wine."

"Yes, if Pabst were a champagne region in France," Mike said.

"Well, nonetheless, I took photos of those paintings, the ones that were street scenes from Paris and the other views. I especially like the one of the two children. We should probably get them appraised. Similar paintings are selling for a lot of money. The one large painting of the children might be a Renoir."

"Not a chance," I said. "They are good quality, but really— French Impressionists? The real thing?"

"Look, I just did some comparisons, nothing more. I'm saying that we need to look at all that clutter with new eyes. We need to be a lot more careful."

"If I see dogs playing cards, I'll yell," Garry said.

"Just saying," Larry said.

With renewed and chastened vigor, we reattacked the house. We looked through the bags of debris more closely, boxes rechecked, folders reopened, and by noon we'd found nothing more valuable than a couple of antique Windsor chairs. We looked at the furniture and guessed some might be Colonial, but these were only guesses. To ordinary people, it was just old furniture.

By the prearranged time of two thirty, we were exhausted by both the work and the expectation of finding treasure. Another full dumpster sat on the driveway. And our hands were empty of any booty. I wasn't sorry.

"So, nothing? No more suitcases, no more paintings?" Tommy said. "I'm disappointed. You guys had all the fun."

"At least the one bedroom is empty, and the kitchen is reasonably clean," I said. There was a debate over tossing the refrigerator and the stove into the dumpster. They were so filthy that both should be declared toxic. We tabled the idea. When we finished, we would revisit the set-aside items. Since Larry did the initial investigation on the paintings, he loaded them in his truck and took them home for more research, maybe contacting a Chicago art dealer. As we walked through our day's work, we were pleased.

"Just Allen's bedroom, the garage, and the basement," Garry said. "If this were a horror movie, it would all happen in the basement. Did you see the movie posters in Allen's bedroom? Some of them had to be sixty years old. Some of them have value, that I am sure of."

"You want them, you take them. That's the rule," I said.

"I think I will. I'm curious," Garry said. "If they're worth something, I'll tell you, and you can tell Barbara."

"The basement?" Mike said. "Yeah, that's where the torture chambers would be, where they buried the bodies maybe, like Edgar Allan Poe's 'The Cask of Amontillado.' I know, I can sense it."

"Do you need to be so vivid?" I scolded. "Tomorrow at nine. Three of us will start with the garage and the others in Allen's bedroom. That will clear the hallway in front of the stairs. We will finally get to Mike's basement torture chamber if there's time."

"It's not mine, it's the Fishers'," Mike said.

"As I said, you want it, you take it," I said.

* * *

Summer 1959

The Marigold Gang stood fidgeting in line at the Lincoln Theater in the mall. Lincolnville's shopping mall was one of the first built in a post-war community. New stores, shops, two department stores (by 1959 standards), and a state-of-the-art movie theater. We'd been to at least six films that summer: *Rio Bravo* with John Wayne; *Some Like It Hot*—we didn't tell our moms and Marilyn Monroe *was* hot; *Warlock* with Fonda and Widmark; *Last Train from Gun Hill* with Kirk Douglas (do you see a trend here?); *The Horse Soldiers* with Wayne and Holden; and *The Tingler*, which to this day still scares the bejesus out of me. I also went singly with my sister, Connie, to keep her company. Admittedly, Sandra Dee did tug a little at my young heart—the movie was *Gidget*. We were in line that Saturday to see *The Hound of the Baskervilles*. We figured any movie with a dog had to be good. It scared the pants off all of us and eventually led to a growing interest in Sherlock Holmes while in high school. You never know where inspiration comes from.

We loved the movies; they took us away. Allen's favorites were the creepy ones, *The Tingler, House on Haunted Hill,* and *The Mummy.* Two of those posters were on the walls of his bedroom. Sixty-five years later, I began to understand the reasons behind his strange fondness for oddity and terror. For boys our age, it was just cool. Horror movies were just pure escapism as long as you could believe they weren't real.

The scariest movie I'd seen as a kid was *The Time Machine,* which came out the following year. It was the scene where, in just six short years into my future, 1966, according to the movie, nuclear war would envelop the world, destroying everything. Six years until the end of time. Mike and Larry saw it with me, and it scared them too. Later, while we were seniors in high school in 1966, the world didn't end. Besides, I discovered girls, and there was more than enough drama in that discovery.

After the movie, we went to the mall's corner ice cream parlor. Chocolate shakes all around. Why is it that bullies hang out at ice cream parlors? Of course, none of us could be considered wimps or even timid. We were the Marigold Gang, and we were the Eagle Patrol. We smoked cigarettes— yeah, we were f'en tough guys. However, that afternoon, Billy Ray Ogden was again hanging out at his usual vantage point near the entry to the mall. His two serious mental-case buddies were with him, Stan and Norm. I was positive each had been dropped on their heads when babies—maybe multiple times. Billy Ray would walk behind the girls as they entered the mall, imitate their walks, tap them on their shoulder, then turn around like nothing was happening. He would often place his buddies to block the walkway, then come up from behind and snap their bras if the girls were old enough. As I said, a real sicko. But he saved his best for the solo boys, those coming in to take lessons at the Music Box, our town's source for all things music. In the shop was everything from sheet music to records. They sold instruments and had music teachers who supplemented their teaching incomes by trying to train young fingers to scratch out a sonata or blow out a march. As far as Billy Ray was concerned, this was the height of foolishness. Every student was a target.

Mothers escorted their prodigies, boys or girls, halfway to the music shop, kissed their future Benny Goodman on the forehead, and sent them on their way, not knowing the gauntlet they faced once around the corner. There, Stan and Norm acted as blockers, and Billy Ray would grab the instrument case and play catch with his henchmen. Sooner than later, it would drop and be dinged. He'd then go apologetic and allow the kid to move on, a kid in tears and fearful for his soul when their mother saw the damaged case of the rented instrument.

Now, how would the Marigold Gang resolve this attack on the high culture of Lincolnville? We began to formulate a plan of attack.

A few weeks later, on a pleasant Saturday afternoon, the mall was busy with shoppers and those enjoying the late June day. The five of us hung out at the ice cream parlor; yes, it was called a parlor. The overhead sign said so. We sat at the window, watching. A couple of girls from school passed by, laughing and smiling. They were hardly prim and proper, as my mom would say, with their skirts rolled up and their socks rolled down. Billy Ray and his minions sat at their usual roost, the end of a long wall that separated the plaza from the lawn that wove through the open landscape. They'd already harassed a couple of the girls, who quickly ran away, their only actual defense. Then a young Asian boy got out of a car; he carried what looked like a violin case. He was mercilessly set upon, first by Stan and Norm; then, like a matador after the picadors had harassed the victim, Billy Ray stepped in. He grabbed the case, tugged it away from the boy, shook it well, and pitched it onto the lawn. The boy was in tears as he walked over and retrieved his case. He then quickly ran across the lawn toward the music shop.

Happy with their triumph, they returned to their roost to wait for their next victim. On cue, Garry rounded the corner and gave us the thumbs-up. Billy Ray knew Garry, but there was little interaction between species: Neanderthal and Homo sapiens. Garry headed toward the music shop like an arrow shot from a bow, and he carried his sister's clarinet case.

"Hold on there, Garry boy," Billy Ray bellowed. "Don't you know there's a toll to pass through this part of the mall? It's a music appreciation toll, fifty cents. Pay me, and you can go on your way."

"Just go away, Ogden, don't be an ass," Garry said, continuing to march forward. "Bug off."

"You hear that, boys? Old Garry the fairy is telling me to 'bug off.' What do we do to fairies not paying the toll?"

"They have to leave something for bail," they chimed back.

"That's right, hand over the case, Garry the fairy."

"I will not—it's a brand-new clarinet. I'm going to learn how to play."

"Garry the fairy is going to play the clarinet? A fairy instrument if there ever was one. Come on, Hughes, hand it over, then you can go."

"Billy Ray, you know that Garry is part of that gang of kids, don't you?" Norm said. "The ones that saved that Black kid from drowning."

"That's two strikes," Billy said. "Fairy clarinets and Black kids. Damn, your bail just keeps going up. Now it's a buck. Now hand me the case."

Garry turned and began to walk away. Stan and Norm stood in his path. Billy Ray grabbed a part of the case and pulled. Garry pulled back hard, Billy pulled again, and suddenly, the case and Garry's hand, still firmly attached to the case and not to Garry, broke off and flew into the chest of Billy Ray. Blood sprayed in great spurts from the end of Garry's sleeve. Blood sprayed all over Billy Ray. Then the clarinet case, with Billy Ray standing next to it, hit the sidewalk. The lid popped open, and a spring-loaded fake snake jumped up, covered in silver and gold glitter. The sparkles flew up in a cloud covering Billy Ray like flies on crap. He tripped and fell spread-eagle on the concrete, still holding the bloody case with Garry's bloody hand attached. He stared at what he'd done and at Garry, who stood there yelling at him and holding up his arm. Blood squirted from the stump. He aimed it a Billy Ray—more glitter fell. Stan and Norm stood off to the side, hoping not to be seen as part of this awful deed and to avoid any glitter caught in the wind.

From inside the ice cream parlor, stunned patrons watched the play. When a man started to rush out to help Garry, I said, "Stop. Just watch; he's okay."

Then Larry stood and deliberately walked out of the shop, his trusty Kodak camera in his hand. Standing over Billy Ray, he took a half dozen photos of the glittered and bloodied bully, then one of the behanded Garry Hughes, a few of the stunned toadies, and then Garry's left hand popping out of the bloody sleeve of his coat. The last shot was Garry's grin.

"We do not want to see you here again, Billy Ray Ogden," Larry said. "If we hear you've messed with anyone else, I will pass these photos around school. Do you understand? Do you, glitter boy?"

Billy Ray Ogden slowly stood. His shirt was now bloodied with catsup (it was the best we could do on such short notice), and enough glitter had stuck to make him a Midwest version of a bad Las Vegas lounge act.

"Well, do you understand?" Larry asked again. Garry stood next to him. I and a dozen others in the parlor were laughing our proverbial butts off. Even some of the adults thought it was quite a triumph in prankstering.

Billy Ray mumbled something.

"What? Louder."

"I understand," came the meek answer.

"Good. Now take those two morons and get out of here, now!"

No one saw Billy Ray or his henchmen the rest of the summer; maybe he moved his act elsewhere, but we never found out. A few years later, I heard his family moved to Kansas City. His dad was in railroads, and I'm guessing he was transferred. There was a lot of that moving around in those days. The other two, Stan and Norm, were good kids. We went to high school with them, and Stan joined our scout troop (but not the Marigold Gang). They even attended our fiftieth high school reunion. It's the influences in life that make the man, and I'm glad we were able to set those two boys on the right path. I still wonder about Billy Ray and what happened to glitter boy. Maybe he found a new direction in life as an entertainer.

CHAPTER 5

Garry carried a cardboard box into the living room. "You have got to see this. I found it in the bottom of Allen's closet. Like most everything, it was under a pile of old clothes."

I looked inside and took a step back. "No way."

Inside was a bleached white skull, not one of those fake plastic Halloween skulls, but a real honest-to-God head. Next to it was the fake hand we used sixty-five years ago to spook what's-his-name. There was also a chrome revolver, a small tomahawk, four small velveteen-covered boxes, and clothing underneath those.

I immediately pulled out my phone and started dialing.

"Wait, Craig. I know we should call the police but hold on just a minute. Guys?" Garry yelled loud enough for Mike and Tommy to hear in the basement where they were beginning their explorations. Tommy was the first to arrive, the others fifteen seconds later.

"What's up?" Mike asked.

"Look in the box," I said.

They all looked in the box; then they all found seats. Larry had taken on his police face, as we called it. He had removed the skull and placed it on a round end table.

"Well, this is a fine kettle of fish we're in, isn't it?" I asked.

Larry groaned; Mike looked at Garry. Garry shrugged.

Tommy said something about staying another week in Alaska.

"The police have to be involved," I said. "Right?"

"Let's all take a deep breath here," Mike said. "And besides, that skull looks weird."

"How many have you seen?" Larry said.

"Look at those teeth. Humans don't have teeth that large, and the sloping forehead and protruding upper jaw overhang," Mike added. "If this is a human, he or she was sure ugly; it looks like a monkey's head."

"Too big for a monkey, maybe a gorilla?"

"Where the hell would Allen find a gorilla skull?"

"Get your phone out, google it," Tommy said.

I typed in skulls, and yes, it was not human. I did monkey skulls, and most of them were similar but smaller. It was not a gorilla's.

"How about orangutans," Mike said. "They are in Borneo and Sumatra, Southeast Asia. Allen spent time there fifty years ago."

We all looked at Mike.

"Yeah, Southeast Asia. Allen was in 'Nam, like me—maybe an orangutan," Mike said.

"Bingo," I said. "Orangutan, so maybe we don't have to call the police yet?"

"Mike, let me see the gun," Larry said.

Mike picked up the revolver, looked it over closely, then opened the cylinder. He handed it to Larry.

"I'll be damned. I haven't seen one of these since 'Nam. It's a Colt 45 with snake rounds in it. Larry, take them out. No need to keep this thing loaded."

"Snake rounds?" Larry said as he dropped the shells into his hand.

"Yeah, the revolver holds rounds that are .45-caliber shotgun shells, like a 410 shotgun, lays out a real nice pattern when you want to blow the head off a cobra or a krait," Mike said. "I hated those snakes. When we were out in the bush, they were everywhere. One guy I know got nicked on the little finger by a banded krait. It wasn't a foot long. He spent weeks in the hospital, damn near lost his hand, and did lose half his finger— nasty buggers. Somebody in the platoon always had one of these revolvers—it would take the head right off. Me? When I saw a snake, I didn't hang around to identify it. They were all poisonous far as I was concerned. The Cong were bad enough. They used snakes in nasty booby traps. The guys going after the Cong in those tunnels would have the bastards drop out of the ceiling. Awful."

"Remember when we used to hunt snakes back when we were kids?" I said. "Garter snakes, green snakes, rat snakes— remember that milk snake? Now that was a prize."

"You guys are creeping me out," Garry said. "Enough about snakes and orangutang skulls and fake hands. I won't be able to sleep tonight."

"See, we were tougher stuff back then." I laughed. "We've turned into septuagenarian wimps, girly-boys."

"Wimps? I am going with smarter and craftier," Tommy added. "Do you know there are no snakes in Alaska?"

"Just stop with the Alaska stuff," Mike said. "I remember it gets cold in Alaska."

"Gets cold here too—maybe colder."

"Your point?" Mike asked.

We dug through the rest of the box. There were two Purple Hearts—each Fisher man had earned one. There were service ribbons, a Silver Star from World War II, and a Silver Star from Vietnam. The uniform was an Army fatigue blouse, and Fisher stitched over the right pocket. A faded corporal's patch was in the left breast pocket. On the bottom of the box was a Conetta Mark 2 fighting knife, standard issue. According to

Mike, the knife and shirt were Vietnam era.

"I'm holding off calling the police," I said.

"Wise move," Larry said. "With what we've found so far, I'd not like to involve them in our treasure hunt. We have a few more hours. Let's see what we can accomplish. I don't know if I can take another full day of this; my lungs are beginning to close up."

I set the memento box on a table in the living room, which we'd begun to call the museum. All sorts of things had piled up: old movie posters, more paintings from the parents' bedroom (some looked interesting), additional pieces of furniture, even English crockery, ceramic dishes, and porcelain. All of it confused me. I never remembered Allen's parents as having any design or artistic sense. After returning from Germany and the war, Ronald Fisher worked for a manufacturing company in Harvey. He was a manufacturer's rep. He'd spend most of the week on the road visiting auto plants: Ford, Chevrolet, Oldsmobile, Nash, and Studebaker. His company supplied parts to automobile companies in four states. I remember Mr. Fisher as standoffish, and I never felt he was warm or inviting. He was big, square-featured, combed-back black hair, and a thin pencil mustache. He favored gray suits and white shirts, silver and black ties. On weekends it was plaid shirts and Bermuda shorts, a sartorial feature Allen inherited. The other guys' fathers were involved with their kids' activities: baseball, dance classes, family vacations, all the usual family things. Not Mr. Fisher. Allen; his sister, Brenda; and his brother, Dennis, were close to their mother. I didn't know much about Mr. Fisher. Brenda took off after her junior year in high school; Allen was in Vietnam then. She just up and left; a girlfriend picked her up. I never saw her again until the parents' funeral. Allen said he didn't know where she was. Dennis, three years younger than Brenda, stayed through high school. Then he disappeared for about ten years. By then, we all had moved from Marigold Court (actually, our parents moved, and we followed). Allen told us that Denny had moved to Wisconsin, somewhere near Milwaukee. I never saw the kid again; he would be maybe seventy-two now. Brenda would be, if alive, seventy-four. Neither came to Allen's funeral.

I called Barbara over the weekend and told her about the money. There was a long silence. "Thank you, I will let you know what to do," was all she said. I emailed her the photos of the money, furniture, and paintings; she was surprisingly circumspect. "Just keep them together," she said in a text. "I need some time to think about all this. Do you know any estate sale people?"

I told her I did not but would check into it.

All families are a jumble of emotions, experiences, rivalries, and even, to some degree, hatred. The adage about being able to choose your friends but not your relatives is as old as Cain and Abel. The Fishers had them all in spades. After Allen buried his parents in 1991, the gang supported him and ensured nothing sinister happened. Murder-suicides have a way of unnerving even the strongest. We gave him some room yet showed him we were there for support. During the last few years, his real heart gradually gave way, and diabetes took its toll. It's a shitty way to die; slowly, as if the body can't make up its mind. Eventually, it was a stroke. When he didn't show up for our Wednesday breakfast, Garry, during a welfare check, found him dead in the debris of the living room. Allen, naked, had been dead a couple of days, according to the ME. To die alone, in that ghost-filled house, we agreed that nothing was worse.

Barbara and Steve came for the funeral and the burial. His ashes were placed near his parents. Then they left. We began the housecleaning three months later. As I looked around that afternoon, I hoped we would finish tomorrow. Like the others, my lungs and back couldn't take much more. Boy, was I wrong.

* * *

Day three, bin three. The garage was the easiest—once we got the door open. Surprisingly, the door was bolted shut with long lag bolts set into the frame. They dropped the new bin ten feet outside the roll-up door. The Studebaker Lark was, surprisingly, in excellent shape. While not a collector's car, there would be somebody out there who'd spring some dinero for a pristine 1963 turquoise blue relic of America's auto industry. While not as stylish as the Golden Hawk, it was in fine condition, with no rust, and the interior was pristine. We left it where it sat; the flat tires made moving it impossible. Garry was disappointed that it wasn't an Avanti. The high-performance Studebaker vehicle still caught the automotive world's imagination.

We rolled Allen's Harley onto the driveway; we would roll it back at the end of the day. We did not try to start it. Larry rode one in Chicago and had experience with Harleys. On the shelves and in cabinets, we found power tools and boxes of the usual screws, nails, and bolts like every other garage in the good old U.S. of A. Hanging on the wall was Allen's steel 26" Schwinn bicycle. I remembered when he bought it used from a bike shop in the Heights. He lovingly sanded it down and hand-painted it bright red, used electrical tape to reupholster the seat, and with some straps and metal strips, constructed a basket he mounted behind the seat. It was a bike design with a triangular-shaped metal filler piece between the knees. He painted the words "Demon" on both sides. Where there was chrome, he burnished it mirror bright. Afterward, he said, "The red Demon is the best damn bike in Lincolnville." None of us could argue. Back then, you had to have a license on your bike, and he still had the metal one issued in 1958 secured to the spokes. Its value was personal, and maybe a kid out there needed a project. He could have it. With some love, a good cleaning, and new balloon tires, the Demon would ride again.

Larry and Mike returned to the basement.

I stood in the garage for a minute after they left. There was something about the Studebaker that bugged me, but I couldn't put my finger on it.. We decided to set up a relay system so we wouldn't have to climb the steps. From the basement to the stairs, the landing, the first floor, and the bin. We'd each take turns at the stations.

Sometime in the distant past, Mrs. Fisher put up preserves—the usual kinds: peaches, pickles, small apples in cinnamon soaked in red food coloring. Many were unidentifiable now that the labels were gone. Some were faded, and a couple of packed pickle jars had the date 9/11/85, almost forty-year pickles—no thank you. There were shelves of empty Mason jars. I feared that if one of the preserves fell and busted open, we would all die of botulism poisoning or some rare fungus or disease. All the jars, empty and full, made it safely to the bin.

Larry, as he passed the last box to Garry on the landing, asked, "Anybody have a tape measure?"

"I've got a twelve-footer in my truck," Tommy said.

"I was hoping for a long one, fifty or sixty feet," Larry answered.

"I saw one in the garage," I said. "Be right back."

When I returned from the garage, I followed Larry down into the basement. The room at the bottom of the stairs was what was affectionately called in suburbia the rec room. It covered half the basement. The walls were wood paneled with that faux knotty pine look, linoleum floor, shag area rug, and dropdown lighting. A heater was installed on the basement wall, and the other wall, free standing, separated the laundry room (and the dozens of canning shelves now empty). The room had a bar, with mirror-type beer signs on the wall behind: Schlitz, Pabst, Old Style, Old Chicago, Meister Brau, and Falstaff. A dozen local beer bottles lined the shelf; I guessed not one newer than 2000. There were posters for the Bears, the White Sox, and the Blackhawks.

"This looks like a thousand other basement rec rooms in Chicago," I said to Larry.

"Remember when our dads would buy a case of beer and religiously put the bottles back into the case, then exchange the case for a full one?" Tommy said joining us. "Hell, they were environmentalists before the word *recycle* was invented."

"Dad kept a couple of empty Meister Brau bottles around," I said, "just in case one bottle would break. You had to have a full case to get the full refund."

"Life was simpler then, right?"

"What do you need the tape measure for?" I asked.

"I don't know; it's been bugging me while I was emptying the place. The two rooms seem smaller down here than upstairs," Larry said. "Hold one end against the rec room wall; I'll pull it through the door and to the laundry room. Then we'll check upstairs."

We did that and found that upstairs was about eight feet longer. The five of us stood in the basement and pondered the discrepancy.

"Why would the basement be smaller?" Mike said.

"It shouldn't be," I said. "It would extend under the entire house. Just a simple concrete box under the house, then frame up, slap on a roof, bingo, suburbia."

"Architects know these things; it is good to have an expert," Tommy said.

"That's what a college degree and a state license will get you," I said.

"Maybe a secret room?"

"Ooh, there's a thought," Garry said. "A secret laboratory." It was said with a thick German accent. Boris Karloff would not have been impressed.

"Outside there's window wells on that wall." I pointed. "None in amongst the shelves."

"And that's the end with the garage," Mike clarified as he pointed.

"Right, no windows," I said.

We walked to the recently cleared wooden canning shelves and began to look under and over the length of the wall; the tape said the house's depth was thirty-two feet. Between the upstairs and downstairs, there was a space about 8' x 32' missing.

"I knew it," Larry said as he slowly inspected the wall. "It's drywall behind the shelves, not concrete block like the other walls." He pointed. "It's just painted drywall."

Mike pointed a flashlight over Larry's shoulder. "What's this?" He reached over the middle shelf. "A handle." He turned it.

The wall and shelf popped and a section about three feet wide moved—it was hinged on the right inside. The hinges were invisible from the outside.

"Does it open?" Garry said.

"It does something," Mike said as Larry pushed. With a creak, a clunk, and a metal-on-metal squeal from the hinges, the door, with shelves, swung inward.

"I told you; I told you. Edgar Allan Poe would be shaking right now," Mike said.

"Just remain calm," Larry said.

The room was completely dark inside; two light bulbs hung from the ceiling on electric cords. Cardboard boxes were piled to the right and the floor was concrete, unlike the rest of the basement, which was linoleum. Two white dust–covered boxes sat against the wall. They hummed.

"Are those freezers?" Mike asked.

I pulled a penlight from my pocket and waved it around. "There's a switch on the wall, Tommy."

The two bulbs cast a stark and sharply shadowed light. It was eerie.

"Larry, take a look in that freezer," I said. I used the flashlight as a pointer.

Larry turned to me and, in the wash of his flashlight, stated, "No way, not a chance."

"Come on. You were a cop. What's the big deal?" Mike said.

"Let's see, a hoarder's house, two people murdered, a secret room, two Sears Robuck Coldspot freezers; let me think. Forty years a cop says nothing good can come out of this."

Tommy walked over to the box on the right. "There's no padlock as you see in the movies—probably nothing more than frozen pies to go with all the canned fruit jars." He pulled up the handle, the lid popped up, white frost rose and turned to fog in the lights.

"Craig, give me the flashlight," Tommy said. He waved the light into the misty void, looked, stepped back, and then at me. His eyes were bugging out of his head. "I think it is now time to call the police."

CHAPTER 6

We reluctantly opened the other box. We had to share the horror in the freezers; the same thing appeared in each. I was shaking. The others looked pale and stunned. We had to look; there was no alternative. Tommy said once was enough—he left and went upstairs. The secret room's smell was dank and musty. The only light came from the two hanging bulbs and the spill through the open door. Inside both Coldspot freezers were large bundles of plastic-wrapped, human-sized pieces fitted into roughly the shape of the number 2. They were stacked one on the other in overlapping layers. We knew they were human bodies because a desiccated face appeared through the plastic in each. How many bodies were in each freezer? It was impossible to tell. The plastic wrap was the kind that sticks to itself as you wrap meat. In these freezers, the plastic-wrapped meat and what was visible through the transparent film was human—or was once human. Now, frozen, dried, and desiccated bundles of what were once human beings nearly filled the boxes. We understood what we saw. Whether the bodies were clothed or not was difficult to make out. Larry whispered that all of us should leave the room and wait outside. "And don't touch anything else." Larry spent a few minutes assessing the scene, then joined us in the rec room.

I called the police; it didn't take additional prompting.

At the opposite end of the narrow room were more than a dozen unlabeled cardboard boxes and suitcases stacked under a folding table. They were the old-fashioned kind, cardboard and covered with fake leather.

"Maybe they are Halloween decorations," Garry said, pointing to the freezers. "Do you remember the Fishers doing Halloween?"

As to decorations, not a chance. We all agreed we'd never seen the Fishers celebrate anything. Allen did not celebrate Christmas, even when we exchanged gifts for a few years. We all had invited Allen over for Thanksgiving at one time or another, and he would politely pass. Eventually, we gave up asking.

"As best as I can make out," Larry said, "at least four bodies are in there, two in each box. They have been there a long time. They might be two men and two women, the men in the right box, the women in the other. I don't know what's in the boxes and suitcases—but I want to find out."

We heard steps on the floor overhead, then a yell from the top of the stairs. "Chief Larry Martini? Police. It's Audrey."

"We are downstairs, Audrey," Larry answered.

Tommy led two uniformed men down the stairs, behind them a middle-aged Black woman in a business suit. A blousy scarf wrapped her neck. She was cute, wore gold wire-rimmed glasses, and her braided hair was pulled back and away from her face.

"Gentlemen, this is Detective Audrey King, lead detective with the Lincolnville Police," Larry said.

"I'm the *only* detective with the Lincolnville Police," Audrey said with a laugh. "Good to see you again, Chief. You are still missed."

"It has been almost twenty years since I left, Audrey," Larry answered. "But thanks. It's probably the Monday donuts you miss the most."

"You left a good impression and even bigger shoes. There have been three chiefs since you retired."

"I know. Maybe next time, you should have me on the selection committee."

"Were it that easy, politics get involved." She looked at us. "So, this is the infamous Marigold Gang you've talked about?"

We made our introductions.

"And what have you discovered?" the detective asked as she looked around. "There's a dank, musty smell around."

"You should have seen the place last Friday," Mike said. "We've taken out four dumpster loads."

"Hoarders?" she asked.

"Yes, and a dear friend. Just awful," I said.

Larry led the detective through the basement to the entry to the secret room. The rest of us civilians gathered on the driveway. There were two patrol Interceptors and a Ford 500 on the street.

"What the hell is going on?" Tommy declared. "Those bodies can't be genuine. Really? Dead bodies wrapped in Saran Wrap? Come on."

Tommy was on edge. It had become clear that Alaska was no longer at the forefront of his thinking. Heather would have a difficult night bringing Tommy down.

"Whatever this is, it took place long ago," Garry said. "Did you notice no footprints in the dust, just ours? No one had been in that room for a long time."

We all agreed to that. As soon as we discovered the bodies, we backed out. There were no other prints in the dust.

"Do you think Allen was involved?" Tommy said.

"Larry will let us know," Mike said. He'd been quiet since the discovery. "They will get to the bottom of this, whatever 'this' is."

"You and your damn premonitions," Tommy said. "I never want to hear about Edgar Allan Poe again."

As we waited, a black SUV parked at the curb. By this time, there was a bizarre mix of police cars, our vehicles, this sinister SUV, not to mention the other residents' cars and trucks parked on the court. Painted discreetly on the door of the SUV was LINCOLNVILLE CORONER.

Delmar Johnson walked across the street to join us.

"What the hell is all this?" Johnson asked. "I finally get a day off, and Rose tells me there are police cars all over the court. What did you guys do?"

"We found bodies in the basement," I said, somewhat more matter-of-factly than I wanted to. "Dead bodies."

"Of course, all bodies are dead," Garry said. "Just that these were wrapped in Saran Wrap and loaded into freezers."

"More than one freezer?" Johnson asked.

"Of course, freezers always come in pairs, like a pair of scissors," Garry said.

"We don't know that for sure. Maybe they are not real— you know, fake dead bodies," Tommy quickly added.

"What else could they be? And if they were fake, why wrap them in Saran Wrap?" Garry said.

I looked at Delmar. I swear the man was having trouble breathing.

"Bodies? Here? No way—any idea who they were?" Johnson said, painfully looking at the house.

"No, and it's in the hands of the police now. Maybe they will finish the cleanout," Mike said. "I know my waning enthusiasm for this adventure has totally dried up."

A tall, thin, gray-haired man exited the black SUV wearing a blue windbreaker that read CORONER on the back in yellow capital letters. He then walked to the vehicle's rear, and the hatch automatically popped open. Two minutes later, with practiced moves, he had slipped off the windbreaker and donned a hood-ed white suit made from paper. He placed a canvas bag over his left shoulder and, with two booties in his right hand, passed us without saying a word. He went to the Fisher front door, where one of the officers had relocated from the rec room and taken up his new position. The officer held a clipboard, and the man wrote something. There the coroner slipped on the booties and disappeared inside. Ten seconds later, Larry walked out.

"Our work is done here, at least for now," Larry said. "Audrey declared this as a possible crime scene. I explained to her why we were there and what we'd been doing. She will have questions for us later. I gave one of the officers your phone numbers. They will call to set up interviews."

"I'm concerned about the money and artwork," I said. "Until now, it was reasonably straightforward."

As Mike put it, this entire undertaking was straightforward until it wasn't. We then deflected questions from the neigh-bors. A young woman, waving what looked like credentials in a plastic pouch, pushed her way to the front claiming she was from the local press. I guess that one of the neighbors passed the word about discovering a heinous crime, bodies, blood, gore, etc. Two other women, claiming to be with the Southside News Blog, began asking questions into their phones and then pointing the phone at us. We all just raised our hands and said we knew nothing—the classic *Hogan's Heroes* Sergeant Schultz defense, which, of course, meant nothing to any of the twen-ty-something news bloggers.

Two hours later, only Larry and I remained. Detective Au-drey King allowed the others to leave. I told them I would keep them apprised of what was happening. Two ambulances arrived, gurneys went in and out, and the Saran Wrap bundles (covered with sheets, to the disappointment of the bystanders, news journalists, and bloggers) were loaded and left. I had seen enough.

"I'm going home. Can I lock the place up?" I said to Larry.

"Audrey is having the forensics guys photograph and do their thing," Larry said. "We all agree the scene in that secret room is old. Only our steps were in the dust, and I assured her we didn't touch anything except the freezer handles. The coroner believes there are two men and two women, but he can't tell their age or race. It will take at least twenty-four hours for the bodies to thaw. How long they've been here, not even a guess. Audrey is one of the best detectives on the Southside, but there are limits. What I learn, I'll tell you."

"And the money?"

"It's fine where it is, for now. Just don't go and remove it. And tell Garry too. I'm sure he won't do something stupid. Tell him that it might be evidence in this case."

"Any IDs?"

"After they thaw. Dick will unwrap the bodies at the morgue."

"Dick?"

"Dick Saperstein, the coroner. Like when I was chief, he had a small staff and just one assistant. Dick is excellent; he came out of Cook County. If there are any identifications, he will make an announcement. Until then, we stand on the side-lines."

Five hours had passed since we made the discovery. I talk-ed with Detective King for a few minutes, and she reiterated what Larry said. She asked me a few questions, all general stuff. She took notes and asked for the phone numbers of Allen's kids. I locked up the house and gave the detective a spare key. Police DO NOT ENTER tape was strung across the doors. A rust-ed-out gray Camry pulled to the curb as she and I walked away from the house. A man about my age left the driver's side and went to the rear passenger door facing us. He helped a woman slowly exit the car. When she stood upright, he placed a cane in her hand. At that moment, more than sixty years flashed by; these were Allen's siblings, Brenda and Dennis Fisher. I had no idea why they were here, but I could guess.

CHAPTER 7

The Fishers slowly walked up the driveway to the three of us. Dennis led the way, and Brenda followed at a surprisingly swift gait, cane and all. Both appeared focused.

"I'm Detective King. Can I help you?"

"Yes, you can get off our property," Dennis Fisher said, a belligerent tone in his voice.

"And what's that damn box doing on the driveway? Anything in that is ours," Brenda Fisher said, using her cane as a pointer.

"And you two are?" King asked.

"I'm Brenda Wysocki, and this is my brother Dennis Fisher. This was our parents' house; I'm here to claim it. It is rightfully ours." She turned and looked at me.

"You a cop?" she asked, pointing her cane.

"No, a friend of your brother's. We are cleaning out the house."

"Who told you to do that?" Dennis Fisher said.

"Allen's daughter, Barbara. She asked us; we were Allen's—"

"I don't give a damn who you are," Wysocki said. "And that niece has no right to do anything with the house. She's out in California or some other goddamn place."

"Allen's will made it very clear about the ownership of the house and all the belongings," Larry said. "His children inherited everything, and there was no mention of the two of you."

"My brother was a bastard. He had no right to any of this," Wysocki said, waving about the cane. "Now that he's dead, I am the oldest, and it should all be mine."

"What do you two know about the bodies found in the basement?" Detective King asked.

"Bodies? In the basement? What bodies?" Dennis said. There was shock on the man's face.

"You are here because of the news broadcast. It was on tonight's early news," King said. She hooked her thumb to one of the white panel trucks with a dish on its roof. The side panel read "WWKW—The Real News from the Center of America."

"After Allen's death, we tried for weeks to contact both of you—nothing," I said. "Your niece had an address, and that's all. If it weren't for the fact I recognized you, we wouldn't be having this conversation. You could be impostors."

"You knew us?" Wysocki said. "How?"

"I lived right over there as a kid, and Larry here lived there. We know you, and we also knew when you left in the sixties. And you, too, Dennis. You couldn't wait to get out of here."

"You were part of that snot-nosed gang that lived around here? I'd have thought you would all be dead by now. This changes nothing, Allen's will or not. The house is ours."

"I will have questions for the both of you. I need your phone numbers and addresses," King said.

"We don't know nothing about no bodies," Dennis said. "Nothing."

"Where do you live?"

"New Lenox since Sis's husband died. I've been using a bedroom and caring for her," Dennis said.

"You were twenty miles away and couldn't attend your brother's funeral. What a hard-hearted pair," Larry said.

"As I said, he was a bastard," Wysocki said.

"And you two are vultures here to pick over the bones," I said.

"The house is a crime scene—no one in or out. Give the police officer all the information he asks for. I will call you to set up an interview," King said.

"We don't know anything," Dennis said.

"I'll determine that."

King and Larry left us and walked to her car, a gray-green Ford 500. I stood there with the Fishers wishing I were home holding that cocktail I'd been thinking of for the last four hours. Taking a few steps away from the Fishers, I called Penny. She laughed in a macabre manner and said she understood why I'd be late. She was intrigued by the bodies in the basement and wanted to hear everything. I said my goodbyes to Larry and Audrey, and before the Fishers could say anything, I walked to my car and drove past the one police car that remained, then my old house at the end of the cul-de-sac. The Fisher siblings remained standing in the driveway.

* * *

Mike said, "Well, that was a fun and bizarre week," as he pulled out his chair at Bell's. "Not every day you find four bodies in a freezer."

"Four dead bodies," Tommy said.

"Again, you are being redundant," Mike said. "Calling them bodies infers them to be dead."

"Just stop. It's too early. As always, you are making my head hurt," I said. I raised my hand and pointed. Karen acknowledged and filled Mike's coffee cup. "I have news."

"About the money? Do we get to split it? There's a finder's fee?" Tommy said.

"No. Good thoughts, though, but no, Thomas. Larry is bringing Detective King here this morning. She has an update."

"I drove by Allen's, and the bin was gone. Did she have it removed?" Garry asked.

"I don't know. You will have to ask her."

"They're here," Tommy said, nodding toward the front door.

Larry and the detective took seats at the end of the table. We hadn't had a guest at the weekly meeting in forever. Karen took everyone's order.

"Detective King is on my tab, Karen," Larry said.

I smiled at Karen. "We'll all split it."

"Damn big spenders here, Detective King," Karen said, looking around the table. "Last time they had a guest, he picked up the tab."

"Right," Garry said. "It was that insurance guy, Harry something; he was trying to sell us annuities."

"Yeah, that didn't go well," Larry said. "Audrey, do you want to start?"

Detective King removed a spiral notebook and flipped through the pages. She stopped and looked at the five of us. "First of all, there was no identification on any of the bodies. The coroner is still trying to lift fingerprints, but all the fingers were so desiccated it might be impossible. Based on X-rays, they are two women and two men. All in their early twenties—one of the women had had a child, or children. He is also processing DNA, but they have been dead so long they are probably not in any database. There might be a chance at a familial match, but that's a very long shot."

"How long does he think they were there?" Garry asked.

"The medical examiner, Dick Saperstein, estimates at least fifty years, maybe longer."

"Good God, since the 1960s?" I asked.

"Possibly. One of my staff, a young recruit, is looking into missing persons from that period, but that's an even longer shot. The bodies also look like they have been in that room that long. Based on the dust and conditions, it is a supposition on my part—no way to confirm it. We are also beginning to go through the cartons and suitcases. There's clothing and personal effects, also old."

"And the artwork on the walls?" I asked.

"Also under review."

"I can't believe that Allen and his family lived in that house with those bodies for fifty years; damn," Garry said. "The paper money and the coins were all dated from around that time."

"Correct. We are trying to find connections if there are any. It will be difficult," King added. "All the bodies had been shot, center chest, excellent marksmanship. They also had broken arms, and two had cracked ribs and lung punctures; Dick believes they were broken to get them to fit into the freezers. The men's legs were severed to get them to fit."

Karen had just walked up, heard Audrey, turned gray, then spun around and walked away.

"Damn," Larry said, watching Karen leave. "If it was from the early sixties, all of us, except Garry, were still living on the court then. Allen, obviously, never said anything about this."

"Assuming he even knew. It had to be his folks or Mr. Fisher," Mike said.

"We are looking at the probability of homicides, even murder," King said. "There were no obvious defensive wounds, but again, it is hard to tell."

"That room, how did Ron Fisher build that room?" I asked. "It took time and effort; you just don't sneak those in."

"He was handy. He was always building things," Tommy said. "There's that brick barbeque in the backyard, and I remember him building that. And he also put that garage addition on in 1962, if I remember right. Then there was the summer we spent at scout camp in Michigan. I was fifteen, and we were camp counselors."

"Right, we were gone from early June through mid-August 1963," Mike said. "When we got back, the rec room was complete. Allen was pissed. He wanted to help his father build it. Then he put that automatic door in when he built the garage. He was the first on the block."

"Then everybody added one," I said. "So high-tech then."

"And it's broken now. We found that out. Then I don't remember the Studebaker. Weird."

A chuckle passed around the table.

"He could have built the room around then, but why?" I asked. "I can't believe we would watch TV in that basement with Allen, those bodies not twenty feet away. Jeez."

"That does help to give me a starting point," King said. "I'll let Albert know."

"Albert?" Tommy said.

"That's my assistant, Corporal Albert Cummins. My boss is concerned this is a very cold case—no pun intended. And, with all that's happening in the village, he's not giving me the resources I need. That's to be expected. Fifty years is a long time, and the prime suspects are all dead. There is very little interest in this case, and resources can be better allocated."

Karen, having recovered, brought breakfast. We ate in silence, each mulling over thoughts of the past half-century.

"I told Barbara what we found," I said. "She was stunned and, I think, afraid. She and her brother had only been in the house several times after their mother moved out in the early 1980s. They never went back, especially after what Ron Fisher did in 1991."

"What happened then?" King asked.

"I haven't told Audrey yet," Larry said. He turned to the

detective. "In 1991, when it happened, I was a captain of the 10th District in the Chicago Police Department. I came to Lincolnville in 1994, but I knew all about it. It was a week before Christmas. Allen came home from work and found his mother in bed, dead. She had been shot. She had had terminal pancreatic cancer. Ron was lying next to her. He'd shot himself. The World War II Colt 45 pistol was lying on the bed. Two bullet casings were found. The bullets and the casing were matched to the pistol. It was declared murder and suicide."

"It was *that* murder-suicide?" King said. "I was about seven then and lived a few blocks away on Lakeside."

"Yes, it shook all of us," Larry said. "We all lived elsewhere then, all married, some with kids. Allen was the only one still living on the court and lived in the house. His parents' deaths broke him. That's when the hoarding began in earnest, I think."

A couple of us remembered that there was a lot of stuff already in the house and that the hoarding may have extended back to his parents. We all agreed. For the last thirty-three years, Allen lived with what happened—if what he was going through was called living. I told Detective King about his parents' funeral; we all were there for Allen. His siblings, the two from the driveway, didn't come. His ex-wife, Bess, came with her husband. They were there with Barbara and Steve for a few hours. Then they all left. We learned in 2012 from Allen that Bess died from cancer. Even after Allen and Bess split in 1982, he kept in contact with his kids. Barbara works for Microsoft. Steve is in Charlotte; and works for Bank of America. I was the only person from the gang Barbara kept in contact with.

"What a mess," King said.

"That's just the half of it," Garry said. "We tried to keep Allen together the best we could. Over the last ten years, his heart began to fail, and his diabetes got progressively worse. I found him in the living room. He had died from a stroke maybe three days earlier. Barbara is the executor of his estate, such as it is. She and Steve came to the funeral. She was the one that asked Craig to close and clear out everything, to put the house up for sale, and get what he could. You know the rest."

"Sad," King said. "And now these bodies. You told Barbara?"

"Yes," I said. "She took it hard. I can only imagine what she's thinking. She said she knew nothing about the basement and couldn't remember even being downstairs. She remembered the furniture and the paintings; she never could figure out where they could have come from. She was sure her father knew nothing about any of it. It was his folks' stuff. Allen's education was high school and the Army; he was forty-three when her grandparents died. She believes to this day that's when everything stopped. She didn't know that he'd become a hermit and a hoarder. His only time out of that house was when he went to work and met us for breakfast."

"What did he do?" King asked as she made notes.

"He was with the school district," I said. "He was a janitor and a bus driver. He lived simply and always seemed to have enough money. We haven't a clue where he got that cash and gold."

"We did a search, and the cash isn't connected to anything in the FBI files, the serial numbers are non-sequential, and the gold is untraceable. Right now, it's not involved in anything illegal—at least so far."

"One hell of a mystery," Tommy said.

"I need your help. I have a small window here; that's my boss's order," Audrey said. "Could you guys meet me tomorrow at the house? We can walk through, and you can help me decipher what's left. I was hoping you could give me an idea about the family, Allen's folks, and the upstairs and downstairs. You knew him back when this all went down. Maybe between the five of you, something will jog."

"You want us to join your investigation?" Mike said, his voice rising.

"Calm down, Kojak. She needs our input," Larry said. "Sure, I think we can help. At least we can't muck it up."

CHAPTER 8

November 22, 1963

It was cold, freeze your ass off, cold. By the time darkness took the woods, we had finished setting up the tents at the Indiana Dunes State Park campsite. The campfire, built by the Tenderfeet, was up and roaring. As the chief cook, I began to get dinner organized. The whole troop was mute and somber. Since the terrible announcement earlier that afternoon, the news of President Kennedy's assassination had seized every American's heart and cut deeply into the blood and bone of America. There was some discussion amongst the scout leaders about putting the camping trip off, but Tommy's dad, the scoutmaster, decided there was little they could do about what had happened in Dallas. We had planned the two-day winter camp at the dunes for months; he would go forward with those that wanted to go. A half dozen boys stayed home, and twenty elected to stay on—the parents of the boys who stayed home understood but wanted their boys to remain close. America was ripe with paranoia about the Russians and what they might do after the president's death.

We assembled at the church school parking lot. Mr. Ellis stood beside the rented school bus and talked to the driver. The driver, Mr. Mathew, would take us to the campground and drop us off. He would be back Sunday at noon to collect us. My dad followed in our Ford station wagon, towing the trailer that carried our tents and gear. Mr. Martini, in his Plymouth, carried a few of the youngest boys. It was Eagle Patrol's job to manage the remaining fourteen boys on the bus.

Our scout troop of twenty-two boys had, for weeks, been excited about this adventure. The president's funeral and memorial events were planned for the following week, and we would be home long before the funeral started. When the news of the assassination reached Lincolnville, the trailer had already been loaded, the food bought, and the rucksacks filled. It would be a costly logistics nightmare if we canceled the trip. We left at four o'clock Friday afternoon, and our short caravan drove north the hour and a half to the campground in amongst the park's dunes. Everyone had their ears glued to car radios and transistor radios.

The troop had two successful campouts that year, in late spring and midsummer. This did not include the time spent at the Southside Council's Camp Betz in Michigan. Our Eagle Patrol was the most experienced and were the camp's leaders. Allen Fisher led our patrol. He was the oldest and biggest and a Life Scout. His backup was the rest of us, the Marigold Gang. Our job was to get the younger boys situated and make sure they remained free of frostbite and hypothermia. Snow was forecast, so tents were quickly set up, wood gathered, campfires started, and the evening meal underway. The older boys worked with the youngsters, Tenderfeet and Second-Class scouts, to prepare for the night. It was dark before we arrived, we finished dinner at eight thirty, and everyone was turned in by ten.

I was the troop quartermaster, and my primary job was cooking. Dad stood back and let me do my best to avoid trouble. While not exceptionally creative, I was good at it. Mike gave me a hand, and I assigned three younger boys to get water boiling, start the dinner fire, and get the various pots and pans out of the trailer. I assigned spots along one of the picnic tables to three of the boys. I laid out carrots and potatoes to be peeled and cut up. I volunteered one Second-Class scout to cut up the onions and another to dust the five pounds of beef cubes with flour, salt, and pepper. They did well. No one lost a finger, though the boys cried during the onion affair. By seven, I was stirring a massive twenty-gallon kettle of Irish beef stew. The aromas filled the campground. Also experienced, Larry and Garry set up the campground tables and ensured everyone had knives, forks, and spoons. The cups and bowls were Army surplus. This was the fourth year for a winter camp of our troop—the gang kept everyone else in line.

A five-mile hike was scheduled for the next morning. We'd hike from the campground down to Lake Michigan, then a couple of miles up the beach along the massive dunes, then wind our way back to the camp. I assigned three younger scouts to make two dozen sandwiches after breakfast. The hike would begin at 9:30 a.m.

World War II veteran Mr. Martini, Larry's dad, would lead the hike. While we cooked dinner, he, Mr. Ellis, and my father hung around a large transistor radio listening to the news, none of it good. Allen's father never joined these campouts; we seldom saw him at scouting events. Mr. Hughes, Garry's dad, was working that weekend; but Garry came. Mr. Jasicki, Mike's father, needed to be home that weekend and had to stay with his family. Mike said his mother was sure the Russians would attack and wanted everyone to stay home. With a bit of hard negotiating, Mike was allowed to go on the camping trip. But if word came that the missiles were on the way, Lucy hoped he could make it home to be with his family when the end came. Everyone understood; those were crazy times.

The Boy Scouts were important to all of us. As far as helping boys grow into men, nothing was and is currently better. Today, I'm not even remotely close to scouting. Penny and I never had children, so my experiences with today's scouting world are through the fellows and their grandkids. I'm pleased that girls and young women can join the scouts and share the adventures, experiences, and knowledge my friends and I gained and enjoyed. Whatever is happening now is not the fault of scouting but the predations of a few disturbed and even deranged individuals. We only have to look at our other institutions—business, religion, and politics—to see that scouting, part of this confused society, is no less sacred than a governor's mansion. Sadly, moral vigilance is critical.

John F. Kennedy's assassination shocked not only America but the world. How much it would change the world wouldn't be understood that weekend. It would be years before the cumulative effects would be comprehended. Mrs. Jasicki was not alone in her fear that the Russians would soon be nuking every major city. That weekend we twenty-two boys managed to retain our innocence. After we returned home, there would be more than enough time to regain our paranoia.

Winter camping requires planning, leadership, and instruction. Wear warm bedclothes, pajamas, socks, and use double and triple blankets if you don't have a sleeping bag. Put at least three layers of blankets under you; keep your clothes dry; damp clothing wicks away body heat. That's why pajamas are necessary. Sleeping in your day clothes will dampen them and, in the morning, can chill you quickly. Boots must also be kept dry—at least you don't have to worry about creepy crawlers climbing into your boots like in the summer.

Dinner was a success, even if I must toot my own horn. We had more than enough, and some of the fellows had seconds. The best part was the dumplings made from dollops of biscuit dough dropped into the boiling stew. The best remedy for the cold is a full stomach. Dessert was fudge brownies baked in two massive Dutch ovens set over the coals of the fire.

Four boys were assigned KP duties. Surprisingly no one complained. Everything was buttoned up by nine. Everyone was snug in their cocoons by ten. I could hear my father, Mr. Ellis, and Mr. Martini talking about the assassination and, in the background, the news on the radio. I also knew they covertly shared a bottle of bourbon my father brought along, no fancy glasses, just tin cups. Later, when I asked, I learned it was for medicinal reasons and to keep away the cold.

Morning unhurriedly appeared as gray light in the winter haze that hung in the bare hardwoods and pine scrub. Larry, Allen, and I were up early to start the fires and breakfast. The boys emerged from the tents like shivering wraiths. Some wandered around, lost in the light fog that hung along the ground, others walked to the campground's communal bathroom a hundred feet away, and others stood next to the fire wrapped with blankets. It would take an hour to get them awake. Nobody froze to death—another victory.

"Coffee smells good," Mr. Ellis said as he zipped his coat and tightened his stocking cap. "Is it ready?"

"Yes, sir, Mr. Ellis. Hot and thick, just the way you like it," Larry said. "Sugar is on the table, and milk is in that small bottle. Sorry, we don't have cream."

"The privations of camping," Mr. Ellis said with a smile.

"Huh," Larry answered.

Mr. Ellis added, "Larry, you might corral the fellows and ensure they get to the restrooms. This winter camp is the first time for many of them. Sometimes you have to remind them of the obvious things to do. Craig, what's for breakfast?"

"Scrambled eggs and bacon; also making some biscuits," I said.

"Need help?"

"You can start cracking the eggs. There are three dozen in the cooler. I'll get fewer shells if you do it than the Tenderfeet. I'll start the bacon; that usually gets everyone going. Hot cocoa is in the pot there."

While Mr. Ellis cracked the eggs, I mixed up Bisquick and punched out a couple of dozen biscuits; they cooked quickly in the Dutch ovens. My father walked by with a cup of coffee.

"Sleep well?" he asked.

"Yes, sir. At about two in the morning, I ran to the restroom. The collective snoring would have scared away the bears, that's for sure."

"Careful there, Son. Your tent wasn't all that quiet."

"I'm putting the bacon on." I saw Tommy stumble out of his tent. I said, "I need your help watching the bacon; hurry up."

He looked at me, then the restroom, then me. "Five minutes?"

"You got three. Move it."

"Slave driver." I heard mumbling.

Breakfast went well, and there was nothing left. A few even scraped the pans for the last of the eggs. The pots for dishwashing were set on the grills. We had a system with two boys scraping the plates, then dropping the dishes into the first pot of soapy water, two boys giving them a scrubbing, then passing on the dishes to two more who would give them a rinse. At the end of the line, two more dried the dishes and stacked the tinware on the table. Last done were the pots and pans. This was required after every meal; we needed the pots for the next meal. I assigned four boys to make the sandwiches, PB&J.

At nine, Allen gathered everyone and checked their backpacks, boots, and gloves. The temperature was in the mid-twenties. There had been a dusting of snow the previous night. Mr.

Martini said that the news predicted snow that afternoon.

"Allen, you watch the weather. Mr. Ellis and I will take up the rear," Mr. Martini said. "It snows more on this side of the lake."

"Yes, Mr. Martini," Allen said, then turned to the troop. "Line up in twos starting here. Get a buddy; he will be your buddy for the whole hike. You go nowhere without your buddy, understood? If you have to pee, your buddy has to pee too. If you get separated out here, you could freeze to death and will not be found until spring. Everyone understand?"

"Yes, Allen, understood," was collectively mumbled.

"Louder, and like you mean it."

"Yes, Allen. Understood," echoed through the woods.

"All your canteens full?"

"Yes, Allen," shouted the reply.

I stayed in the camp with my father and the two youngest in the troop. Both were ten years old and had just joined. They had older brothers going on the hike, and I'd keep them busy in the camp. Dinner would be a hamburger patty, sliced potatoes, and vegetables, all wrapped in aluminum foil and baked in the campfire coals. I needed twenty-six bundles. The two fellas would give me a hand.

At precisely nine thirty, Allen called everyone into ranks and headed out. Mr. Martini and Mr. Ellis took rear flanking positions. Mr. Martini had been in the Army and had fought in Europe during the war—Bastogne had taught him the trials of winter hiking. Our scoutmaster, Mr. Ellis, a doctor and pediatrician, was responsible for the maps.

As they hiked out, we began assembly of the hamburger bundles and stored them in the aluminum coolers. Again, everyone was careful, and all fingers accounted for.

Two hours after the troop left, it began to snow. It was in the forecast, but this was worse, much worse. Today the weather is reported with almost scientific accuracy, even down to how many tenths of rain or snow will fall, the hour it would start, and when the storm will pass. Back then, it was a prediction, an informed guess, a hope. Nonetheless, if the suitable parameters and the local geography were met, a storm might put five inches of snow on Chicago's Northside and two feet of snow on the windward side of Lake Michigan along Indiana's shoreline. Then, as now, it was infamously called the snow belt.

By noon, eight inches had fallen, and it was not letting up. Dad built up the fires. "When those boys get in, they will be cold. Craig, get the boys and make cocoa. It will keep them busy. Also, keep the snow off the roofs of the tents. I don't want them collapsing."

The hike was to take five hours, an hour a mile. Under normal conditions, the troop could march two and a half miles in an hour, give or take—they would have plenty of time. Dad looked at his watch. "Jim and Adam will turn them around and head them back. This snow does not look like it's going to stop. They are already four hours into the hike. We should be seeing them soon."

Eighteen inches of snow was on the ground at two, and the boys did not show. Dad went to the pay phone on the wall outside the restrooms at three thirty and called the sheriff. It was more to alert them to their conditions and that the boys were late returning from their hike. The roads were becoming impassable. Dad went to the trailer and pulled out three folding shovels.

"These aren't going to be a big help, but they will have to do," Dad said. "Start clearing away the snow from around the sides of the tents. We will need the room when we knock the snow off the roofs. Also, keep the tables clear and the fires up. When they get in, they will be cold and wet."

We were all cold and wet; I could only guess what the hikers were going through. The snow was now past my knees, light and puffy. Through the haze of snow, we heard the roar of a massive truck. It pulled into the campground next to the cars. A V-shaped plow, taller than me, was mounted to its front bumper. The driver, dressed in an insulated orange jumpsuit, climbed out and waded to us.

"The sheriff sent me over to see how you guys are doing," he said. "I'm Dutch, Dutch Elgin. I plow the roads in this part of the county. The sheriff said you have a couple of dozen Boy Scouts in this shit?"

"Mr. Elgin, we do," I said. "They went out for a hike before the snow started. We expected a little—not this."

"I know what you mean. Our guys said maybe six inches. There're some spots I've plowed where it's almost three feet. I can get on the radio and have a dozen men and women on snowmobiles here in an hour to look for them. Should I give them a call?"

A marching song drifted through the woods. It sounded like the "Heigh-Ho, Heigh-Ho" song the dwarves sang in *Snow White*. Through the gray of the falling snow, I saw Allen and Mr. Martini. Behind them marched the troop, a rope tied between them from the right wrist to the next.

"That them?" Dutch asked, a big smile on his face.

"Yes, sir. That's them," Dad said as the boys entered the camp. "Put more wood on the fire. I want you all warm and dry."

Mr. Ellis leaned up against one of the benches. "Lucky, we were damn lucky, Chris. Allen and the boys kept their heads about them and looked for the trail signs; the snow almost covered most. They got us back."

"All accounted for?" I asked.

"Yes, Craig, all here," Mr. Ellis said. "The last mile was the toughest. The falling snow was so thick we couldn't see a hundred feet ahead. It was Allen's idea to tie everyone together just in case, even us old guys. Tommy, Larry, and Mike led the way, breaking the snow. I took up the rear making sure we didn't lose someone. Skill and patience won out, though a little luck was helpful."

A couple of the boys were close to hypothermia. We got them out of their damp clothes and into dry pants and shirts. The driver said he'd call the sheriff and tell him all was good. Mr. Elgin said he would be up all night, but he would keep the road to the campground open. We started dinner early; the aluminum foil hamburger packs were massive hits. I could have made a dozen more. Mr. Martini suggested a Chianti would be a great addition to the meal. I had no idea what he meant.

The morning sky was a brilliant blue, and as with most winter storms, a cold front followed. The sun rose and provided no heat. The temperature dropped twenty degrees during the night, and Dad guessed it to be just above zero. We stoked the big fire. Everyone stood in a circle and, like roasting chickens, continuously turned about on their boots. Breakfast was a reprise of the morning before, scrambled eggs, bacon, and bread toasted quickly over the grill. Our snowplow driver, as promised, kept the road open, and at ten, our bus driver pulled into the parking lot. Quick work was made breaking the camp down. Dad said something about drying out the tents when we got home. All the pots and pans were loaded, and the gear stowed away in the trailers. Forty gloved hands made quick work of clearing the cars. The Marigold Gang volunteered to stay behind to help with the last of the packing and cleanup. Everyone else got on the bus. It was an adventure we talked about for years, and nobody lost a finger or froze to death.

CHAPTER 9

July 2024

Tuesday morning, two weeks after we'd discovered the bodies in the freezer, the six of us met in the living room of the Fisher house. Leading this meeting was Detective Audrey King.

"I am on a tight schedule," King said. "My chief wants this case closed as quickly as possible. The problem is the who, what, why, and when, a classic detective's dilemma. So far, we got nothing. We still don't know who the four people are. How they got here is a mystery. The same gun killed them. Why? Then there's the when and where this happened and who did it. So far, we have nothing."

"There is the money and artwork to consider. Maybe it was involved," Larry said.

"Possibly. How important they are, I'm not sure—yet. I don't particularly appreciate having unidentified bodies in the morgue. Not because I need to know who killed them, since whoever did it is most likely dead, but to clear up the bigger mystery—who are they? Evidence may have been tossed during your cleanup. And, more importantly, the chief told me he is not paying for a crawl through the dump looking for something we don't know we are looking for. However, there may be something left in the house that may help us. I want you to look around. If there's anything out of the ordinary, let me know."

"You are recruiting us in the investigation?" Mike asked. "Do we get badges?"

"No badges, no swearing in, and no, you are not an official posse," King said, smiling. "What I see are five interested guys that can help me solve my problem."

"Five retired geezers who have nothing to do. We work cheap—free. And can't apply for overtime," I offered.

"Exactly," King said. "You guys willing?"

"Damn straight," Larry said, standing up. "I'm back in the saddle!"

"You've hated horses since scout camp when that horse bit you," Garry said. "Never seen anyone so afraid of a four-legged beast after that. You would have been a terrible cowboy. I remember that time at the dude ranch in Montana—"

"Are you both done? Any shiny object, and you guys are off to the races. As we say in the business, we are burning daylight," King said.

"Ouch," I said. "I've been clichéd ."

We started in the corner bedroom and reexamined the shrine Allen had created for his parents. I told Detective King what we found here thirty-three years earlier. I remember it like yesterday. That memory, once burned into the brain, is hard to put out—the frantic call from Allen, his voice, the fear, the tears. "I need your help, Craig," was all he said. Then, walking into the house, the intense quiet, the smell of gunpowder, the nastiness in the bedroom, the violence, blood, and death. Allen stood with his back against the wall, staring at his parents. "He was there." I pointed as I explained. "Mrs. Fisher was lying on her left side, looking toward the window. Red goo was across the bedsheets and against the wall behind her. Mr. Fisher lay sprawled on his back, legs over the edge of the bed, left arm to his side, right arm and hand on his chest, and a huge pistol on the edge of the bed. Blood and gore across his chest."

"Jesus," Audrey said as she imagined what I recalled.

"Larry—it was his day off from the Chicago Police—was the second to appear at the scene. The first Lincolnville police officer soon joined us—I called the police on Allen's house phone. Within an hour, Tommy and Mike arrived. Garry would arrive later in the day; he was in Chicago when his secretary passed on the message. Later I called Bess, Allen's ex-wife. I remember her saying she felt sad for Allen but nothing for his folks, Ron and Lois. 'There was something off about the two of them,' she said. I didn't ask what she meant."

Since then, it was obvious Allen had cleaned the room; none of the residual carnage was apparent. It appeared painted. The photos on the dresser were of his family, the Fisher family. None of their expressions were pleasant or warm. We inspected the photos, looked behind the backing in the frames, searched under the carpets for loose floorboards, and searched anything that might hold a clue—nothing. We went through the last two rooms; one was Brenda's, his sister's. Before we started to clear the house, we found Brenda's room packed fuller than the others, as if Allen had intentionally used it for trash. We reinspected it to the paint on the walls—again, nothing. Allen's room (which, as a child, he shared with Dennis) still had the movie posters on the walls, a single bed, dresser, two bedside tables, two lamps, faded yellow curtains, and a cheap-looking worn carpet. I was surprised since there were at least four other valuable oriental rugs in the living room and dining room. The closet was now empty. A yellowed, tinted, and faded newspaper photo hung on the wall of the six of us and the two Black kids from 1959—"Young Heroes Save Kids," was the title, our names listed. I remember there was a short article. It was not attached to this photo.

"I wonder what ever happened to those two," Mike said,

inspecting the photo. "They would be in their late sixties or early seventies. Their names are here on the photo; maybe we could chase them down."

"Put that on your To Do List, Mike," Larry said.

Detective King studied the photo, then looked at us and said, "You guys were heroes way back then. Damn—the first adventure of the Marigold Gang."

"The first of many, individually and as a whole," I bragged.

"What doesn't kill you makes you stronger," Garry said.

"Considering the moment, that's dark," Tommy said.

We worked our way back into the living room—what we called the museum. We showed Audrey the box with the presumed orangutan skull (she said she'd have Saperstein look at it and confirm the species), the Army ribbons, and the remaining paintings and furniture. Garry told her he had half a dozen recovered paintings at his home. We needed to do something about security.

"We were confused by all this," I said. "Some of these paintings may be valuable, maybe very valuable. There's a chance even some of the furniture pieces are worth money. Then there's half a million dollars' worth of cash and gold coins. All this money, and yet, Allen did nothing with them. It is bizarre."

"Did you chase down any of Allen's bank accounts?" Larry asked.

"First thing we did," Audrey said. "Barbara, his daughter, was helpful. As executor, she has control over everything. There are five accounts, three with almost no money. Each month for the last twenty years, they were dinged a few bucks by the bank for management fees. There had been no activity. One of the two remaining accounts has over one hundred and forty-nine thousand dollars. There were no co-signers on that account, just Allen Fisher. Barbara said she was surprised by that account; she knew nothing about it. Nothing had been taken out for the past three years. The last account surprised us; it has had numerous monthly direct deposits and deductions for bills and direct expenses."

"Barbara said she set up that account to do just that," I said. "The Social Security and his pension checks were directly deposited into that account. She had access to that account. She told me she would watch to make sure he got his money. He never asked her for money."

"The man was as rich as Croesus yet never lived like it," Tommy said.

We searched through the kitchen for hidden cans or boxes and behind the cabinets (like with fake back panels)—nothing. The refrigerator, as ghastly as it was, had been emptied. We checked the freezer and the back of the oven (favorite spots, according to Larry)—more nothing.

The forensic unit of the Lincolnville Police had searched the basement. We went through it again. Tommy and I walked into the freezer room, which it was now called, more out of morbid curiosity than actual detective work. Finding nothing new, we gathered in the garage and spaced ourselves around the light green Studebaker Lark.

"Tommy, would you open the garage door?" Larry asked. "We need more light."

The add-on garage was two cars' wide with one large garage door, unusual for the early sixties when remodeled. America was still mostly a one-car-per-family world then. Inside, on the far side of the Studebaker, were boxes stacked against the wall. The dust was so thick you could drag your finger through it. The packaging tape had dried and released from the boxes; again, there were no labels. Earlier, we had cleared out the bags of garbage. They were in the last dumpster that eventually ended up at the forensics lab. They found nothing except old books, clothing, and garbage (tossed there by us). Allen's dust-free Harley-Davidson Sportster sat uncovered behind the car. A white cloth tarp lay bundled next to it on the floor; Garry had removed the bike's cover when we started to clear the garage. Allen's red bicycle hung on the wall beside the mounted license plates. The tools and jars, filled with nuts and bolts, littered the workbench, and more dust-encrusted power tools sat on shelves underneath. The overhead cabinets at the end of the garage were full of paint cans, turpentine cans, and plastic multi-drawer organizers. Along the back wall sat a gas-powered push mower, garden rakes and shovels hung from nails, and a double-door cabinet filled with light bulbs, more paint, gardening supplies, and terra-cotta garden pots. It was like any other American garage.

"Did you find keys for the car?" Mike asked as he peered through the fly-specked garage window at the back. It looked out onto the backyard.

"No," Detective King answered.

I walked around the Studebaker. "The license plate is Illinois, 1964. That was back when we got a new plate every year. I'd guess the car was from around 1962 or '63."

Mike squeezed the door handle, and the door popped open. "Amazing," he said.

All the doors opened. I noted that the mechanical odometer read 648.

"That's almost no miles for a sixty-three-year-old car," Garry said. "That will definitely increase its collector's value. The interior is pristine, and the dash isn't cracked. A little spit and polish, and it would be an interesting addition to a Mecum's auto auction. Can you pop the trunk?"

"It has a key lock," I said. "No popping trunks in those days."

"Damn," Larry said. "Look around; maybe there's a key.

You never know."

Above the workbench, a precise line of finishing nails had been set on a board nailed between studs. A key hung on each—five nails, five keys.

"Those are house keys, old ones," Garry said. "Try the last one."

Larry pulled the last key off. "There are two keys, and one's smaller."

"Those days, the larger key was usually for the doors and the ignition and the smaller for the glove box and trunk," Garry said.

"You know that, how?" I asked.

"Muscle memory, I guess. Back then, there were two keys for everything, not the fancy-schmancy, push-button fobs we have now. Try the smaller one."

Larry tried the smaller key in the trunk lock. He engaged it, there was a slight pop, and with a finger tug to release old rubber seals, the lid sprung open. I swear ghosts rose along with an oily smell; it stank of rotted rubber and a mustiness that comes naturally with old automobiles. Inside there was nothing but brittle, yellowed newspapers.

"There should be a spare tire in here. It has been removed," Garry said.

I inspected one of the pages of the newspapers. There were dark stains on parts of it, the same for most of the other pages.

"This reads the *South Bend Tribune*, June 20, 1963," I said.

"South Bend, what the hell?" Larry said, peering over my shoulder.

Tommy reached past me and removed a couple more pages. "Yes, this page too—*South Bend Tribune*. Somebody spread the newspaper across the floor of the trunk."

Detective King slipped herself between Tommy and me.

She looked around and quietly said, "Step back, boys. I'm certain that's dried blood on those pages."

Tommy and I delicately dropped our pages back into the trunk. King pulled a small flashlight and slowly scanned the interior. She then snapped on a pair of blue rubber gloves, reached into the far back corner, and pulled on a piece of loose carpet. A moment later, she held up a large automatic pistol.

"A Colt 45. Looks old, at least fifty years old—or more," Larry said.

"Holy crap," Mike said.

"Chief, would you look at the registration plate? It should be on the door column," King said.

A moment later, Larry said, "It has been pried off, just holes where it was mounted."

I looked around the garage, unsure exactly what we'd discovered. I pointed to the top license plate in the stack of plates nailed to the studs.

"That top plate is from Indiana, the year 1963," I said. "I wonder if that plate and this car once went together?"

"Interesting idea," King said. "I'll get the forensics people out here before we mess with this any further. Do you guys have any ideas?" She was smiling.

"Maybe this car, and those bodies in the freezer, arrived on the same day?" Larry said. "And if that plate belongs to this car, then maybe those four bodies are from Indiana. We have someplace to start."

"Hold your horses, Chief," King said. "Let's get some forensic evidence; see if this is blood. I have a pistol and four bodies that the ME says were shot. He found two bullets in the bodies, and we need to do the ballistics."

Mike, who was standing back from the group, boldly declared, "As Sherlock Holmes said: 'Doctor Watson, the game's afoot.'"

The Marigold Gang

* * *

The game *was* afoot, and we split the detective tasks among us for the next few days. Detective King was more than willing to allow us the opportunity. She was busy, and having five retired quasi-detectives with nothing to do working for her was, as she put it, "A perverse and awkward treat." I wasn't exactly sure what she meant. Nevertheless, we did have a lot of time on our hands. Larry was familiar with tracking license plates through other states. The more important question was could someone find, after sixty years, information on the license plate's owner, and could the plate be tied to this Studebaker Lark? We inspected every inch of the Studebaker again and found an identifying vehicle number on the gas tank (thank you, internet). The other places—where they were supposed to be—had been stripped. Maybe a search through Studebaker's sales records might turn up something. A quick Wikipedia check said that the company closed the South Bend manufacturing plant in late 1963, and the whole Studebaker operation slowly disappeared and was gone by 1968. The chance of finding sales records was remote, at best. Our quickest bet for identification was the license plate.

A few days later, I did look again through the narrow freezer room with Tommy. An unpleasant odor drifted about in the still air. The freezers (now off, open, and unplugged) still sat against the foundation wall. Both were covered with fingerprint dust giving a bizarre patina to the white enamel. Audrey said they found no fingerprints of value. Both were commercial waist-high freezers with a large single door on the top. They were about thirty inches deep and five feet wide. Both were identical Sears Coldspot units. Sears was America's most important retail store in the early 1960s, their appliances second to none. Under the company's current financial diffi-

89

culties, I was sure they would not like to hear that their freezers continued to run after sixty-one years.

Detective King said they had asked Sears for any records on the sale of two identical freezers in the summer of 1963 in the new store that opened in Lincolnville in the early 1960s. She doubted that they would be found.

The interior shelves of the room were now empty. When we found the room, it was stacked with boxes. Detective King said they found jewelry and two dozen expensive watches, Rolex, Omega, and Cartier. Many of the watches were still in their presentation boxes. Some of the jewelry appeared valuable; the rest was the costume kind, not worth much. There were silver plates, pitchers, and cups. Her team had boxed these up for further study. They also found additional bundles of money amounting to almost two hundred thousand dollars. All the bills were twenties, fifties, and hundreds, and like the suitcase of money we found, all dating from the late 1950s and early 1960s. There were no newer bills. There were a dozen polished wooden chests that contained silver flatware, real silver. All stored as evidence. For all intents, the room was both a crypt and a treasure room. Their ownership was in question, but there was a chance that Barbara could claim them if there were no satisfactory answers.

"This is bizarre, macabre, something from a horror movie," Tommy said as he poked around. "Allen had to have known, don't you think?"

"I've come to the same conclusion," I said. "He had to have known. Why he didn't tell anyone—he took that to the grave. Was he protecting his father, his parents? This is inexplicable."

"And his sister and brother turn up like vultures to pick the bones. I'm not sure anyone would buy this place now. Not worth much as is, let alone with this horror hanging over it.

Somebody named it that in one of the podcasts: the Horror House on Marigold Court. I hope that Barbara understands."

"The money, the valuables, the art, I figure it is loot from dozens of thefts," I said as we walked to the stairs.

"My thoughts exactly. It boggles the mind," Tommy offered. "I'm going upstairs. I'll meet you out front."

"I'm done."

We walked through the house and looked at the furniture and things we had placed in the museum. With a different perspective, we agreed that much of this, like the things in the freezer room, had likely been stolen. It was one thing to conclude about the loot and an entirely new thing to add the four bodies.

As we stood on the driveway, Delmar crossed over the cul-de-sac and handed each of us a beer.

"Something straight out of a B-movie on TCM," Delmar said. "My wife is creeped out."

"We are all creeped out," I said. "Detective King has asked for our help chasing down some leads. Could be interesting."

"The Marigold Gang is now private investigators?" Delmar said. "Yep, getting creepier by the day."

We clacked our beer cans together in salute.

CHAPTER 10

We elected Larry as the lead investigator. He had a leg up on us with over four decades in the policing business. The Fisher Case, as we called it, had caught the imagination of the local bloggers, podcasters, and even the Chicago newspapers for a week. The newspapers had the memory of a goldfish. After a week of updates, it disappeared from the news.

Three weeks after finding the bodies in the freezer, we gathered at Garry's country club, where we had access to both privacy and the bar. While Bell's would have performed adequately, the thought of someone overhearing our conversations about Saran-Wrapped bodies in Sears freezers might have put some patrons off their meal. And besides, Garry had a vested interest in keeping the restaurant free of potential scandal.

"How could there be a scandal over what we are doing?" Mike said. "We are just a bunch of old codgers, and I use the term affectionally, having a conversation. This certainly beats sitting around watching the White Sox—jeez, what a terrible team this year."

"I understand, Mike," I said. "What would happen if one of those bloggers comes in and tags us with the sobriquet 'Bodies in the Freezer story talked about over bacon and eggs'? Karen would never forgive us."

"And besides, Bell's doesn't have a liquor license," Garry added.

"Yeah, there's that too," Tommy added.

We held the first official meeting of the Marigold Gang investigating the Fisher Case in the wood-paneled clubroom behind the bar at the country club. It began precisely at 4:00 p.m. I would take notes. Club sandwiches on a tray, and each of us held our preferred beverage. Thankfully, none of us got to that stage where we'd sworn off liquor (or, for medical reasons, stopped drinking altogether). Liquor, tobacco, and women were the topics of our youth. Then our marriages and jobs changed our collective minds; time and families brought us back together for important events, but this was the first time since our high school days that we worked together with a specific purpose and goal.

"First of all, I suggest a toast to Allen Fisher," I said. "He left us too soon."

"I hope that he's finally found peace," Mike said.

"Amen to that," we agreed and clinked glasses.

"Now, let's get this meeting started," I said.

"Maybe we can apply for a 501(c)3 tax designation and set this up as a foundation," Garry said with a laugh. "Any money we spend can be deducted."

"Interesting idea," Larry said.

"No, it's not. It is stupid. I remember when we opened that first freezer, not one of you was thinking about setting up a nonprofit company. We need to keep our eye on the ball here," Mike said.

"Well said, considering where we are," Garry said. "Okay, let's tee it up."

"Just stop, both of you," I said. "I ask, what will constitute a success in this investigation? Usually, for the police, it's finding the bad guy, arresting him, and getting a conviction."

"The problem here is that it's a good bet that the bad guy is dead," Garry said. "And there's nobody to arrest and convict."

"And that is why Audrey's chief doesn't want her to waste her time," Larry said. "I get that. Spend hours, and what do you end up with? Zilch—nothing to show. Maybe some answers, but who cares, now."

"This is a mystery, fellas. Plain and simple, a whodunit," I said. "I've given this a lot of thought."

"See, Craig does have a plan," Mike said. "Lay it on us, brother."

"Really? You are a big *Law & Order* show guy, right?" I said. "This is more like *Twin Peaks.*

"Those were good programs; I learned a lot. And *Twin Peaks*, yeah, bizarre, so, so bizarre. Good points here: everyone dead, bodies in the freezers, and a Studebaker—nice script."

"You can apply that TV training to this case," I continued. "Here is what I see we need to find and resolve. I've written them down and stuck them on a board."

"No PowerPoint? I'm disappointed," Larry said.

"Maybe later, if we are successful, we can make it a TED talk, a podcast." I stopped and let that sink in. "Here, at the start, there are five major questions to answer. The first is who are the people in the freezer, two identical twin women and two men? All in their early twenties. Second, where did the Studebaker come from? There is the possibility that the four arrived at the house in the trunk of that car, but when and why? Third, where did all the art and money come from? I suggest that it is stolen."

"Well, duh," Tommy blurted.

"Yes, I know it seems obvious, but this needs to be confirmed. Fourth, what is the involvement of the Fisher family in all this? Who did this and why? Don't forget about Allen's parents."

"His father kills his mother, then himself, and Allen finds them," Mike says. "And it appears that the bodies and the money and art were in the basement at the time, big miss by the police."

"In their defense, finding a murder-suicide doesn't give the police carte blanche to do a cavity search of the house," Larry said. "Looking back, maybe they should have. You said five major questions, Craig."

"The last, what have been the repercussions to all those involved?"

"Like what?" Tommy said.

"I'll give you a few, but there will be dozens more before we finish. According to the coroner, one of the girls had given birth within the past year—what happened to the child? Are the victims related? We know two were, but is one of the men the father?"

"A stretch," Larry said.

"Yes, but can we find that out?" I added. "And the artwork, they are worth millions. They belong to someone. If stolen, then what happens to them? And the cash and gold. Who does it belong to—and how do we or they prove it belongs to them? If this goes public, we will have dozens of people claiming it. Barbara wants it put someplace safe, and a self-storage unit in the Heights won't work. We need a large safety deposit box, which is not cheap. And can we use this money to pay for it? That is both an ethical and legal question."

"Use the money. Somebody will thank us," Tommy said as he looked at his phone. "There's a walk-in vault security company here on the Southside, high-security, and not far away."

"Your first assignment, Tommy. Check them out. We can move it all there if they have space. Audrey would be pleased."

"Regarding the bodies and DNA," Mike said. "The testing isn't cheap, and how do we pay for it—if and when we need it?

Lucy is reminding me of the costs. Legal? Does that mean we need an attorney? Our little band of merry woodsmen could become a small army of paupers."

"We don't need an attorney—yet," I added. "Barbara is looking into it; her hands are full with her aunt and uncle. They've taken a keen interest in this. They have been calling her, making threats."

"Damn, I forgot about those two, Brenda and Dennis," Garry said. "Not surprised, the parasites. Lady Macbeth and Iago come to mind. Maybe we'll find out they are the ones that put the bodies in the basement."

"They would have been what—ten years old?" Mike said.

"One can hope. I'll work with Tommy on the vault logistics, Craig."

"Scary thought, Mike, but they will be here every step of the way," I said. "That's why the vault. They see it all as theirs, every Canadian Maple Leaf, every dollar, every piece of art. We all agree that this is one seriously messed-up family and has been for a long time."

"I'm thinking of going on another cruise," Tommy said.

"You can go when this is over, lover boy," Garry said. "We owe this to Allen and whatever all this turns out to be. Somebody out there needs closure and answers."

"Thanks, Garry. That said, Larry and I have assigned additional jobs for each of you. Sometimes you will be a pair, other times working on your own. This is just the first stage. As we get into this, our work will expand, as it always does. Look at my five big points; we will find dozens of the things under each heading."

Everyone nodded. "I'll get right on the vault. That's a priority. Once everything is there, our worries will drop," Tommy said and gave a thumbs-up to Garry.

"I'll let Barbara know," I said. "Mike, art like this must have a track record that suddenly stopped years back; maybe there were news articles, something in the art world about thefts. Find out what you can about the pieces, take photos, call galleries, and maybe we can find the owners."

"Got it. Garry has a few pieces; the rest are at the police station. He can bring those to the security vault. I'll start an inventory spreadsheet."

"Excellent. Larry and I agree that the first place to start is the Studebaker. It is the one thing completely out of context. Allen drove that old Ford truck for the last fifteen years, and before that, another Ford for God only knows how long. It was always on the driveway. I don't remember the Studebaker, and if it was about 1963 when it arrived here, that means a few of us were still on the street."

"And that means . . ." Larry started to add.

"Those bodies were here when I was here," Tommy said. "Damn and sick."

"Larry asked Audrey to request registration records for the license plate from Indiana BMV."

"It's a 1963 plate, blue with yellow letters and the numbers 71 H 417," Larry said. "The plate looks brand new, and they issued plates annually back then. It's a place to start."

"The bloody newspapers in the trunk, didn't they have 1963 dates?" Tommy said.

"Yes, from South Bend. And that's a place you, Garry, can start. Newspapers on and around those dates from South Bend. Were there some big news items, something that might connect to this? Maybe there's a service or an app out there with access to past issues. What did they call the archives in newspapers?"

"The morgue," Mike said. "How appropriate."

CHAPTER 11

Summer 1965

I hefted our aluminum canoe to my shoulders. They said it weighed sixty-five pounds; by this time, our third portage, it felt like two hundred. Larry carried it on our first portage, Mike the second, and now it was my turn. They were not getting away with anything; behind me, they each carried double rucksacks of clothes, food, and tents. There were five canoes in our armada, three boys each. In two of the canoes, our leaders were the third seat.

This June afternoon, we were now a half dozen miles north of Gunflint Lake and well into the Boundary Waters Canoe area. Four hours of hard paddling and portaging put us in the Canadian province of Ontario and the Quetico Provincial Park, one of North America's most spectacular wildernesses overwhelmed by granite cliffs, winding rivers, tumultuous waterfalls, and clear, pristine lakes. The region, scraped by glaciers fifteen thousand years ago, has miles of meandering waterways connecting hundreds of pristine lakes, large and small. Our goal that first day was the isolated wilderness high above the largest lake, where it was impossible to portage a motorboat. As a result, these lakes were isolated and tranquil. After our early morning start and three downriver portages around tumbling cascades, we neared our goal. The first day's destination was a ten-mile paddle to Gneiss Lake, where we would rest and set up camp for the night. The next day we would push farther north into Canada and hopefully reach a Canadian outpost on Saganaga Lake. Our destination was a campground we'd found the year before on a singular granite island nestled within a bay of an unnamed lake. We would spend three days fishing and exploring there before continuing clockwise through a series of unspoiled lakes and portages back to Gneiss Lake and then home to Gunflint. All in all, two days of hard paddling, three days of exploring, then three days back to our jumping-off point.

Our group of fifteen adventurers included all those in the Marigold Gang, two parents, and our post's leader, Bob Hunger. They were there to ensure we didn't get lost. I have to say there were times when we knew where we were, and they didn't. Also, on our trip up from Chicago was another group of younger and newer members of our Explorer post. That group of ten had three adult leaders. They also had a more manageable itinerary.

I forgot to mention that we were a Post of Explorer Scouts, the next rung up the ladder of Boy Scouting in those days. We were older boys, most over fifteen, who participated in activities more strenuous than those for younger Boy Scouts (I also admit that we didn't have to deal with ten-year-olds, either). Later, the Boy Scouts split into more focused programs in the late twentieth century. The closest to our Explorers became Venturing Scouts. The scouts have been through so much in the past thirty years; I'm not sure what all this means in these early years of the twenty-first century.

Back then, there was no freeze-dried food; everything we ate or needed for shelter we carried on our backs: cans of beans, hash, vegetables, and condensed milk; anything you can think of was in a tin can. Loaves of bread were crushed accordion-like into dense six-inch bundles; you peeled the bread from the bale to make a sandwich. We packed fresh eggs in hard-shelled containers that eventually assured their destruction. We ate the eggs, scrambled, of course, the first two days to reduce our egg anxiety. Most of us were good cooks. In the rucksacks were flour, baking powder, salt, sugar, and all the necessary ingredients to prepare meals. And, of course, we ate off the land. There were fish everywhere—northern pike, smallmouth bass, and the tastiest, walleye. We would skewer a whole walleye on a stick and slowly cook them over a hot bed of coals. We would drizzle them with butter and salt; it was as decadent as it sounds.

The morning after we set up our three-day camp, we crossed the lake and headed up a river that coursed through a wide gap between flanking granite cliffs. We guessed their height to be a hundred or more feet. Thick stands of white and red pine sat high above the groves of birch, aspen, and red osier dogwood growing along the water's edge.

Tommy was the first to spot it.

"What the hell is that?" he yelled from the bow of the lead canoe. He pointed to a large brown mass in the middle of the river.

"Just a boulder, Tommy," Larry yelled.

"Boulders don't have fur," he yelled as we slowed and slid up next to the hump.

The water was clear and maybe ten feet deep. As we gathered around Tommy's furry rock, we were amazed to find that it was the carcass of a bull moose, antlers and all. The animal was at least half the length of our canoes.

"Are those tires?" I asked, using a canoe paddle to push against the body to expose what I saw.

"Well, I'll be damned. Yes, those are tires," Mike said. "Goodyears, the lettering as plain as the nose on my face. What the hell?"

"A mystery, I'll tell you that," Larry added. "Nothing we can do about it. Onward, boys."

The mystery was solved a week later when we stopped at the Canadian ranger's office and country store on our way back to Gunflint Lake. We were picking up some eggs and fresh milk when Tommy told the woman at the counter that we'd seen a dead moose in the river.

"Lots of dead moose, fellas," she said. "That's the way of life up here after a hard winter. The wolves and other critters will care for the carcass, but sometimes they end up in the rivers."

"Well, ma'am, this one had four Goodyear tires," Tommy said.

"Tires? Well, damn." She looked across the store to the office area set aside for the park ranger. "Officer Timmons, do you remember those hunters that lost that moose in December?"

"Yes, I do, Laura. Why?"

"Seems these boys found it." She looked over at us. We knew a story was coming. With a big grin, Ranger Timmons walked over to us. "Fellas, four hunters on snowmobiles came across the lake last December. They were heading over to Trafalgar Bay and up the Weikwabinonaw River."

"We called it Floating Dead Moose River," Tommy said.

"Good name. I like it," he said with a smile. "I can pronounce it; its real name, well, good luck with that. Four days later, these fellas came back with a tale that was hard to believe. They shot this big bull moose and used the tires they brought as skids to tow the carcass out. So, they tied the tires to the moose and made a kind of sled—been done before up here. Then they secured the animal to two of the snowmobiles and began to drag it out across the ice. Not fast and not too slow, and all was going well. An hour or two in, they stopped in the middle of the river to rest. The moose was maybe thirty or forty feet behind them. They heard a crack and a pop, and immediately the moose tipped and began to settle through the ice slowly. It seems they stopped over a weak spot. They gunned the motors to try and pull the carcass out of the hole. It was too heavy. Within seconds, the moose slipped under the ice and was caught by the current, and now began to pull the two snowmobiles toward the hole in the ice. One of the guys says the ice was so clear they could see the moose sliding toward them as their gear skidded in the opposite direction to the hole. Quick thinking, they pulled their skinning knives and cut the ropes. The lines snapped in the ten-below-zero air and nearly winged one of the fellas. Then they heard the moose bouncing along under the ice. My guess was that nature would take care of the carcass. It would find a spot along the river in the spring, and the bears and wolves will get into it."

We all just stood in wonder, thinking about what the ranger described. He turned to us. "Good trip, fellas?"

"A great trip," Allen added. He'd been quiet through this exchange. "We found a waterfall, more like a cascade, I guess, a few miles from where we found the moose."

"I know the spot, one of the prettiest places in the park, almost magical."

"Yes, it was. Mystical and stunning. The boulders all covered in moss and lichen and the birch trees reaching over the river—it was almost like a church."

"And good fishing, right?" the ranger added.

"Some of the best," Larry said. "Every cast, we caught a fish. Craig there caught a two-foot northern pike. But mostly nice smallmouths and even a few big walleyes. All in all, a great day."

"Good for you, fellas. Glad we could help."

On the long bus ride home, we all agreed it had been a trip of a lifetime. Nobody died or even put an axe in their knee, which was a great success. We heard a sad story the last night at the outfitter's lodge from a group of canoers that passed through. It seems that a couple hadn't respected the river and what could happen if you did foolish things. They tried to run a particular series of rapids and cascades in their canoe. Halfway through, they overturned. They recovered the man's body but hadn't found the woman. There were three canoes in their group. It took two days of hard paddling to reach the government house to find help, not that they could do anything about what happened. Nature demands respect.

During the last afternoon at our three-day island camp, we climbed the granite mountain above us to a wide ledge that looked south over the verdant country. The sky was as brilliant blue as genuine turquoise, whisps of clouds offered perspective and distance, and the warm sun reflected off the water like a trillion mirrors.

It was cigar time. We sat there, all of us feeling grown-up, for all our sixteen years. We'd conquered the wilderness. We talked of our futures; you did those things then. Not sure about fifteen-year-olds these days; the evidence seems to point to severe phone separation anxieties. Out there, back then, deep in the wilderness, there was not a cell tower or even a phone. Help was paddling till exhausted and then paddling more.

Those ten tumultuous years of the 1960s had serious and profound impacts on all of us. We all started the decade as whimpering twelve-year-olds. At the decade's end, Mike had had his turn in Vietnam, caught a bullet in the thigh the second week in country, and was shipped home with a shattered ilium. By 1970 he was married and had a child on the way. Allen was drafted out of high school, sent to Vietnam, awarded for his heroism, and the rest of his life, fought another war with

PTSD and himself. Larry, the sizable Italian kid who played defensive end and offensive tight end in high school, won a scholarship to Northwestern, blew his knee out the last game in a loss to Michigan State, and in 1970 was walking a beat as a Chicago cop. Garry went from an intelligent, gangly kid with a sense of humor to a class leader and the quarterback of his high school team. He played for Illinois (and against Larry at Northwestern three times). He spent his summers working for a housing contractor and, by 1970, knew he wanted to be a developer. By way of the Illinois Institute of Technology, Tommy became a graphic designer at the Disney Studios in Los Angeles, a far cry from the Southside suburbs of Chicago. And I went from the cute towheaded twelve-year-old, to a stint in high school politics as class president, to college with Tommy at IIT. I studied architecture. When the seventies arrived, I was a junior draftsman at the vast architectural firm of Perkins and Will in Chicago's Loop. Ten years go by so fast. Then again, looking back fifty years, we all wonder where those five decades went.

Sitting on that polished glacierized rock, none of us knew what lay ahead. The smoke from our cigars drifted out over the pine trees. Above, a bald eagle screeched and unhurriedly turned to catch a look at us interlopers. Beyond the trees, the three-note song of a loon's call echoed. A mournful answer rose in the gathering evening mist from the other side of the lake. For us, it was complete.

CHAPTER 12

August 2024

The Indiana Bureau of Motor Vehicles' answer was both a surprise and a shock. The initial request for information came through Lincolnville's police department and Audrey King. It was a simple request: What automobile was registered to Indiana license plate 71 H 417? Audrey called Larry and passed on the information emailed from Indiana. I was with him when he answered his phone.

"Larry, the plate was for a 1963 green Studebaker Lark owned by Walter Paine. The address is in South Bend, Indiana. They have no other information; it is sixty years old."

"But our Studebaker is blue—robin's-egg blue," I told Larry.

"A vehicle number?" Larry asked.

"Yes," Audrey said and started to give out the numbers.

"Hold a sec. I need paper and a pencil." He looked at me. I shrugged.

"Audrey, please email me the information. Our only number is on the fuel tank, and we aren't sure if it is the same for the vehicle."

She agreed, and Larry hung up. When Larry took Audrey's call, we were at the house taking photos and generally talking about what-ifs. We headed straight to the garage with the same idea.

The 1963 Studebaker Lark, it was hoped, would save the Studebaker company, at least for a couple more years. Nonetheless, within a year, the South Bend assembly lines were shut down, and manufacturing moved to the Canadian facility in Hamilton, Ontario. Eventually, the company closed in 1968; it wasn't a swift and merciful death. It was a slow and painful end to the oldest production vehicle maker in the world. After World War II, the company was called the Studebaker-Packard Corporation. In 1962, it returned to its original name, the Studebaker Corporation. The 1963 Lark VIII Regal model in the garage—which we'd confirmed through online sites—had morphed into a luxury sedan. From all appearances, our car in the garage fit the Studebaker moniker of "America's First and Only Limousette." After lightly scratching the right quarter panel, we discovered that our pale blue car was, underneath, iridescent green, the color noted on the Indiana BMV confirmation. We were sure that the license tacked to the wall was the plate for this car.

Audrey confirmed that the Illinois license plates currently on the Fisher Studebaker were for a blue 1961 Studebaker owned by Ralph Peete with an address in Gurnee, Illinois. Even as rookie detectives, we concluded that they were stolen. None of us remembered this automobile out on the street; it makes you wonder what your neighbors are hiding in their garages—or basements. And at the time none of us remembered our past connection to the car.

I called Garry and told him about the information from the Indiana Bureau of Motor Vehicles and the name Walter Paine. He would dig into it later that evening. He had a tee time at two. There was no way I could make an issue of his time. After all, we were all volunteers, and besides, what was the rush?

I talked with Tommy. He had contacted the security company and was astounded by the rental price for a vault, with three months up front. I told him to hold and that we would discuss it later.

"They want ten thousand dollars up front," I told Larry. "Three months' rent."

"To just store the art and money?" he answered.

"They don't know what we are storing. Tommy says they do not want to know. The only prohibited item is drugs."

"How would they know; do they sweep the vaults with dogs?"

I raised my hands in surrender. "No idea, but this must be stored somewhere. I'll propose we use some of that money to cover the costs, and I'll talk to Barbara. She and her brother are the owners until it's decided what is legal or illegal."

"Then there are Allen's siblings."

"Another battle, another time."

We stood at the back of the garage, admiring the car. We had decided not to clean it or attempt to make it drivable. All four tires were flat, the battery was dead, and the dust was measurable. The proper procedure would be fingerprint dusting. To what end, though?

Larry said, "Whoever pops up must be dead. That car arrived in 1963. That was sixty-one years ago. Whoever it was, and for argument's sake, let's say it was Mr. Fisher. He would be well over one hundred years old. And we know he's long dead."

"Are we looking for a living killer or trying to find out what happened?" I asked. "Maybe bring some closure to someone."

"You said it best," Larry said, "when you talked about those left behind. Somebody knew those four in the freezer. Something happened back then that had an impact on those living today. I suggest a road trip."

"South Bend?"

"Where else. I'll bet you didn't know I was offered a scholarship to Notre Dame."

"No shit. I did not know that," I said, impressed.

"Yes, but Dad thought that Northwestern was a better school. I should get a business degree. He envisioned opening a dozen dry cleaner shops around Chicago, maybe a master plant to handle them all. We'd become partners, dry cleaner moguls. He even had a name: King Cleaners. So, naturally, I became a cop; it was a thing between us for a long time. Mother was sure I'd be shot, killed. You never get shot running a dry cleaner's, she'd say. You know Italian mothers."

"Your mother was great. I never ate as well as at your house," I said.

"But when I became chief of police, at least they lived long enough to see that. He was so proud."

"Your sister never had any desire to take over the business?"

"No, she wanted to teach, and after Rose divorced, she continued teaching. She's got her pension, and with the trust that Dad set up, we are fine."

"He did have six locations, right?"

"Yes, he lived a good life considering he nearly died in Italy during the war—if that had happened, I wouldn't be here."

"Here's to Naples and near misses. So South Bend?"

"I'll call the police department, schmooze up the chief or someone, tell them what we are after, then you and I will pay them a visit."

"I can't do tomorrow or Thursday. Penny has me painting the extra room," I said.

"Come on; you're a big-time murder investigator. House painting is not in your job description."

"You tell Penny. I'll stay outside when you do, then come in to pick up the pieces."

Larry smiled. He'd known my wife for almost as long as

she and I had been together. Penny and I went to the same high school. Then she went to college, and I lost track until she walked into my senior studio at IIT one day. I was completing a scale model for a housing project. She was still cute and funny and was in mechanical engineering. I didn't realize, until it was too late, that she'd pegged me to be the one. That came out a few years after we were married, not that I minded being the one. We graduated, we got married. I worked at Perkins and Will, and she worked at an engineering office a few blocks away. We rented an apartment on the near west side and lived the Bohemian life—come to think of it, we still are.

Larry went home, and I spent another half hour wandering the house, wondering if the ghosts would make an appearance. I count at least seven dead people in this house, including Allen. The doctor believed he lay there a long time before he died. Garry found him a day later when he hadn't appeared at breakfast. It broke our hearts. For twenty years, our fearless leader, as kids, had been slowly fading away. After his folks' deaths, he became a shadow. His PTSD would kick up, and we'd make sure that he didn't harm himself. We were thrilled when his daughter or son would return for a visit. He'd brighten up, dress better, and again look you in the eye. He even remembered a few jokes. He loved those kids, but he wouldn't leave the house. More than once, they tried to have him move nearer to one of them. Barbara was in California; Steve was in North Carolina; for Allen, it was hard to choose between the door on the right or the one on the left. He stayed put.

As I took another look around, the creepiness of it all weighed heavily on me. For four people, sixty years frozen, stuck in a box, and entirely ignored. These four ghosts were the most demanding. Every creak or whistle through a crack was a cry, an admonition, a pleading for justice. It is easy to slip into an eerie melancholia when you know there must be ghosts. Did they force Ron Fisher to shoot his wife and then himself? Were they standing in the bedroom taunting him that night thirty years ago? Did they applaud as he pulled the trigger, not just once but twice? And, most of all, did they, now six phantoms, drive Allen further into his hell?

We had millions in art, half a million in cash and gold, boxes of trinkets and watches, and one sprayed-over Studebaker. I took a deep breath and walked slowly through the empty rooms to the front door; reaching it, I pulled on the handle. The next moment, I looked up at Garry's and Tommy's faces. Penny was standing behind them, tears in her eyes.

The back of my head pounded; point in fact, my whole head hurt. I was sitting on the hallway floor near the front door to Allen's house. It was the last place I remember.

"You okay?" Garry asked as he held a cold compress to the back of my pounding head.

I looked up at Penny. "I'm good, honey, just fine. I have no idea what happened." It was dark outside. Just one light over the entry hall and another from the kitchen ceiling lit the empty house's interior. I saw the flashlight in Tommy's hand.

"Did you see who hit you?" he asked.

"Somebody hit me? What do you mean?" I mumbled.

"From the looks of it, something hard hit the back of your head. Someone knocked you out," Garry said as he handed the cloth to Penny. He stood. "I talked to Larry, and he said he'd left you in the house just before five. It's now 8:35, three and a half hours. You didn't come home; Penny called me. I called Tommy, and the three of us came here."

"Police? Did you call them?"

"No, but if you weren't here, it was our next call," Tommy said. "What happened?"

"I have no idea," I said. "One minute, I'm walking through the house to the front door; the next, I see your faces."

"Wallet, watch, you got those?" Garry asked.

I checked; they were all there. "What the hell? Point the light, there." I was looking at the wall across the living room. In black spray paint, it read: *God will punish all—atone.* The opposite wall read, *Demand vengeance,* and *Proverbs 11:21.*

"What do those mean?" Penny asked.

"I have no idea."

CHAPTER 13

September 2024

Larry was at a village function he couldn't leave; he called and was very happy that I was alive. So was I, I told him. Coincidentally, the village safety committee he was chairman of had gone late. No cell phones were allowed during the session, and after the meeting, he got a text message about my assault. Mike was with three of his nine grandkids; he was babysitter that night. Lucy, his wife, was with her girlfriends playing mahjongg. For Mike, nothing was greater than playing video games with their son's three boys.

I didn't begrudge any of them for not dropping everything and coming to my side. I was pissed, so pissed that I'd almost forgotten the lump on the back of my head—not at them, mind you, at myself for being bushwhacked. Someone had forced our small detective operation to the dark side—that was Garry's assessment. Later at home, after an uneventful visit to the hospital, Penny told me we should drop this "shit." "There is absolutely nothing good that can come out of this, Craig. I was going to say that someone would get hurt. Well, we are now beyond that. What is the point?" She didn't wait for an answer but stomped off to bed. Unable to sleep, I sat in the living room, lights off, sipping bourbon and cogitating.

She was right, as Penny was most of the time. What was

the point of five old men trying to chase down the answers to four sixty-year-old murders? Our lives were already a geriatric hodgepodge with family traditions, anxiousness, anxieties, and medical issues. Penny's question was a real one: Why do this? My answer was simple—the thrill of the chase. I'd seen the excitement in the faces of the gang; this was unique, exciting, and employed skills they seemed to have lost—or at least that's what I told myself. The next morning, I told Penny I would be more careful. She answered with a smirk. I'm not too fond of her smirks.

Larry called me later in the day and said he had talked with the chief of police of South Bend, Indiana. The chief was stunned after Larry told her about what they had found and the possible connection to South Bend. The chief invited Larry and me to her office for a sit-down to discuss the crime. She added that she'd ask her chief of detectives to dig a little and see if anything pops. "I can't promise you much," she'd said. "To be honest, all this happened fifteen years before I was born."

We scheduled the meeting for 10:00 a.m. at the chief's office on West Sample Street in South Bend. We pulled into one of the visitor's stalls in front of the building. Larry stood beside his Ford F-150 and whistled. "Now, this is a nice building. We could use one half this size in Lincolnville."

Before we arrived, we took a tour of the neighborhood. We were surprised that the multi-story brick building behind the station and the county jail was the original Studebaker factory. I had expected something more significant. Larry hadn't been in South Bend since he was offered the scholarship to Notre Dame, so I promised him a drive around the campus after we met with the chief.

We waited in the spacious and officious lobby as the desk sergeant buzzed the chief. What Larry hadn't told me was the chief of police was a woman, tall, athletic, and blonde, not that I was paying all that much attention. With her was another woman in civilian clothes; a shield hung on the belt of her slacks under her suitcoat.

"Chief Martini, Chief Linda Bellows." She put her hand out to Larry. "And this is Detective Amanda Brandt. Unfortunately, my chief of detectives is on vacation. But I believe you will find that Detective Brandt is an excellent substitute."

"Chief, this is my friend and fellow investigator Craig Martin," Larry said.

We shook hands, engaged in small talk as we crossed through the outer office, passed a secured door requiring a card key, and entered a hallway. The second door down was the chief's office—the sign on the glass door read CHIEF OF POLICE LINDA BELLOWS, in neat gold-painted letters. I could feel my detective skills growing.

"Were you on the force with Chief Martini, Mr. Martin?" Bellows asked.

I must have blushed.

"I'm sorry, was that a trick question?" she said.

"Chief Bellows, I was an architect for fifty years," I said, chagrined. "Our gang of detectives consists of four retirees and this guy, the only one with formal police training. We volunteered for this gig, as one of us put it. To us, it is a great mystery in need of solving. There are more than a half million dollars in cash and gold, valuable art and sculpture, and fine jewelry. We have four dead found in a Sears freezer and a Studebaker with the blood of the dead in the trunk. Let's say our curiosity got the better of us."

"You know about that cat and curiosity?" Detective Brandt said.

The back of my head throbbed as if cued. I told them about my ambush.

"Now that is interesting," the chief said. "Who would care that much about all this to whack you across the back of the head?"

"It's a mystery," I said.

The police officers smiled. "However, Amanda did a little digging. She has some things to show you."

We sat at a conference table that took up a third of the chief's office. On the tabletop were three binders. They were old and worn. I looked at Larry; he was smiling like a kid at Christmas.

"These are just the top of the pile; we pulled them from boxes in the evidence locker. There's a lot more to go with this. As far as cold cases go, this one is the coldest—and it is all sparked by your license plate request and the Studebaker."

"So, there is a crime?" I asked.

"Yes, and it is brutal and evil as well," the chief said. "My parents were teenagers when this happened, and I wasn't even a glimmer in their minds. When I joined the police department, the crime was a forty-year-old mystery. Leads had run out, people had moved on, grown up, or died. It all had dropped off the face of the earth."

"Our interested is piqued," Larry said. "What do you have?"

"I know what I've read in the reports and seen in the evidence; that's what's in the files there. I suggest that you meet with another retired detective, Dexter Millhouse. He was second to the lead detective, Walt Buchanan. Walt died in 1978."

"Dexter Millhouse would be, what, in his nineties?" I offered.

"Yes, Dex is ninety-one. I attended his ninetieth birthday party at the retirement home where he lives," Bellows said. "I try to see him a couple of times a year. I hope I'm as sharp as he is when I'm that old."

Both Larry and I had exasperated looks on our faces.

"What is this cold case you seem to be dancing around?" Larry said.

"On June 21, 1963," Amanda began, "a senior executive of the Studebaker company and his wife were brutally murdered in their home. The killers also shot their son, who lived but was paralyzed. Two other children hid and survived. Valuable art and jewelry were taken, and their car, a Studebaker Lark Regal VIII, light metallic green."

I looked at Larry. He nodded.

"What?" Amanda asked.

"The car we found in the house with the four bodies was metallic green but painted over with light blue," Larry said. "There had been Studebaker VIN plates; they had been removed. We found a license plate in the garage that your BMV identified as belonging to a green 1963 Studebaker. We assume that the plate belongs to the vehicle. We were also informed that the car was registered to Walter Paine."

This time Bellows looked at Brandt, and they both nodded. "The murdered couple were the Paines, Walter and Clare. The boy is Louis. He was seven at the time. The other two children are Janet and Mark. I am unsure about their current locations or whether they are alive."

"Were there suspects in the killings?" I asked.

"They found fingerprints that identified one of the possible killers," Bellows said. "They were from a right hand and were left on the frame of the jimmied-open sliding door. They were for Tobias Wozniacki. He was twenty-four. The report says he lived in Warsaw at that time. He had a record for petty crimes and a sealed juvenile report. There's nothing in the files about associates or where he lived at the time of the killings. The report states that he was never found or arrested. We followed up for a few years, but nothing ever popped. Millhouse might remember more."

"I assume you have the fingerprints for this Wozniacki?" Larry continued.

"They are in the files, photos of the originals on the door, and copies from his arrests."

"May we take these?" I said, looking at the files.

"Detective Brandt will make you copies—can't see any harm after all this time. Like everywhere, we are stretched thin, and this kind of cold case can eat up hours of time. I appreciate your help. The killing of the Paines reverberated through the community for years. My father told me that the Studebaker company was on the edge of collapse during this time and, within five years, failed here in South Bend. The death of one of their senior executives may have had an impact. Again, that was a long time ago."

"This Wozniacki kid—known associates, girlfriends, anything?" I asked.

"For a rookie, you ask good questions," Bellows said. "The report names about a dozen people he knew from Warsaw. They wouldn't appear in the reports if he had any connections in South Bend."

"Now that we have some fingerprints to compare to," Larry said, "we'll take a good look at the car. See if they are on it."

"I assume you will also check out the bodies?" Amanda asked.

"First thing. Our medical examiner thinks he can pull prints. It took a while to slowly thaw the remains. He also had to figure out which leg and arm goes where; the bodies are well desiccated. He has some ideas about regenerating the fingerprints. He is certain they are two women and two men."

"Maybe these will help," Bellows said, pointing at the files.

"We hope. Where is Mr. Millhouse?"

"Dex lives at Golden Living Estates, about fifteen minutes from here on the north side near the campus."

CHAPTER 14

Larry and I planned on heading home by two. After Penny's pointed remarks following my bushwhacking, I needed to be sure not to push the envelope too far. Terry, Larry's wife of forty-nine years, was used to a cop's hours, but I'm sure she'd had similar conversations with her husband. Larry said nothing as we drove north through South Bend and past the Notre Dame campus. One remarkable thing about Notre Dame University: at any time, at any public gathering in America (like a dinner at a country club or a church social), at least one person who went to Notre Dame will be there. The Irish seem to involve themselves in every part of Midwestern life and, most likely, American life. I also imagine the school's endowments are pretty lucrative.

"I'm glad I went to Northwestern, Craig," Larry confessed. "I'm a Big Ten guy. I've always thought that Notre Dame should have been in the Big Ten instead of their strange relationship with the conference. Now that the Big Ten extends from coast to coast, I'm not sure what it all means."

"Money. It means money," I said.

"Cynical bastard." He laughed.

"It's just the way it is. It's always about the money."

Larry's phone rang, and Big Ben booming came through the truck's speakers.

"Really? London?"

"My favorite city outside of Chicago." He punched the button on the steering wheel. "Larry Martini."

"Hi, Larry, Garry here. You and Craig still in South Bend?"

"Yes, just left the chief of police. Amazing information, big surprises—we'll bring you all up to speed."

"How's the muggee?"

"He's good, no aftereffects."

"I guess we found out how hard Craig's head is. I always knew it, but this confirms it."

"Ha ha," I offered.

"We are on our way to interview a detective who may know more about the people in the freezer. The registration name that came with the Studebaker . . ."

"Walter Paine?"

"Yes, he and his wife were murdered, and their car stolen. Their children were involved."

"Damn. Were they also killed?"

"No, they survived. We can go over all this this weekend. What do you have?"

"Both interesting and surprising. This feature in Google lets you drop an image into their program, and Google's AI will find similar images. I dropped a couple of the photos I took of the artwork from the house. They were part of a home robbery in 1962 in Kenosha, Wisconsin. An executive with American Motors owned the Picasso. It was reported stolen in a newspaper article connected to the image."

"Do we have a theme developing here?" I asked.

"Theme?"

"Garry, we are a few blocks from the closed Studebaker plant. Walter Paine worked for Studebaker; he was a senior executive. Your man in Kenosha was an auto executive?"

"Looks like it. I'll let Mike know. He's chasing down news

articles—another app and informative source. You said you are interviewing a detective?"

"He retired thirty-four years ago, and he's ninety-one."

"Good luck with that," Garry said. "I usually can't remember what I had for breakfast. Let's meet up sometime this weekend. I'll send you all a text about time and location. Drive safe."

* * *

Retired Detective Dexter Millhouse sat in a black vinyl lounge chair in the library of the senior home. When he saw us, he waved us in. I've not seen a bigger smile. Dexter is a small man now. But there was a robustness that hung about the guy like an aura. His smile radiated warmth, his once blue, now bluish-gray eyes twinkled, and his pinched-up cheeks were pink, not the usual trappings that one sees in a person who has survived the vagaries of life into his nineties.

"You must be the detectives from Illinois," Dexter said, still waving us in. "Linda called and said you would be over. I don't get a lot of visitors, and I've outlived my old friends. It's the youngsters that come around now and then, mostly out of curiosity, I think. I do have some great stories. The chief said you had information about one of my old cases, the Paine murders. I am glad to be of help."

His eyes sparkled, and I thought I saw a tear. "Thank you, Mr. Millhouse," Larry said.

"Please, call me Dex. Sit, sit. You there, and you, there." He pointed. "I've got some vision issues, macular something or other, so the closer you sit together, the easier to have a conversation."

When we sat, I noticed a couple of binders, like the ones at the police station, on the low table next to him. We'd only left

Chief Bellows an hour earlier; this man was organized.

"The chief mentioned that you are interested in the Paine killings. There hasn't been a week that I hadn't thought about those deaths. It was the one that got away. So where do we start, Detectives?"

"First of all, Dex, we are not detectives," Larry began. "We are helping our local police department sort out what we found and its connection to a friend. We are all amateurs."

"Dex, Larry here is a retired cop. Me, I was an architect for fifty years. He is Larry Martini, and I'm Craig Martin; glad to meet you."

"And me you. Now what is this all about?"

We spent the next thirty minutes telling Dex everything that led up to our trip to South Bend. He said "no kidding" a few times, "you cannot be serious" twice, and punctuated the discovery of the bodies with a hearty, "I'll be damned." When we got to the Studebaker, he said, "For sixty years, I've believed the car had been dumped into the St. Joseph River that runs through town."

When finished—it was a tag team description and bounced back and forth between us, Dex sat there, took a deep breath, contorted his face, and looked out the window to the garden beyond. One of the staff looked in and asked if everything was all right.

"We are just hunky-dory, Doris. Can you have the kitchen make us a big pitcher of iced tea? We are going to be here for a while. And a half dozen of those chocolate chip cookies." He looked back at the two of us. "Yes, I believe it will be a while. I have had over sixty years to sort this evil out and was stymied at every significant lead. And you come in and drop the big one on me, which upsets everything I thought I'd worked out. I'm about to pee in my pants from the excitement."

"Dex, we have no idea what you are talking about," Larry

said. "We have what appears to be a stolen car, four mutilated bodies, and they seem connected to this man Walter Paine."

"Not seem to, Mr. Martini. They are connected directly and murderously. Evil walked that Friday night in June 1963. I was there, and I saw it all."

Doris walked in carrying a tray. She placed it on the low table and poured us all tall glasses of iced tea. A lemon slice was offered, and we accepted. The cookies, our first food since breakfast, were delicious.

"Here is what I know," Dex began. "Most of what I will tell you is in the files, but some is conjecture and even speculation. It is hard to connect the dots when many are missing." He slowly took his glass and sipped.

"Walter and Clare Paine lived on Oak Road in a subdivision of nice homes southwest of South Bend. Mr. Paine worked for the Studebaker automobile company. That night Walter was forty-eight years old, and Clare was forty-three. They had three children—Janet was fourteen, Mark was eleven, and Louis was seven. Walter had worked in the automobile industry since he returned from World War II. He was a captain in the Army. During the war, he had been in logistics and supply. He never fought but was based in England before and during the invasion. When he returned to the U.S., he was hired by the Studebaker-Packard Corporation and worked in their shipping department. Eighteen years later, he was in charge of all part supplies for the company; he was a senior vice president, and some told me in follow-up interviews that he was on track to become its president. Sadly, the company quickly imploded after his death, and by 1966 disappeared as an automobile manufacturing company. Did you see that big building downtown? Hard to miss. It has been an empty shell for more than sixty years. Maybe someday it will be something, but right now, it's a reminder of when South Bend was great." He took another long sip of his tea.

"The Paines married a couple of years after the war ended. Clare—excuse my familiarity; I've been carrying this a long time—grew up on the University of Michigan campus. Her father was an economics professor that focused on the automobile industry. It was at a symposium on the future of the automobile where he was speaking that Clare and Walter met. It sounded almost idyllic, as their daughter told me a few months after the murders. They were a well-known and respected couple; she was the ultimate business wife—back when that was as critical as the man's job. I could go into everything that went on at the business and all Studebaker's ups and downs during those days, but it distracts from the story. So, as we say in the detective business, I will cut to the chase.

"Just before midnight on Friday, June 21, 1963, the station received a phone call. The caller complained that they had heard gunshots. The caller said the location of the gunshots was near the Paine house. They were specific. Dispatch sent a prowler out to investigate. By this time, it was almost one o'clock in the morning. The patrolmen could see that the lights were on inside the Paine residence, and they investigated. They walked the perimeter. Mr. Martin, you said you were an architect?"

"Yes, I was, fifty years," I said.

"You've not been to the house?"

"No, this is all new to us."

"You should. It is a Frank Lloyd Wright design, one of his last. Walter commissioned the work in the mid-fifties. They'd lived in the house for eight years. Very nice; even an old fart like me can tell. The officers walked the perimeter, saw what looked like two bodies in the living room, and entered through a broken rear slider door. Walter and Clare were dead. Clare lay on her husband. In the hallway lay a child, unconscious. Blood covered his pajamas. The officers immediately called it in. The medical techs got the boy, Louis, to the hospital. He survived, but his spine had been severed, and he was paralyzed from the waist down. The parents were dead, the woman had been shot in the head, the man in the back."

"You said there were two other children?" Larry said.

"Yes, Janet and Mark. When the robbers broke into the house, Janet took her brother and hid in a closet. She couldn't get to Louis. It appears he wandered into the killings and was shot. He was lucky. I'll get more into that later."

"Robbers—there was more than one?" I asked.

"Let me finish the setup, and then I'll answer those questions. It was two in the morning when my partner and I got the call. He was Detective Jack Buchanan. We arrived just after two thirty. I had been on the force for eight years, two as a junior detective to Jack. He was a mentor and father to me. He died of a heart attack in 1978. This case tore at him as much as it did me. The children came out of hiding while the police were investigating. We barely had time to cover their parents' bodies with sheets. Trying to question two terrified children in the middle of the night is not something I want to do again. They said they heard yelling, then gunshots, when Janet tried to find Louis. Later we determined that he had just walked into the murder scene looking for his mother; we can discuss the kids later. I talk to Janet every few years or so to keep her up to date, such as it is. She lives up in Lansing and is an attorney. Nice lady.

"Janet told us why they were home that evening. The family was supposed to be in northern Michigan that Friday night, but Mark's Little League team had to play a rain-delayed game that afternoon, so they decided to head up the next day, Saturday. They have a family cabin on Torch Lake, Clare's family summer residence. Her grandparents were there waiting for them, but they never arrived. It was then that she told us about the Studebaker Lark. It was in the driveway that night and was a new car. She said her father was thrilled to have one of the latest models to drive. He was optimistic it would turn the company around. She said she liked the color, sort of an iridescent green. We didn't learn any of this until past six o'clock Saturday morning. I wanted to press the kids more. Jack would have none of it. Give them a couple of days, he said. They'd been through too much to press this. He was right, but maybe we would have found it if we'd called for a statewide all points."

After another mouthful of iced tea, Dex opened one of the files. "We found evidence everywhere, bloody footprints on the floor, blood in the entry hallway, one bullet casing for a .45 automatic, later determined to be a 1911 Colt."

Larry looked at me and nodded.

"What?" Dex said. "What was that nod?"

"In the trunk of the Studebaker, we found a 1911 Colt automatic. The magazine was empty. A bullet recovered from one of the bodies in the freezer was matched to the gun."

"No shit. Interesting. In addition, five valuable paintings were taken." He looked at the file. "Two small Renoirs, two Pissarros, and a Matisse portrait. These paintings belong to Clare's family. Her parents collected French Impressionists."

"Wealthy, right," Larry said.

"I interviewed Clare's parents, the Hineses, in their Ann Arbor home. Mr. Hines's family collected the paintings well before World War I. Yes, they were well situated but hardly rich by today's standards—art was cheaper then. The robbers also took two boxes of quality silverware—real silver, mind you. They also took an unknown amount of money, jewelry, and watches from a wall safe; the guess was about fifty thousand dollars cash. The jewelry was expensive. Janet was little help; she didn't know about the contents. We assumed the safe was unlocked. There was no sign of force on the lock."

"They could have been forced to open it," Larry suggested.

"I agree, but we had no supporting evidence."

"And they took the Studebaker," I said.

"Yes, that was weird. They obviously arrived in another vehicle but then left in Studebaker. I've maintained that they split up, one or more to one car, the remaining robbers in the other. We found evidence to support my theory, but it was inconclusive. More on that later."

"You said others; how many?" Larry asked.

"The bloody footprints were for three different pairs of feet. Based on their size, two men and one woman. The killings were messy, blood sprayed everywhere, and the killers weren't too concerned about their feet. And one set of fingerprints was found on the edge of the sliding door. Three neat fingerprints from a right hand matched a small-time juvenile delinquent from Warsaw, Indiana. His name is Tobias Wozniacki."

"And did you ever find him?" I asked.

"No. Our follow-up put him with another kid who went to high school with him, also from Warsaw. We discovered that they were in South Bend during the robbery and killings. The other kid was Joseph Slauger. Both boys were twenty-four. We canvassed the bars and made connections to both. We also found they knew two women, identical twin sisters, Sheila and Gloria Lingermann, both from South Bend and twenty-two. A couple of the local bartenders reported that they strung along guys at bars, and then the boys would take over and rob the marks. The girls were pretty, according to reports. We couldn't put them in the house, just Tobias."

"Well, damn. All this adds a few more pieces to the puzzle," Larry said.

CHAPTER 15

"What do you have, other than the Studebaker?" Dex asked. "You mentioned bodies, and sixty years is a long time. They couldn't be in good shape."

"Yes, there were four bodies," Larry said, "They had been cut apart and wrapped in clear plastic. It still amazes us that they could last that long through blackouts and mechanical failures. We don't know if others in the Fisher family knew about the bodies, money, or art. Allen, our friend, died three months ago and is survived by two siblings. We are looking into all that."

"Fisher's?"

"That is the name of the family that owned the house with the bodies and the Studebaker. Allen Fisher, the son, was a friend of ours. His death got this all rolling," Larry said.

"Interesting. Families—you know the adage about choosing friends but not your family. For many, it is a sad yet true story."

"True," I said, agreeing. "Did any of your interviews or evidence collecting lead to a man, Ronald Fisher?"

Dexter Millhouse scrunched his face and said, "No. That is a new name for me. I've been through the files and the interviews so many times I believe I'd remember. You said this Fisher house is where they found the Studebaker?"

"Yes, actually we found the car, the money, the art, and the bodies," Larry said. "His son lived in the house his whole life. He inherited it when his father, Ronald, murdered his sick mother and killed himself in 1991. Allen Fisher lived alone in that house for the last thirty-three years."

"Now, that is bizarre and difficult to believe. The connection to all this is the car. The bodies you found?"

"Two men and two women. After he put the pieces together, the ME says they were in their early twenties. The girls were harder. They were identical twins."

"My Lingermann twins?"

"Possibly. There were no identifications, and we need to get corroboration with your crime, somehow," I said. "And we have no other DNA sources to compare with. You mentioned you had evidence of another car."

"This is not in the Paine files," Dex said, tapping the stack. "This happened three days after the murders. One of our patrols in town found what they assumed to be an abandoned car. When they tracked down the license plate—it took some time, it's not like today with computers in patrol cars—it came back registered to Tobias Wozniacki."

"From Warsaw, Indiana," Larry said.

"The same. The empty car was parked in an alley behind an old brick warehouse. No keys. That warehouse is a few blocks from the police station. With Wozniacki as our identified person of interest in the killings, we began a building-to-building search—there were mostly warehouses in the area. We got a search warrant; in one warehouse, we found what we determined was a crime scene. Inside were tire prints in the dusty floor leading from the roll-up door, footprints, and four distinct pools of blood. There were obvious signs of bodies being dragged across the concrete floor, loaded into a vehicle, and removed. We found a single bullet casing under a rack of shelves. Whoever did the shooting policed his brass but missed one. It was for a .45-caliber pistol; it did not match the caliber of the bullets that killed the Paines. Our only connections to Wozniacki were his abandoned Plymouth and fingerprints at the Paine house. We could not match anything or anyone else. This was long before DNA was a thing, so there was no positive identification from the blood and tissue we found. We did type the blood—two pools were identical and for females, and we know why, now. The others were for males; again, not much else to match. We also found in an office a recently cut rope. It appeared as though someone had been tied to a chair."

"Who owned the warehouse?" I asked.

"A local fellow owned the building; he was out of town that weekend. He leased it to a manufacturing company that did work with Studebaker. He never met the contact. The lease had been through a local broker and was for one year. The company that leased the warehouse was in Racine, Wisconsin. The lease expired the same month as our discovery. There was no answer to the phone number on the warehouse lease. The owner speculated that someone may have broken into the warehouse. It was a dead end."

"I'm guessing that that contact was Ronald Fisher," I said. "I remember he worked for a manufacturing company located in Harvey. It's a town about twenty miles from Lincolnville. I guess he stored parts there but didn't want it connected to his company."

"Damn. That's a reach but plausible. But as I said, Ronald Fisher's name came up just once."

"Excuse me, but you said you didn't recognize the name Ronald Fisher. The Fisher name never came up," Larry said.

Dex stopped and stared for a moment at Larry, then blinked. "You are right. My mind jumbles some things up. Too much sometimes."

"It happens, Dex. Too much to do and so many directions. Ronald Fisher—when did you hear Ronald Fisher's name?"

Millhouse picked up one of the binders and flipped through the pages. He stopped and ran his finger down a long, typewritten paragraph. "There he is—good God, I am becoming forgetful." His finger tapped the copy. "Ronald Fisher attended a dinner party the Paines threw the previous week at their house. He was on a guest list that the caterer helping Clare Paine still had. There were ten other names on the list; with spouses, there were maybe twenty guests at the dinner." He looked at the copy and flipped the page. "Here it is, Ronald Fisher, phone interview. He was two hours away at his home in Illinois the night of the killings. According to the notes, he seemed distraught when told about the Paines. He said that the Paines were longtime friends, and he was at the dinner. There are no other notes."

"Who was to know back then? It would be hard even to speculate," I said.

"That was my job, Mr. Martin, to speculate. However, you are correct. Nevertheless, right now, if I had connected this to Fisher, his employer, and the warehouse, who knows."

"Yes, that's true. The twins?"

"The Lingermann twins, yes—the girls, as I called them."

Dex picked up another of his binders and carefully flipped through the pages. He stopped and again read something, then looked at us. "When we followed up on the Lingermann twins, we learned that Sheila had a baby boy about a year earlier. We met with the girl's grandmother, who took over raising the child—the twins' mother died in 1960 from a drug overdose. Later, I learned that an aunt raised the child after the grandmother passed. The girls disappeared the same weekend as Tobias and Joe. We watched the Lingermann house for a while, wondering if they might return. Blood tests on two of the pools in the warehouse matched the blood type for the girls, which we got from the hospital where Sheila had the baby, but we couldn't match the specific blood pool since they were identical. As I said, we had nothing to compare to the men."

"Your assumption?" Larry asked.

"Based on the amount of blood, someone killed the four people in the warehouse, policed the scene, missed the shell, and removed the bodies. And now, it appears, they used another car to take the bodies to Lincolnville, Illinois."

"The car being the Studebaker?"

"Yes, it may have been the Studebaker. I now have more dots to connect. The killings had quite an effect on the survivors."

"I can only imagine," Larry said. "They are the forgotten in cases like this."

"I've kept in contact with Janet Paine. She lives in Lansing, Michigan. The maternal grandparents raised the three children. Janet is an attorney and is married to a federal judge. They have a couple of adult children. Her brother Mike lives in Colorado. I only know about him through Janet. He's married and has a car dealership in Colorado Springs."

"Louis, the child shot?" I asked.

"Louis died in 1995 from complications due to his injury. Janet was heartbroken. It has been a lot to carry around for sixty years."

"You said Sheila Lingermann had a child?" Larry asked.

"Yes, the child, a boy, was eight months old when Sheila disappeared. He was named Henrik Lingermann. The aunt did a good job taking over for the grandmother. The wildness of Sheila and her twin missed a generation."

"How so? You've kept in contact with the child?" I asked.

"All I know is that he is a big-time mucky-muck in the automotive world."

"You know a lot about him. Why?" I asked.

"We keep an ear to the road, so to speak, here in South Bend when it comes to the automotive world—leastwise some of us do, especially when the man's face appears in national magazines."

"And who is that?" Larry asked.

"Henry Lindeman, the electric car guy."

"No shit," I said.

We were silent for the first twenty minutes of our ride home on the Indiana Toll Road. When we passed La Porte, I couldn't hold it any longer.

"What the hell went on back there, Larry? We go to South Bend to chase down a license plate and return with six murders. Good God!"

"Six murders that we know about," Larry added. "All we added are two more, the Paines. We already had four in the box."

"That's sick."

"Police humor, Craig. But yes, to your point, this has just become much bigger. The robbery, the Paines' murders, Walter Paine, and the automobile industry. And now the possibility that the Paine killers were also murdered and taken to Marigold Court, chopped into pieces, and stuffed into Sears Coldspots. It's both overwhelming and scary. All this went on in our quiet little court, and no one made any connections to any of it."

"That we know of," I added.

"Yes, that we know of."

Ahead, the toll road disappeared into a dark wall of advancing clouds; a Midwestern storm was about to slam into us.

"That front is moving in fast," Larry said. "It will hit before we reach home. Why don't you call the fellas and set up a time this weekend where we can bring everyone up to speed."

"I'll ask Garry if we can use his club. That worked out fine last time."

"Perfect."

I called Penny first.

CHAPTER 16

June 1963

The St. Joseph River starts in the highlands of Michigan near the Indiana border and flows generally westward, turning south briefly into Indiana, twisting through the town of South Bend, Indiana, and then returns to heading north, eventually entering Lake Michigan at the twin cities of St. Joseph and Benton Harbor, Michigan. During its 206-mile course, the river drains some of the finest fertile farmlands of southern Michigan, northern Indiana, and Ohio. For thousands of years, before the Europeans' arrival (or invasion, according to some), the river was an important canoe and trade route east and west between Lake Michigan, Lake Huron, and Lake Erie. It augmented the famous Indian Sauk Trail that crossed this river at several locations.

Twenty miles north of South Bend, on the western shore of a small lake formed by damming the St. Joseph River near Berrien Springs, Michigan, sits Camp Betz, a fifty-acre scout camp. The camp is about eighty miles northeast of Lincolnville and is the year-round campground for the Boy Scouts of the Scouting Councils of Cook and Lake Counties in Illinois and other scout councils from the region.

The gang had spent a few summers as regular camp scouts. We worked on merit badges, camping skills, and woodsmenship. Our cabins were wooden barrack-styles with bunk beds. We called our cabin the Eagle Perch. The camp's showers and bathrooms were communal and located central to the rows of cabins; it was more than three hundred feet away for the campers. If you had to pee at night, you did it as a bear would. Two football fields away sat Thunderbird Hall, which contained the kitchen and dining facilities. The woodland grounds gradually sloped down to the lake, swimming pool, canoes, small sailboats, and other watercraft.

That June 1963, the Marigold boys were not just campers; we were camp counselors and assigned separate living quarters in tents with wooden floors and beds. They were far better than the stuffy cabins that became stagnant ovens at night during the hotter summer days.

Our duties were assisting the younger scouts, managing the lifeguard stations at the pool and the lake, helping in the dining room, and doing whatever the camp director needed. For us six boys, it was as close to heaven as possible. We were independent, set our hours (to a point), and were free of overbearing parents and annoying siblings—as said, it was paradise to fifteen-year-old boys.

One evening, after the first week we spent preparing the camp for the first summer scouts, we built a campfire that looked out over the lake, sat on logs that half-circled the fire, and for the first time, enjoyed an hour to ourselves. Lights sparkled through the trees from across the lake. The rumor was that the lights were from a Girl Scout camp.

"What do you say we take a couple of the canoes, paddle over there, and see what's up," Mike said.

"That is not a Girl Scout camp," I said. "I asked the head counselor, and he laughed. It was always a rumor, but the lights are just houses. And if you take the canoes without permission, they will send you home."

"He wants to keep the girls to himself," Garry said. "Got to be a camp. Who else would be out here? We're a hundred miles from any city."

"Look, lame brain, we are only eighty miles from Lincolnville," Allen offered. "I checked it against the odometer on Mr. Martin's station wagon, eighty-three miles exactly."

"See, almost a hundred miles."

"There are hundreds of cities and towns between us and Lincolnville. I'm going with Allen; you are a lame brain," Larry said. Changing the subject, he asked, "I haven't seen your dad around much this summer, Allen. What's he up to?"

There was a long pause as Allen, sitting at the end of one of the logs, looked off into the dark. The waning moon sat just above the black wall of the treetops on the opposite side. It threw a silver strip of light across the lake's glass-like surface.

"He's been busy," Allen answered. "Summer is the busiest. The auto plants are retooling and getting ready for the winter. They plan ahead more than a year."

"So, what's he doing?" Larry pressed.

"He was in Kenosha a couple of weeks ago, then up to Detroit, then back to South Bend. He sells his company's parts to all the car companies. He's always on the road, two, three days at a time, sometimes a whole week."

"I saw your mom heading out with your sister and brother," Tommy said.

"Yeah, she was driving up to Milwaukee to stay with Grams. Mom likes it there. It's a place along the lake, peaceful, she says. That way, Dad doesn't have to worry about getting back home. I'm up here, and they are there. It works out well."

"But you never see him," Larry added.

"I see him enough."

Three of us had moved off the court, or more correctly, our parents had moved from Marigold Court. Garry Hughes's family now lived in Chicago Heights, my family was in a larger house also in Chicago Heights, and Tommy Ellis's folks had moved to what the boys called a mansion in Olympia Fields. Mike Jasicki, Larry Martini, and Allen Fisher still lived on the court. We still lived less than four miles from the center of Lincolnville.

The six of us sat quietly watching the moon dapple the water; Mike broke the silence.

"It's a shame. We only get one father. He's important—parents are important."

"Stay out of it, Mike," Allen said. "It is what it is. I remember your pop on the lawn in front of your house. We all got shitty families to deal with."

None wanted to start an argument, especially this argument. It is a no-win. Every family has issues, conflicts, successes, and failures. Allen's father's long absences, traveling, and rumors of a short temper. Mike's alcoholic and now divorced father. Larry's father, who lost the fingers on his left hand in Italy during the war—all had personal and physical issues.

In contrast, Tommy's father's pediatric practice did well, catering to the crop of Baby Boomer babies. Garry's blue-collar father worked in the steel mills and still could afford a new house in Chicago Heights, and my father had just told us that he would be starting a manufacturing business to cater to the appliance business. All families are different—yet I remembered what my sophomore English teacher told us when we studied the arcane Russian authors.

"What do you think of this first line in Tolstoy's *Anna Karenina*?" she asked. "*Happy families are all alike; every unhappy family is unhappy in its own way.*"

Barbara Stastic, the well-appreciated and -endowed young woman in the front row of the class, raised her hand, was acknowledged, and agreed. "Yes, I believe that Tolstoy understood families quite well, and there is truth to what he said."

"Is this opinion based on your own experience, Barbara?" the teacher asked. "The happy or unhappy part of the sentence."

There was a slight tittering among some of my classmates. They had recently learned that Barbara's mother had left their house in Flossmoor and gone to California to join a commune.

Barbara looked around the classroom, brushed away strands of her blonde hair, and then back at the teacher. "Some families can become happily unhappy, Mrs. Wiltz."

Mrs. Wiltz studied the girl, not sure how to answer. "Happily, unhappy?"

"Maybe Tolstoy was too engrossed in his own unhappy family and had trouble projecting outside of it. Sometimes an unhappy family becomes happy with just a single move of a chess piece."

Mrs. Wiltz was happy to have the discussion ended with the bell ringing. She wasn't sure how to answer such a profound statement like that or even if she could.

"I wish I had a cigarette," Mike said, adjusting his butt on the log. "I heard they sent one of the other counselors home for smoking—strange if you ask me. Everyone smokes."

"We are supposed to be upright and act like gentlemen," Larry said. "That's the reason behind scouting, to help us follow the twelve principles."

"Not one of them says, No Smoking," Mike continued. "You tell me, which one covers that sin?"

The others mentally went through the twelve principles: trustworthy, loyal, helpful, friendly, courteous, kind, obedient, cheerful, thrifty, brave, clean, and reverent. Yes, we all agreed to smoke or not to smoke was not one of the principles.

"Maybe it falls under the clean principle?" Tommy said.

"Not sure that's what they had in mind," I said. "I think

that's for a clean mind and body."

"That's a tough one. I've heard you talk about Barbara Stastic," Garry said. They all thought about Miss Stastic for a moment.

"And there you go, the whole clean thing is down the drain," I said. The boys all laughed. Yes, Barbara Stastic could do that.

"Dad's been talking about fixing up the basement for a recreation room," Allen said. "I'd rather he find a bigger house. I'm tired of living with my brother. Brenda has her room, and I don't know why. I'm the oldest. Maybe I can make myself a room in the basement."

"Made a difference when we moved," Tommy said. "I have a room, and my sister has hers."

"Your dad is a doctor. They get paid more than a plant foreman," Garry said.

"I wouldn't know about all that. I don't understand why someone gets more than someone else," Mike said. "A job is a job. Is your dad making steel more important than a doctor or a salesman, or even a dry cleaner owner?"

We thought about the statement. Soon, during our years in college, we would learn those thoughts had bounced around intellectual circles for the past hundred years and led to three major world wars where millions died.

"Some jobs are more important," Garry said.

"It's all conjecture and opinion," Mike continued. "Yes, if you break your leg, you need a doctor. You need a dry cleaner if you need the spots on your coat removed. Society makes those distinctions; a leg is worth more than a spot on your jacket. But why does one need to be paid more?"

"You sound like a communist," Larry said.

"I wouldn't know a communist if he walked out of the woods. I'm just wondering about families and money and where we are going," Mike said. "After my dad came back, it was good. Then he fell apart, and Mom said it was enough. The war messed with his head, he told us. It took a long time to get it straight. So, yes, a family can become happy and then unhappy."

"Let me cover a few of those principles, guys," Allen said, sticking his big right hand in his breast pocket and pulling out a package of Camel cigarettes. Garry lit a long twig and passed it around. A cloud of sweet smoke drifted out toward the lake. We resolved nothing and evaluated no new evidence—only re-affirmed our friendship.

CHAPTER 17

September 2024

The gang and Detective Audrey King sat around one of the bridge tables in the corner of the bar lounge at the country club. We each had short stacks of folders and papers in front of us. After drinks were served, the work began.

"You fellas have been busy," Audrey said, looking at the papers. She had asked that they keep her out of the day-to-day hustle. Her plate was full. These weekly or biweekly updates would suffice to keep her abreast of the investigation, an investigation that she believed would lead to no arrests, indictments, or prosecutions. She needed clarifications and identifications to clear her paperwork and hopefully answer the big question: Who were the four dead people in the freezer?

I looked at Larry. He nodded, and I began, "Audrey, it looks like the four were involved in the brutal execution murders of an important executive of the Studebaker Company and his wife in their home on June 21, 1963. Their son was also severely wounded but survived, and two other children survived uninjured. They were there to rob the house. The family, the Paines, were supposed to be away on vacation. They delayed their departure by a day and surprised the robbers. They were then murdered."

"Good God," the detective said. "This was what you found

after you chased down that license plate and the old car?"

"Yes," Larry said. "One thing did lead to the next."

I continued, "The retired South Bend detective, Dexter Millhouse—the junior detective on the case at the time—remembered it well; he even had copies of his notes. This unsolved crime has been grinding on him for sixty years. When we told him what we'd found—the car, the bodies, the stolen goods—he was like a guy who'd pulled a winning lottery ticket."

"I can imagine. I've got a few of those cases myself," Audrey added. "Identifications?"

"We believe so," Larry said. "Millhouse believes another crime scene, found a few days after the Paine murders, was connected to the original crime. In a South Bend warehouse, they discovered four blood pools, and based on blood types, they were from two men and two women. This was years before DNA testing, and there is nothing they can test today in the evidence boxes. One set of fingerprints was left at the Paine murders; they were matched to one Tobias Wozniacki, twenty-four years old, from Warsaw, Indiana. We have copies of his prints in the folder. He was a minor hooligan and grifter."

"Till he went big time," Tommy said.

"Yeah, till he went big," I said. "Millhouse, after exhaustive legwork, found a friend of Wozniacki named Joe Slauger. They were both identified by a couple of local bartenders. The two were from Warsaw, Indiana, and they hung out together. There's been no hard identification of Slauger connecting him to the crime, but the two men had not been seen for a few weeks when Millhouse tracked down the connections. Millhouse said they were often seen with a striking pair of twins, the Lingermann sisters. One of the bartenders confessed that the girls would solicit male patrons, then the boys would step in and rob them. The twins, like Slauger, had not been seen since the killings of the Paines. South Bend police could not place the others at the murder scene, just Wozniacki's fingerprints. However, the ME who tested the blood pools in the warehouse determined that two were from the same person."

"Or an identical twin?" Audrey asked.

"Or identical twin," I said, agreeing. "One more thing. Millhouse said when they chased down the Lingermanns, they discovered that one of the women—they were twenty-two at the time—had a baby boy; the child was eight months old. When they interviewed the twins' mother, she was beside herself. She had no idea where the girls, Sheila and Gloria, were. And she didn't know what to do with the baby. Millhouse could see this was not a good situation and called in what was then child protective services. We want to confirm what happened after that, but we have a name."

"Good job. A name?" Audrey asked.

"We are chasing that down. When we have more, I will let you know," I said.

"You believe that the bodies are these four?" Audrey asked.

"Yes, but we need more information to identify them positively," Larry said. "There are no fingerprints for three of the four people in the files. And, if the Lingermann child is still alive, and Millhouse said he is, he'd be sixty-one. We could ask for a DNA match. But that's a long shot."

"Agreed."

"We will continue investigating," I said. "Our collective curiosity is raised. Garry has some interesting news."

"Just a minute, you said there were three Paine children?" Audrey asked.

"Yes, three. Janet was fourteen, Mark was eleven, and the wounded boy was the youngest at seven. His name was Louis."

"Are they still alive?" Audrey asked.

"Millhouse says yes, two of them are still alive. He keeps in touch with Janet. She is seventy-five and lives in Lansing, Michigan. The youngest, Louis, died almost ten years ago from complications from his paralyzed condition. That's all he knew."

"So, could a third death be attributed to the robbery?"

"Yes, according to the law," Larry added.

"Craig, you started to say something," the detective said.

"It's what Garry found," I said and looked at Garry.

"I've been tracking down the paintings and artwork through various artificial intelligence programs on Google," Garry said. "I was shocked when some of the images popped up and matched the photos I took. They were all reported stolen during robberies in the early 1960s. The robberies were of automobile executives throughout the Midwest, from Kenosha, Wisconsin, to Detroit, Michigan. Three are the Paine paintings. They were photos in an *Architectural Digest* article about the Paine house published a year earlier, 1962—Frank Lloyd Wright designed the house."

I looked at Garry. "That's what Dexter Millhouse said—there's an article?"

I could have wiped the grin off Garry's face. "I was keeping the news until the right moment. I know you worship Wright; we've put up with your commentaries for fifty years. Yes, images of the paintings were in the article, and you confirmed they were stolen. We've got them in the storage unit along with the other paintings. With more time, there's a chance we can find the owners of the others and get them back to them."

"One thing we have a lot of is time," Mike said, holding his glass up for the bartender to see.

I looked at Larry. "I'd like to get back there; I would love to see the house."

"Assuming that it is still there," Audrey said.

"You can bet I'm going to find out."

"A question that hasn't been asked," Mike said. "We got the bodies, the car, the artwork, and the ludicrous amount of money and gold. My question is a two-parter: Who killed the four robbers, and how did they and all that loot get here? It appears we are missing a crucial part of this story."

"It has to be Mr. Fisher?" Tommy said. "If I remember correctly, he was into automobile parts."

"That's a leap. I'll agree it's not a long one, but the evidence is circumstantial," Audrey said. "Any ideas?"

"I say a lot more than circumstantial," Larry said. "The car—with blood in the trunk—was found in the Fisher garage. The car belongs to the Paines, and so do the paintings."

"Larry and I are going to contact Janet Paine," I added. "She lives in Lansing, Michigan, and her husband is a federal judge. We have her information from Millhouse. He offered to contact Janet and prepare her for our call. With her approval, we will talk to her."

"And this would help, why?" Audrey said.

"First, to confirm the artwork, maybe the car, anything to help fill in the story. We think that somebody set these four up for the robbery—they had no clue as to the value of the artwork—but the money was something else. Maybe she remembers something. Besides, we'd like to talk to her and tell her what we have found."

"You mentioned the son of one of the twins. Is he still alive?"

"Yes, and Millhouse filled us in," I said. "Mike and Garry are chasing records and anything else they can find through the local police to confirm it. The South Bend chief of police said she would help as much as possible. However, she is concerned that there could be trouble if the word gets out."

"I talked with Chief Bellows. She called me; we had a

pleasant conversation," Audrey said. "She wanted to check on you boys and make sure you are who you say you are. She was surprised and impressed that you guys were taking on this task. Like me, she doesn't have the resources to follow up on this cold case. What kind of trouble?" She looked at me.

"The Lingermann child, according to Dexter, has grown up to be some big-shot entrepreneur, wealthy. However, there is a name change, so we will confirm what we can."

"Well, damn, this snipe hunt only gets better and better. How's your head, Craig?"

"Still hurts, but I'm good. Whoever hit me is also on my list. I will find the asshole—I don't like being cold-cocked. Anything on the graffiti, Proverbs 11:21?"

"I remembered it from bible school," Audrey said. "*Assuredly, the evil man will not go unpunished, but the descendants of the righteous will be delivered.*"

"Interesting, especially the descendants part," Tommy said. "You must have pissed somebody off, Craig."

"As I said, if I find them, I have a score to settle."

* * *

Tommy gave me a tour of the storage unit they'd contracted. It was in Burr Ridge, about ten miles away, in an industrial park near the intersections of Interstate 55 and 294. Only an address, painted gold over the glass doors, identified it outside. To the side and on the glass, there was a small, discreet sign: PRIVATE FACILITY, PLEASE CALL AHEAD FOR AN APPOINTMENT. No phone number was on the door. I figured if you were there, you already knew the number. A key card was required to access the first room, a mantrap. This compact, secure vestibule faced another glass door. The enclosure was just large enough for four people. I also assumed that the glass doors and walls were bulletproof. A biometric reader that scanned Tommy's face and the right eyeball was mounted on the second door. He also placed his left hand on a flashing wall plate. Watching Tommy, I had the gory reminder from a dozen movie thrillers, where they popped out a guy's eye and used it to access the main entry—that wouldn't work here; you needed at least three or four other body parts. Two guards sat at a desk facing us. Only after Tommy performed the appropriate rituals did they open the interior door.

"Good morning, Mr. Ellis. It is good to see you again," the uniformed guard on the right said, checking the monitor built into the desk. "Would you please have Mr. Martin present his identifications?"

Tommy, who had called ahead, made sure that I brought my driver's license and passport. I passed them to the guard. The man on the left sat quietly watching me, then glanced at his monitor. That's when I caught a peek at the full body scan images of two people on the monitor. We had been scanned while waiting for the second door to open. I didn't know whether to feel safe or violated.

After checking and scanning my documents, I was asked to place my left hand on a flatbed scanner. Tommy had already done this next step during the security protocols.

"One moment, Mr. Martin," the right-hand guard said. "I am required to take a scan of your face." He stood and raised a small Go Pro camera and quickly took a photo, or I assumed it was a photo. For all I knew, he was looking into my soul. I remembered that Indians feared cameras; they would steal their souls. At this moment, I wasn't too sure they weren't right.

"Please wear these. They must be returned before you leave," our talkative guard said. He handed us elastic wristbands. "Mr. Jones will lead you to your locker, Mr. Ellis." A door opened behind the seated guards, and another uniformed guard walked out. He wore a Taser on his belt and a black collapsible baton. "Please follow him. I again warn you not to step off the pathway. Alarms will sound."

A couple of minutes later, we stood at a stainless-steel door along one wall of a well-illuminated hallway. There were six other identical doors, but none had numbers. Tommy's wristband glowed bright blue when he stood at the front of one door. Three feet away, the band had been dark gray. Standing there, a small panel on the door began to glow with the number 1367.

"They tell me that not placing numbers on the doors adds to the difficulties of locating the appropriate locker," Tommy said. "Only with the wristband can you positively identify your locker's door."

"Makes sense, I guess." I was impressed. "What about other aspects of the security?"

"I asked—they said it was not my concern."

"For the price they charge," I said.

"If you have to ask, then you can't afford them, was the answer."

"No kidding."

Below the glowing number was a simple key card entry slot, not unlike a hotel room entry. The only difference was that the hand plate next to the slot scanned your left hand while you ran the card through the device. When completed, the door popped open an inch.

"Mr. Ellis, I will wait at the intersection," Mr. Jones said. "If you need anything, double-click the button on your wristband."

There was a red button on my bright blue band. Mr. Jones smartly turned and walked to the intersection of the two corridors. Tommy pulled open the door. I'm guessing it weighed a couple of hundred pounds of stainless steel. It swung open easily and silently. Inside were steel shelves with boxes that held the jewelry, the cash, and the gold from the Fisher house. Stacked neatly against the walls on the left side were the dozens of artworks and graphics collected in the secret room and the house. I mused that this was probably one of Chicago's finest private collections of Impressionist and early modern art, worth whatever the market could afford. I also knew the money and jewelry were worth over a million dollars.

"Well, what do you think? Is it worth the ten thousand a month?" Tommy asked.

"Glad it's not my money."

"Me too."

CHAPTER 18

September 2024

At Bell's the following Wednesday, I was the first to arrive. I ordered a cappuccino and a croissant. Karen and Garry elevated the hash house's menu during the last few years. They now had a small counter out front that offered a selection of French and Italian pastries, a barista, and more coffee drinks than I'd ever heard of. Lincolnville may be a small-time suburban village, but Starbucks and some other local coffee brands forced the local foodies to better their usual fare of donuts. Karen's pastry chef was a young woman from the Chicago Culinary Institute, and she'd learned her art well. I was halfway through my pastry when Larry and Tommy rolled in, and Garry followed a few minutes later. Mike had called and said he'd be late but not to worry. He had exciting news—we were to start without him.

"Chief Bellows called," Larry began after we ordered our usuals. "Dexter was able to contact Janet Paine. She has agreed to meet with us. She lives just outside Lansing; she asked if her husband may join us. I agreed. I also talked to Dexter. He said that Janet is a retired prosecuting attorney for Michigan. And her husband is the current chief federal judge for the Western District of Michigan."

"Really? Judicial royalty," Garry said. "Considering what

happened to her, she seems to have accomplished a lot."

"I set up an appointment at noon this Friday. Craig and I will drive up. It's just a few hours each way."

"No problem; I can't go anyway. The club championship is this weekend," Garry said. "Someday, I hope to regain my past glory."

"Good luck with that," Tommy said. "Just remember that two weeks ago, that Ping driver had become your worst enemy. I think you called it a worthless shit-ass snake killer."

"I've been practicing."

"You need more than practice; prayers to the golf gods would help," Tommy continued. "Maybe sacrifice a chicken or something."

"And I understand that the defending champion is just twenty years old, plays on the University of Illinois golf team, and is a woman," I added. "I also understand she drives the ball three hundred yards."

"I will use my eleven handicap to its full advantage."

"And your snake beater?" Tommy offered with a grin.

Breakfast was served, and for a few minutes, it was quiet, each of the gang in their thoughts. Mike walked down the aisle with a folder under his arm, sat at the head of the table, and waited. His grin was as wide as that comic from the forties and fifties, Joe E. Brown—all lips and teeth.

"Well, Senior Cheshire Cat, what's got you all wound up?" Garry asked, pointing his fork at the man.

"I think I found him," Mike said. "It took a few hours of chasing down news articles in the local papers from 1963 and tapping into my Ancestry.com account to follow up some names, but then, bingo, there he was."

"Who the hell are you talking about?" Larry asked.

"The son of Sheila Lingermann, one Henrik Lingermann. Born December 20, 1962, in Memorial Hospital, South Bend,

Indiana."

"Damn—you think that's him, her son?" I asked.

"Not completely, but everything fits. But that's not the punch line. He goes by the name Henry Lindeman."

"Not Henry Lindeman, the electric vehicle guru?" I asked. Mike had just confirmed what Millhouse had told Larry and me.

"Yes, the same. Henrik Lingermann is now, sixty-two years later, the uber-businessman and chief prophet of the American EV company Jager."

"Or, according to some in the *Wall Street Journal*, the chief bullshitter. I'll be damned," Garry said. "There has to be a story there."

"His offices are in downtown Chicago. His manufacturing plant is in Whiting, near that old Ford plant."

"Now, that's irony for you. He's in the automotive business," I said.

"No kidding. The Jager website notes that he has been married thirty-eight years and has two grown children. There is nothing about them."

"Understandable," Tommy added.

"He is a force of nature. There is a lot out there," Mike continued. "*Wall Street Journal*, YouTube, *New York Times*, *Forbes*, TED Talks, and dozens of other articles. He sees himself as an American Elon Musk."

"You believe that this is the same person?" Larry asked. "We could be opening ourselves to serious embarrassment if he is not the right guy. And considering his public presence, he might not take kindly to answering our inquiries."

"Everything points to him. He notes in his autobiography that his grandmother raised him after his mother abandoned him—he's used that as his Horatio Alger story during some of his business speeches. He points out that he was not born with a silver spoon in his mouth. The theme: 'How I overcame the loss of my mother but found love from my grandmother.' He talks about how he taught himself business, voraciously read, and worked through the University of Michigan on a scholarship earning a master's and eventually a doctorate in economics."

"Another strike against him," the Northwestern and Wildcat grad Larry said.

"Parents?" I asked.

"Yes, it's implied, but not said directly, that his parents disappeared when he was a baby—no names given. His birth name, Lingermann, is not mentioned. He is also a leader in the business world in climate change and has sponsored international conferences on poverty and global warming."

"And his political support for anything Democrat," Tommy added.

"Yes, there's that—aren't you a Democrat?" Mike said, pointing a finger.

"There are Democrats, and then there are Democrats, just like Republicans."

"Why would we want to meet with him?" Garry asked. "Does he add anything to our investigation?"

"No more or less than what Janet Paine has," Mike said. "It's just one more detail that would help us complete the story. At least, that's my thinking. Garry and I are also chasing down the other artworks, and we have a few leads but nothing significant—yet. I'm close to confirming the victims' names in Kenosha. I have some names; I need confirmation. Then we'll chase down next of kin and relatives."

"Who have no more connection to the money or the art than we do, but that's how it will have to be, I guess," Larry said.

"As I was going through the images and getting a picture of

the artworks' past," Garry said, "I had an important thought. If these paintings were so valuable, even for 1963, these people would have had them insured. A friend here at the club is the president of one of the biggest insurance companies in the country. I asked him, 'What would your company do if items you had paid settlements on were eventually recovered, like expensive pieces of art or jewelry?'"

Garry continued, "'It has happened lots of times—there're precedence and legal cases that have defined the process,' he said. Simply put, the original and rightful owners or their estate have a right to the paintings. In most cases, the owner signs a subrogation agreement with the insurer that releases their rights to the piece of art just before they are paid the appraised amount of the lost artwork. If the piece is later recovered, the insurance company might claim the artwork and hope to sell it to recover their payment. However, the courts have held that subrogation is not a transfer of title or ownership of the piece. What typically happens is that the insurance company and the owners, or their estate, try and find an amicable solution. The original owners may elect to take the recovered artwork and pay back the insurance company for the money the insurer paid out when the settlement was made. Sometimes the owners don't want the piece but elect to have it sold, and the proceeds split with the insurance company, who would receive their original settlement and the owners the remainder. He is unclear on what would happen if the original owners or their estate no longer existed and who would own or control the artwork's fate. He was leaning toward the idea that the insurance company might be the rightful owner then."

"Is there a database for stolen artwork?" Mike asked.

"My guy said yes, it's the Art Loss Register. I'm chasing them down," Garry said. "Their website says they have been around since the early 1990s; they are in London. Our pieces date from the 1960s, and I'm hoping that older stolen pieces are in the system. Till then, all we have are a few names from newspapers. I'm guessing that some of the stolen pieces were from people who did not want their names out there. This database might help."

"And the money and the gold and the jewelry?" I asked. "There is a lot there. We can't keep it, and Barbara has said more than once, 'If it's from where it looks like it came from, it's stolen,' and she wants no part of it."

"It's a good bet that Allen's sister and brother have designs on that loot, all of it," Larry added. "I bet the brother is the one that clipped you over the head and left the biblical phrase as both a warning and threat."

"That thought has crossed my mind," I said. My head still throbbed, especially when I had to think. The phrase from Proverbs stuck with me. *Assuredly, the evil man will not go unpunished, but the descendants of the righteous will be delivered.*

After some research, Penny interpreted the phrase: "If you believe in the Lord, then you will be saved and be with him. If the evil person continues in his way, he will be punished for his deeds."

"You think there's a connection to these two siblings?" I asked.

"Yes, they know a lot more than what they let on, I'm sure of it," Larry said. "Even when we were kids, those two seemed broken. They were strange, and certainly now, in this context, more than interested in what has gone on. They believe that what was in the house is theirs. Did you talk to Barbara about them?"

"I did, and she said, 'They have no legal right to any of it.' That was the way Allen wrote his will. He paid a qualified attorney to put it all down. And he specifically said they were to receive nothing."

"Did the will mention the money, the art, the bodies?" Tommy asked. His smile had a ghoulish look to it.

"No, it simply reads, 'All possessions, goods, properties, assets, and currencies found in the house are to be shared equally between his two children, Barbara and Steve.' Carte blanche. After all this, they both told me that this needs to be sorted out—and that we must keep Brenda and Dennis as far away from all this as possible."

"They remind me of yellow jackets," Larry said. "Once they get a taste of the fat, there's no way to get rid of them."

CHAPTER 19

September 2024

Larry and I pulled into the circular driveway that led up to a stylish glass-enclosed modern house with windows that reflected the dense greenery of the woodland neighborhood on the east side of Okemos, Michigan. The house, hidden from the narrow country road that wound through the neighborhood, was engulfed by hedges, privets, honeysuckles, and hydrangeas. If you didn't know, you would drive right past.

Before we could dismount Larry's truck, an older couple strolled out the front door and engaged us with smiles and a wave. It was unnerving; the tall, striking woman about our age in a summer weight suit in light blue, soft yellow blouse, and matching blue shoes walked toward us. The man, robust and sporting a mustache and goatee, wore a black polo shirt and khaki dress pants. As I said, I was uncomfortable—we were dressed in polo shirts and dark slacks and felt underdressed, and we're here to discuss the most traumatic event in Janet Paine LeBlanc's life. It had the opening visuals of a summer afternoon social; cue the mint juleps.

Since I'd made the contact, I extended my hand. "Craig Martin, Mrs. LeBlanc. This is my friend and fellow investigator, Larry Martini."

"A pleasure," Janet LeBlanc said, introducing her husband,

Bernard LeBlanc. "Please, let's go inside; the humidity is less humid. I've refreshments in the screened-in porch, and it's quite comfortable—iced tea, lemonade, and cookies."

I looked at Larry, and he gave me a look that said what I was thinking. "What the hell?"

Judge LeBlanc pointed to the padded wicker chairs, then poured us iced tea. The cookies, I swear, were Girl Scout Do-si-Dos.

"These are from our granddaughters. We have three," Janet said with a laugh. "Cookie time puts a serious hit on our budget, and we must treat the girls equally. And if you gentlemen eat your fare share, there will be less to tempt me."

"I understand, Mrs. LeBlanc," Larry said. "I have two granddaughters. Young capitalists all."

"Please call us Janet and Bernie," Janet said. "There's been enough of the formal stuff of judge and madame prosecutor to last us a lifetime. We've both retired. Informality is just fine. When Dexter Millhouse called, I was astonished by his story. After all these years, this sadness returns and is far too bizarre to make up. He said that we had to hear the story directly from you. He couldn't do it justice. I'll tell you, to shock Dex is quite a triumph. I've known him for almost sixty years, and he is as hard-boiled as they come. As a prosecutor, I would have been thrilled to have that detective on my side."

"He is impressive," Larry said. "And sharp. We should all be so lucky at his age."

"Now, what is this about a Studebaker and a freezer?" Bernie asked as he bit into his cookie.

An hour later and at the end of our story, the LeBlancs just stared at the two of us. Larry and I had developed a tag team in the story's telling, but each time, even to us, it sounded more bizarre than the last telling.

"You believe that Ronald Fisher was behind all this?" Janet

said. "He planned the robberies using his business clients as targets? And he kept the loot?"

"Yes, but we can't entirely confirm it," I said. "He may have fenced some of the artwork, but sixty years have passed, and any past connections are probably lost. He may have spent some of the money or sold some of the gold; again, we have no way of knowing. The physical evidence, artwork, jewelry, and money are substantial. We have stored them in a secure location under the direction of the Lincolnville Police."

"Good, I am always concerned about evidence," Janet said, "especially when it gets lost."

"Can you tell us what happened that night?" Larry said. "We understand your reluctance, but it may help us tie together some issues, especially regarding the car."

Janet looked at Bernard, and I saw her eyes tear up. She took a tissue and quickly blotted her cheek.

"I have gone over that night a thousand times in my mind," Janet said. "I don't celebrate our survival that June 21, the day of the murders. I try not to think about it. Nonetheless, when the first day of summer comes, it is impossible not to remember what my brothers and I lost—that night, it was more than our parents. It was our childhood, our future, and most of all, our parents' love for us and each other. We were a very happy family.

"Since Christmas, Mother had planned our annual summer vacation to our grandmother's cottage on Torch Lake north of Traverse City—the cottage is her parents'. We always spent at least two weeks, sometimes more. There was the lake, boating, waterskiing—I was getting good at it. My brothers loved to fish and go to Lake Michigan with our grandfather. I believe Dad was just glad to get away from all the automobile business in South Bend for a while. We were supposed to leave early that Friday; that was the plan. However, it was the end of Little

League, and Mark needed to make up a rain-delayed game to make it to the championship game. With one more win, they were in the championship. That game was Friday afternoon. Father decided to leave on Saturday. We weren't supposed to even be at the house that night.

"We came home about seven and had a light dinner of leftover hot dogs and potato salad. Mother wanted us in bed early; we would be up at five o'clock. She wanted to get going before the heat and humidity. Father's new Studebaker was going to be a moneymaker for the company. He was so proud; however, it did not have air-conditioning. At midnight I was awoken by yelling. I recognized my father's voice and another man's I didn't know. Then my mother screamed. I jumped out of bed and ran to the boys' room; our rooms were at the end of the hallway. Mark, frightened, was sitting up and staring at me. Louis was not in his bed. I returned to the hallway and looked toward the living room; Louis was standing there—he didn't move. Then there were gunshots and flashes, and I saw Louis fall to the floor. I wanted to run to him, but instead, I returned to Mark and pulled him into the closet. It was large, and we hid behind the piles of clothes in the back. I remember the smell of laundry soap to this day. I heard more yelling. It was a woman's voice, and she was laughing hysterically. Then two other male voices; one yelled, 'Shut up!' I did not recognize any of the voices.

"We waited another twenty or thirty minutes. Mark was shaking and crying. He held a tee shirt to his face to muffle his sounds and mask his fear. Me, I have never been so afraid."

"You did not see the people in the house?" Larry said.

"No, I believe there were at least three because of the voices. A few weeks later, as the investigation continued, that's what Dexter also believed. They found fingerprints of this guy named Tobias Wozniacki. They also connected three others to

160

him. They hung out together at bars in South Bend. Neither Mark nor I saw them. Louis did see them, but he was so traumatized by being shot, even when they showed him photos of the people a few weeks later, he could not identify them."

"That's understandable," I offered.

"Later, as a prosecutor, I saw the same thing time after time. Reliable people, devastated by what they saw, could not identify the bad guys. Larry, as a former cop, I'm sure you've seen that."

I looked at Larry. He was surprised by Janet's comment.

"Yes, ma'am, I have seen it."

She smiled at Larry's propriety. "Dexter told me you are a retired cop. I called the South Bend police chief, and she confirmed it. I figure this has all the markings of a cold case."

"It does, Janet. It is interesting being back in the game. Even us amateurs have tools now I would have been pleased to have when I was a cop."

"Dex said that there are others in this group of yours," Bernard said.

"Yes, there were six until Allen Fisher's death," I said. "As I said, Allen was the son of Ronald Fisher. We aren't sure now what Allen knew about his father. The five of us are doing this as a favor for his kids. It started as a simple housecleaning."

"And no good deed goes unpunished." Bernard laughed.

"It is beginning to look that way," Larry said. "What happened after they left?"

Janet stopped and gazed out the window. The deep woods, dark and cool, filled the view through the picture window. "It was all bloody and messy. After about ten minutes—it seemed like hours—Mark and I went to the front of the house. I will never forget what I saw. My parents lay on the floor on one side of the living room. Blood was everywhere, and bloody footprints were all over the wooden floors. Louis was unconscious but breathing; a pool of blood was under him. I learned later that he had been shot in the lower back, and his spine had been shattered. He never walked. Mark was crying. He still held the tee shirt from the closet. I knelt next to Mom; she had been shot in the head. Father's white shirt and chest were soaked red with blood. I later learned he'd been shot in the back trying to protect Mom. I called the police, but I heard the police sirens almost at the same time as I called. There was no 9-1-1 back then. It took time to get through to the police, and we were in the county. The sheriff had jurisdiction. Later, I learned that somebody called the crime in from a pay phone downtown. Who it was that called was never solved. Dexter told me a year or so later that there were attempts to connect our crime to another crime scene near the pay phone that was used, but the evidence was thin. The police believe the killers took Father's Studebaker and put the art inside. The car was never found—until now."

"We are so sorry," I offered.

"Thank you, but so much time has passed. I have to admit there are days when I never think of it. Then it comes back, even nightmares. And all this over some paintings and artwork."

"The artwork, was it insured?" I asked.

"My grandparents handled all of that. When I was older, they told me the insurance paid for our college. Our grandparents arrived the next morning, taking us to their Ann Arbor home. We lived with our grandparents near the University of Michigan; both of Mom's parents were professors at the university. I eventually went to Michigan State. That's why I got into law, and so did Mark. He's a corporate lawyer with an EV startup in Detroit, and before that, he spent thirty years at Ford. Sadly, we lost Louis ten years ago from complications due to his injury. As a prosecutor, I thought if I found the killers, I'd also charge them with his death. Now you think somebody killed the killers?"

"Yes, it appears so," Larry said. "Who killed them? We don't know. Tobias Wozniacki, Joe Slauger, and two identical twins, Sheila and Gloria Lingermann, have been missing since that night. We are close to confirming they were the bodies in the freezer."

"Those names are vaguely familiar. Dex probably mentioned them to us at some point," Janet said.

"What a sad story," Bernard added. "The paperwork about the insurance settlements—not sure where that all is, but we have it. It took a few years, and I remember it was with a big company. They insured all the Studebaker executives—and the company is still around. I will check our files and send you any information I find. The insurer might have a list of the artwork pieces and the payouts. Not sure if we want the pieces back, but Janet and I will talk about all that. We are travelers, not collectors, so we must consider it. I know the law regarding these things, even adjudicated on a few similar cases in federal court. We will let you know; thanks for keeping them safe."

We stood to leave. "A lot of money was found inside the house and dated from around that time, and there were hundreds of gold coins."

"And there is no way we can put a claim in for any of it," Janet said. "If I had my druthers, I'd send the money to pediatric hospitals. They would make better use of it than we would. I'm just speaking for us, and I'm certain Mark would agree. What the other victims involved in this would do . . . I can't speak for them."

"We understand and thank you. I will let the Lincolnville detective know."

* * *

It was after seven when Larry dropped me off at the house. I'd called Penny several times after we left Lansing and kept her up to speed on our progress home. The weather held; another front was moving in that evening and would delightfully push out the heat and humidity—all standard fare for a late Midwestern summer.

Penny handed me a gin and tonic, and we headed to the screened-in porch. Larry and I stopped to grab a hamburger at Burger King outside Kalamazoo. Larry needs to manage his blood sugar; he can't go too long between meals. All of us in the gang have our infirmities: Larry has Type 2 diabetes. Mike has a heart issue he's monitoring; it is an electrical problem, not a plumbing one. Tommy has Heather, and we are always concerned about what she is doing to him, though I admit he does look healthy and happy. Then there's Garry's heart, not that he will talk about it; his *is* a plumbing problem. I'm the picture of health, though a picture is worth a thousand words; my PSA number is rising, and Penny is concerned.

"This is taking up much of your time," Penny started.

"I have absolutely nothing else to do, and besides, this is interesting," I said. "We are hoping to find answers to some difficult questions."

"You found bodies in a freezer. Can't the police deal with all this?" she asked again.

"They are too busy with important matters that are happening now. These crimes are sixty years old. And now it appears that six people were murdered, and there may be more. We don't know."

Penny stopped mid-sip. She set her drink on the table and pointed her finger. "You didn't say these were murders—now, I definitely want you out of all this."

"Everyone connected must be dead, except those that were children. There's no killer out there trying to protect himself."

"Children? What children?"

It was ten o'clock when I finished telling Penny about Janet LeBlanc, what we'd discovered, and what was happening with the investigation. I hadn't realized how much I hadn't told her; that was on me. I promised to keep her informed—she deserved it. How much the others told their spouses, that was up to them.

"So, the bottom line, what is it?" she asked.

"Confirm the identities of the bodies, find the owners of the artwork, come to a resolution on the money, and maybe bring closure to Janet and Mark."

"And this billionaire son of one of the killers, what about him?"

"I have no idea."

"And Allen's siblings?"

"Now, that is a whole and scarier other matter."

The front struck at precisely ten fifteen; the wind picked up, and the rain pelted the porch roof. Penny and I sat there enjoying the welcome change. Flashes of lightning, followed by drumrolls of thunder, troubled the night. The temperature dropped fifteen degrees. I filled my glass for the third time and settled in for the show; Penny decided she'd had a long enough day and headed off to bed. No severe weather was predicted, just an agreeable cooling front. Fall was marching toward us.

CHAPTER 20

Summer 1968

Thunder and lightning exploded and echoed off the granite cliffs as the sharp edge of the cold front crossed the lake and headed directly for us like avenging demons. We lashed the five canoes in our small squadron together for safety, two in one pair and three in the other. The hastily joined canoes looked like Polynesian outriggers and, with the increased stability, helped us cross the lake before the severe wind hit. Then, with heaven's raw fury on us, we dragged the canoes up the bank and took shelter under the trees. We had no other option. High above us on the cliffs, lightning struck the tall pines and hemlocks; the thunder churned my gut. After we tied up the boats, we pulled our rain gear and strung up canvas tarps to counter the heavy rain. The storm raged for two hours; then, as follows these phenomena, a cool, almost cold, wash of air passed down the lake and over us. The gray pall of clouds separated, and the blue sky revealed itself. The sun's rays lit the lake's far side like a stage show. Being late June, we had another four hours of daylight and decided to set up camp here on this peninsula. The breeze off the water would keep the mosquitoes away.

By then, we knew our assignments well; four set up the tents, two were assigned latrine duty, and the rest built a fire.

Tommy and I got started on dinner. We had saved the cans of stew for such a night. Tommy got the stew into the Dutch oven, and I mixed up dumplings that would steam up in the stew. Later, dinner was lauded as a success, though we all were tired of the powdered fruit flavoring used to brighten the boiled water.

Some said the lake water in this part of Canada was as clean and pure as any in the world save for what washed out of mountainous snowmelt. We still didn't trust it. While you could fill a cup directly from the lake and drink, we advised everyone to keep that to a minimum. Getting sick on the water was not fun, nor were the runs. In some locations where we camped, the water for cooking and dishwashing contained tiny black bugs, thousands about the size of the head of a pin, all furiously swimming in circles. We would strain the water through cheesecloth and then boil it for use. Somebody in the group called them jobbies, and the name stuck. No one knew how many of those bits of protein we eventually consumed, but the thought, sixty years later, still gives me the willies. Luckily none got sick or contracted typhoid, giardiasis, E. coli, or salmonellosis. As far as we knew, the water was clean, and there were almost no humans upstream from where we were. Now, bears, moose, white-tailed deer, and fish (God only knows what they were doing in the water) were enough to ensure our desire to keep our drinking water as clean and purified as possible.

Four short years later, Allen and Mike were in Vietnam. They applied their experiences in Canada and struggled with new diseases: liver fluke, schistosomiasis, malaria, and a dozen other wormy things. Allen got malaria, and it was years before the bug was finally washed from his system. It was just one more thing added to his PTSD hit parade.

* * *

October 2024

Mike and I were unanimously selected to meet with Henry Lindeman. It was hard to argue with the verdict of the guys. Mike's extensive research and knowledge of the entrepreneur sealed it for him. I was there for continuity and my recent conversations in Indiana and Michigan. Larry had family issues, and he bowed out. Mr. Lindeman filled our conversation as we drove downtown. This time, I drove; Mike had a stack of files on his lap and would often refer to them.

"Henry Lindeman is sixty-two years old and is married with three children. His wife is seldom seen and keeps out of the limelight that her husband enjoys. He joined JP Morgan's research department—directly out of college in 1987. He then moved on to Ford for fifteen years. He was on track to be its president, then abruptly left the company in 2017. That same year he announced the formation of Jager Motors and declared this venture his Midwestern American dream to build America's first all-American electric vehicle for the regular guy—Tesla notwithstanding. He amassed a remarkable collection of investors and venture capitalists. In 2020 he rolled out his first EV vehicle, the Celerity. Then COVID struck and put a damper on everything. *Forbes*'s story that summer was about his intentions to have the largest IPO in the history of the markets, produce one million cars a year by 2026, and do it all without government subsidies. It took Tesla fourteen years to reach a million sales, helped by government payments, tax incentives, and carbon credits. Lindeman promised his million in less than seven years."

"Ambitious," I said.

"He also shows up at every international environmental conference, talks about saving the planet, and then flies off in his jet plane. He is careful to announce that it uses recycled oils and hydrocarbon waste as the fuel source."

"How nice for him."

"He has three floors of the Willis Tower, the old Sears Tower. When I called, I told his associate that we were investigating a murder under the supervision of the Lincolnville Police. It was related to events in South Bend, Indiana, and may involve people he may know. I left it cryptic enough to ensure his assistant would pass along the information. He called back an hour later and said we have the ten-thirty slot today. Mr. Lindeman is only in town today, and we have fifteen minutes."

"Maybe after what we tell him, he might give us five minutes more."

We waited fifteen minutes in the executive office lobby, well past our ten-thirty time slot. At ten minutes to eleven, a middle-aged man in a nice suit and modern haircut crossed the lobby and greeted us.

"Gentlemen, I am Tad Unger. Mr. Lindeman will see you. As you can see, we are running late. Please be precise and to the point. After passing on your comments in the call, he was extremely interested in what you said. He has asked me to sit in and take notes. These days he's not comfortable taking one-on-one meetings. I will be there in the capacity of a court reporter."

"Do we have a choice?" I asked as we hurried to keep up with Tad.

"No."

We walked a long hallway that cut through the eighty-second floor of the tower. Behind the flanking glass walls were dozens of offices. We reached the southeastern corner; the door read MR. LINDEMAN. Inside we crossed an outer office. A Black woman sat at a desk that flanked the double doors to the private office beyond. Tribal artwork from multiple continents hung on the walls directly behind her.

"Miss Flowers, I want to introduce you to Mr. Martin and Mr. Jasicki. They have an appointment with the boss."

Miss Flowers, a lovely woman in a peach-colored suit, smiled and tapped a button on her desk. The double doors clicked, then swung open; Tad led the way into the inner office. The view was east out over Lake Michigan. This morning the horizon lay clear and sharp. More than thirty miles away, a portion of the Indiana shoreline was visible.

Leaning against the inch-thick glass desk the size of a sheet of plywood stood a sunburned man in a black polo shirt and black slacks with sandy blond hair and dark gray eyes. He looked fit. I felt like sucking in my gut. He also had no shoes on. The only touch of flare was an Apple watch with a red band. He smiled and scanned us like a Xerox copier.

"You are not what I was expecting," he said. "Who's who?"

I paused. So this was what it was going to be. I had dealt with wealthy clients during my architectural days, most of whom were less than twenty years from celebrating significant events at the Olive Garden. I knew Mr. Lindeman's type; I'm guessing they didn't have an Olive Garden in South Bend when he was growing up.

"I'm Craig Martin, and this is my associate Mike Jasicki. We only want a few minutes of your time; we are working with the police in Lincolnville. It concerns multiple murders."

"And how does this concern me?"

"One of the bodies, we believe, is your mother's, and the other is your aunt's. They are Sheila and Gloria Lingermann and have been missing since 1963."

The arrogance and swagger Henry Lindeman showed when we walked in disappeared in the interval of one breath. He turned to Tad. "Tad, please leave us for fifteen minutes, then return. I will talk to these gentlemen in private."

"Mr. Lindeman, you have an eleven o'clock."

"They will wait. They need me a lot more than I need them. Change lunch to one thirty. I will join our guests in the restaurant. Now, git."

Tad gitted as quickly as we entered. Lindeman crossed his office to a sitting area and offered us seats. We all sat.

"This is quite a shock, gentlemen. How do I know you aren't feeding me a line of bullshit?"

"You don't," I said. "Mike, please tell Mr. Lindeman what we have learned."

Uninterrupted for the next ten minutes, Mike told Lindeman what we found, why we found it, and where. I then filled in the bits about South Bend, the robbery, and the murders. With each revelation, he became more agitated. He stood, walked to his desk, and clicked an old-fashioned intercom. "Miss Flowers, hold all my calls for the next hour. And tell Tad to be patient. I do not need him having another of his anxiety attacks."

"Yes, Mr. Lindeman."

He turned back to us. "What's your game? Why all this . . . bullshit? My mother and aunt disappeared before I was a year old. I didn't even know my mother was my grandmother until I was nineteen. Are you telling me my mother's body was found in a freezer sixty years after being murdered? And three others, including her twin sister, were also found with her? Good God, why the hell should I believe any of this? What do you want? Money? Is this extortion? Some gotcha from the usual wacko nutjobs? You two don't look like that crowd."

"Thanks for that," I said. "All we are trying to do is help our local police and put this all to rest. There're millions in cash, gold, and artwork also at stake. If we can find the rightful owners, it will be returned. The only way of confirming the women's identities, assuming one of them is your mother, is through DNA. It will confirm it. It would be helpful if you could tell us what you know."

Lindeman walked to the window, looked eastward, and took a deep breath. "My grandmother Anna Lingermann raised me. As I said, I believed she was my mother until I was nineteen. Anna died in 2000; she was eighty. She was my strength, my compass. She lived long enough to see me become successful. I was able to make the last years of her life comfortable. I owed her that. That was all she wanted; she helped me excel in high school and acquire a full-ride scholarship for soccer and my math skills. It was then that she told me about my mother and her sister. My mother was Sheila Lingermann, and her sister was called Gloria—you know that. She said they were beautiful, tall, smart, and at the same time incredibly irresponsible and wild. My mother got pregnant in early 1962. That was me, and I was born. She never told Anna who the father was, but Anna believed it was a guy named Toby Wozniacki. I never met him."

"He is connected to the South Bend murders. His fingerprints were found at the scene," Mike said. "We believe he may be one of the other two bodies in the freezer."

"Good God, after sixty years? Seems too far-fetched to believe."

"We agree with you on that," I said. "Would you allow us to take a DNA swab? It will help to confirm the identities."

The phone on Lindeman's desk buzzed. It was the third time.

"I told them not to disturb me; it seems they don't believe me," Lindeman said with a smile. He walked to the phone. "Yes, Miss Flowers." He listened while she talked. "Please tell the governor's chief of staff to pound sand; I will get back to him this afternoon. And please ask Mr. Rodgers to come to my office right now."

He walked back to us. "I will agree to the DNA test, but you two will sign a non-disclosure to receive it. I obviously had nothing to do with the events in South Bend or my parents' disappearance. No one is alive who could be responsible. However, I am in the middle of important negotiations with bankers, investors, an IPO, and the state of Illinois worth potentially billions—not billions to me, but to two thousand employees and my investors. Any word of this whole . . . whatever this is . . . could dramatically change the deal. So, will you sign a non-disclosure?"

"How could this affect those deals?" Mike asked.

"If the word gets out that my parents may, and I mean may, have been responsible for the murder of two people and the injury to a child, the whole conversation changes from one that deals with the merits of Jager Motors to me and my family's past. Many years ago, I guessed some of it after my grandmother told me what happened around my mother's disappearance. I found out that the police interviewed Anna about my mother. She never told me why. Later, I hired an investigator who found a possible connection to the deaths of the Paines. But there was nothing I could do, and my mother was gone. Anna told me that my mother loved me more than life itself, so I accepted that she was dead. What does the swab give you? Confirmation? What?"

The intercom buzzed. "Yes, Miss Flowers."

"Mr. Rodgers is here."

"Please tell him to wait." Lindeman turned to us. "Gentlemen?"

My head buzzed. With this non-disclosure statement, we couldn't reveal anything we said or learned during this meeting."

"Can we use the DNA results in our investigation?" I asked.

"Yes, you can use the results to confirm the identification of the female remains to the DNA of Henrik Lingermann, my birth name given to me by my grandmother Anna Lingermann. You cannot tie those results to me, Henry Lindeman. If there is any release of this information or there's the chance that the release of the information has connections to either of you, I will sue. You will not win. You can identify the remains somehow, but that's up to you. I believe I am your only direct biological connection. So, do we have a deal? Can I call in Mr. Rodgers?"

CHAPTER 21

October 2024

Mike and I were beat, or truly beaten. Either way, we were exhausted after the hour with Mr. Henry Lindeman. We left with a DNA swab and an NDA. We would hand over the swab kit to Detective King, and she would have it processed. Maybe we would confirm two or three bodies that Dick Saperstein, the ME, still held in his morgue. What Mr. Rodgers would do with our NDA, I wasn't sure. He would likely stick it in a folder, and only when we did something stupid would it reappear. We liked Henry Lindeman. He seemed genuinely concerned about global issues, his company, and the people that worked with him. Guys like him often received unfair and biased reporting, which told me more about the reporter or the institution they worked for than the truth. Lindeman seriously wanted to help the world and make a profit at the same time—who didn't?

We stopped at the Lincolnville Police Department and talked to Audrey for a few minutes. She had a village council meeting that evening and needed to prepare. We brought her up to speed on our latest interviews with Janet Paine LeBlanc and Henry Lindeman. I could tell she was impressed; I'd pass the word on to the boys. She'd get the DNA done on the sample. Since we were doing the heavy lifting, she said the village could afford the test. She still didn't know what to do with the

Gregory C. Randall

bodies, but maybe Henry Lindeman, after we had confirmation, could be encouraged to cover the burial costs. I told her we'd wait to read the results, then take her lead.

Four hours earlier, Mike and I had put our phones on mute before we met with Lindeman and forgot to turn them back on. We both had three messages. The first was from Penny.

"Call me as soon as possible. Garry Hughes had a heart attack on the golf course. Please, call me."

The call was from two hours earlier. Mike had one from his wife, Lucy. We quickly called.

"Where the hell have you been?" Penny yelled.

"You know I was in Chicago with Mike chasing down the kid. I'm sorry, I'd turned my phone to mute. What's happened with Garry?"

"He was on the twelfth hole; it has that steep slope in front of the green. He was walking up the hill and just collapsed. Luckily, his playing partner was Doc Greene. They stabilized him before the EMTs arrived. He's at Ingalls. I talked to Angela; she says he's doing okay; he was lucky. When are you coming home?"

"Mike and I are at the Lincolnville police station; I need to drop him off. I'll be home in fifteen minutes," I said.

"Angela said that he was to have no visitors for at least a few days. They want to keep him calm. I will see you soon. Love you."

"I love you."

After dropping Mike off, I sat in the car for five minutes, thinking. This was Garry's third heart attack. Each was more challenging than the last. The second attack required a double bypass. We would soon find out what plumbing work was necessary after this event. At our age, medical problems lined up like ducks in a row. We prayed to avoid them, hoping to put them off for another, more convenient time. Life didn't do

176

that. It seemed to glory in the sucker punch, the slam to the heart as you walked to your ball on the twelfth hole during the club championship, the hip broken when you stumble putting on your shoes. The light-headedness after a heavy dinner and the trip to the emergency room due to a sugar incident; I was there when Larry had his due to his diabetes. Considering the list of medical issues in the gang, we probably should have a doctor on retainer.

Penny was calm. She understood why my phone was off, but accepting the reason was still not the same as understanding it. "Leave the damn thing on all the time; important stuff happens, Craig," she said. I could not, and did not, disagree.

I talked to Angela, Garry's wife, at length. She cried for half the call. They were one year short of their fiftieth anniversary. She was always calm and maternal and there to hold hands when the others went through the crap in their lives. She was a substitute teacher after her two kids were old enough to attend school. Now, both boys were in their forties with kids of their own.

"He's good, Craig—better than he has a right to be," she said. "After the last attack, the doc ordered him to get in shape and watch his diet. Lord knows I've tried to do my part, but he's always out there, doing his thing, being the ringmaster."

"I understand. He has always been stubborn," I said.

"Stubborn? I've known mules half as obstinate. This time, he's in for it. You know helicopter moms? Me? I'm going to be that helicopter wife."

And she would be. She was that type of woman. Garry would complain, yet he would follow her directions—or else.

I talked with Larry and Tommy and told them what happened in Chicago and where we were with Henry Lindeman.

"We are getting close, Craig," Larry said. "I'll follow up with Audrey on the DNA. The sooner we can confirm these identifications, the sooner we can move on to the money and the art. Garry had kept Tommy and Mike in the loop; he set up a shared file on his Dropbox account. They have access to what he'd found about the paintings and jewelry. There are a lot of loose ends."

"Too many to resolve them all," I said. "I'll call Barbara and bring her up to speed. This is getting weirder, don't you think?"

"Weird is selling it short. I also got an email from Dexter—the guy is ninety-one and uses a computer. We should be so lucky if we make it that far. He said that he found another file, one he'd forgotten. He scanned the information and sent it to me."

"Applicable?"

"Yeah, looks like it. Dexter believes that the other man in our freezer foursome was a friend of Tobias Wozniacki. They are from the same town; they went to high school together. Like the other three, Joe Sauger has been missing since the night of the robbery. Dex interviewed a fellow a few weeks after the murders who lived in Warsaw, Indiana. The guy was Robert Sauger. He was twenty-one in 1963. He was Joe's younger brother. Dexter thinks the guy may still be alive. He'd be eighty-two. The last address was a trailer park outside Plymouth, Indiana."

"Interesting. Any help with Audrey, maybe doing a little checking on Robert Slauger in the criminal database?"

"I'll ask. You're beginning to think the way I think."

"You are a good teacher."

* * *

Two days later, I spent a few chaperoned hours with Garry. He looked good and was his usual self. When we started to talk about the case, Angela quickly ended it.

"I want no discussion on those bodies in the freezer. Do you two hear me? Talk about the weather, the grandkids, whatever. I want nothing about golf, those bodies, or anything to do with the Marigold Gang." She turned and walked out of the room.

"She knows that we will talk about it. She just needed to say her piece—and she won't tell me who won the championship," Garry said. "Do you know?"

"Your twenty-something super-golfer babe, Stacy Kline, from the University of Illinois. I read it in the paper. She shot a two-day total of 137."

"Seven under, good God. I'll bet her dad is bust a button proud of her. Like me—my two boys knock the ball around. We enjoy the camaraderie but have not accepted the game as a religious pilgrimage to a place you will never arrive."

"Lucky them. Surgery?"

"No, they tell me more blood thinners will do the job. Then some relaxation and peace and quiet. No business. The orders have been given."

I smiled. "Are you sure you can do that?"

"We will find out or die trying."

"Gallows humor."

"Craig, as I lay on that hill, I was wide awake, my heart pounding erratically—I felt every hammer blow. I was sure this was it. I even said some prayers. The grass was comforting, like a warm bed, the sky above a sharp flawless blue, and the breeze just right. I tasted my life. I believed, and still do, that if God just picked me up and carried me away that moment, I couldn't have been more at peace. Then, old Doc Green started pounding on me, sucking my face, and all sorts of rude things. They got a defibrillator from the cart girl, and bam, here I am. But I'll tell you, buddy, that moment I was alone and with nothing but the sky and God—that was the most peaceful I've ever been."

Old age ain't for the young, the aphorism goes. Only those who have put in the years can understand the feelings, the racing mind, the minor panic attacks, the fears, and mostly the memories of a life well-lived. The boys and I are lucky. We have had each other's backs for over half a century. None of our marriages are as long as our blood brotherhood. Allen's death put us on alert. We learned his secrets were onion-like; as we peeled away each layer, there were tears and pain, and then . . . another layer. What we found to be a treasure trove is now a burden of sorrow and death. Could any of this be made right? Did our volunteer army even have the right to be involved?

CHAPTER 22

October 2024

There is this archeological discovery that has intrigued me since college. More than a hundred years ago, they found the bones of a man in a cave in Yorkshire, England. They determined he lived more than ten thousand years ago and called him Cheddar Man. Why the name, other than the obvious—he was found in Yorkshire—I don't know. I am sure, though, that there was a marketing guy involved. An early Green Bay Packers fan, a cheesehead? I digress; I apologize. Since unearthing his bones, the poor fellow has been the serious subject of studies, stories, and speculations about who and what he was. They scanned, reassembled, and analyzed every inch of his shriveled carcass. Of course, no one will ever know why he was there in that cave. Time does eventually hide almost everything. However, they were able to extract DNA and determined that there was a direct genetic ancestor to the man living just a few miles away from Cheddar Man's cave. For some, they are comfortable where they live, I guess.

This is the thought I had as Tommy and I stood outside the single-wide trailer in the Shady Haven Trailer Park on the north side of Plymouth, Indiana. Would ancestors of some of these trailer dwellers still be in this area of central Indiana ten thousand years from now? Robert Slauger was at least rooted.

Dexter said he'd lived at this address for the last forty years. Audrey came through with a benign report of the criminal past of Robert Slauger. He had a couple of juvenile arrests when he was in his late teens, an arrest for check fraud (two rent checks bounced in 1973), and a felony arrest for assault and battery (while drunk) on a police officer that got him a year in Indiana's state prison in Michigan City in 1975. Since then, he'd been clean. When I called, he was both surprised and wary. "Why the hell do you want to talk to me? That's so long ago I can't remember nothing." Yet, after all that, he still agreed to meet with us.

I brought a bottle of WhistlePig rye as an offering and a bribe. Robert Slauger was eighty-two and surprisingly didn't look that old when he came to the aluminum screen door of his trailer.

"Just a second, fellas, let me get the boys settled. We don't get many visitors—I'll tell you that," he said through the screen door. Through it, we heard the strident barks and yips, then three faces appeared at the bottom of the door's frame—three Chihuahuas puffed up and throwing attitude.

A minute later, Robert Slauger came through the door and pointed to a picnic table under an awning extending from the trailer. While I held the door, he carried out a tray with a pitcher of iced tea and plastic cups. He set it on the table. I introduced us and briefly told him why we wanted to talk. I offered him the bribe.

"Thank you kindly, but I don't drink," he said. "But a few of my neighbors do, and they will thank you most profusely this evening when I tell 'em all about our visit. One rule here at Shady Haven, we keep no secrets. So, you want to know about my brother. Now why would that be? He's been gone now sixty-one years; when he walked out, he left a big hole in my family."

"You believe he walked out, Mr. Slauger?" Tommy asked.

"Please call me Bob since we be drinking buddies." He winked. Along the road walked an elderly couple; the woman pushed a four-wheeled walker. They looked questioningly at us; Bob waved.

"That's the Aimeses. They've lived here almost as long as me. So, you want to know about Joe? But I need a trade, and the bourbon is a good start. Your phone call, I'll tell you, out of the blue, left more questions than answers. So, why are you here?"

Tommy and I told him about what we found in the Fisher house, the Studebaker's connections to South Bend, and the bodies in the freezer. He listened intently and never interrupted.

"I'm an old shit, worked as a tradesman and fixer-upper most of my life—never found anything I couldn't repair. Never married and didn't even get close. I like my independence. Do you think that Joe is one of the dead? Sad, I'll tell you that. I been wondering about him for a long, long time. Yes, this seems inevitable. I was more prepared never to learn what happened to him. Joe was three years older than me, always in trouble, and broke our mother's heart more than once. He hung around with tough guys and others from town. I tried to follow in his wake but failed miserably. I was too nice a guy. I didn't have the baggage he did or claimed he did. Said he was owed it, life owed him, us being without a father and all—it was all the government's and the war's fault. Mom lived off the insurance from the government for a few years, then that was gone. She remarried; the guy turned out to be a bum. He and Joe got into it a few times, then he up and left. Joe was the provider then; any job that paid was okay by him. Joe was the breadwinner. After he left, I took over. I wasn't surprised when he disappeared. We lost our father in the war, the one we old guys know about, right? Joseph Sauger Sr. died on Okinawa on April 10, 1945. They buried him in the Veterans Cemetery down in Madison. Only been there once—when Mom was alive. I never met the man. Mom left us in 1990; she was seventy-five, heart still broken. She lived with her sister over in Leesburg." He took a sip of his iced tea. "I digress. My apologies."

"None needed. Did your brother hang around with a guy named Tobias—"

"Toby Wozniacki? Sure as hell did. They were together all through high school, and luckily both missed getting drafted. The Cold War was starting to heat up. Back then, whenever they could put a handful of extra money together, Joe and Toby wasted it on girls. In the early 1960s, they spent a lot of time in South Bend. They both worked on the Studebaker assembly line, which was hard work. He sent money home. He was a good son for that. Other than that, he didn't include me in his circle—maybe that was a good thing. Then he got laid off—more likely fired."

"Do you remember anything about the girls they dated?" I asked.

"Not really. As I said, he was living in South Bend when he disappeared. I borrowed a car and drove over and asked around. I even stopped at the police station and asked if anyone knew about him. Mom was freaking out. A detective took a serious interest in my questions. I spent an afternoon talking to him. I can't remember his name, but I gave him all my particulars. Never heard from him."

"Is that all you can remember?"

"Lot of water under that bridge, Mr. Martin. I got a call from his landlord two months after he disappeared. Joe and Toby shared an apartment, barely more than a trailer like this, really. They hadn't paid their rent, and he was going to toss the few things they had left in the place; he wanted to know if

I wanted them. I borrowed the car again and picked up what Joe left. Mostly I wanted the cigar box of medals that Dad received for bravery in the Marines. A Purple Heart, Navy Cross, ribbons, and some letters Mom wrote to him. There was also a picture on the dresser; I took it. I also filled a couple of boxes with their clothes."

"You took Toby's stuff?"

"Yeah, the landlord had people waiting to move in. I had to pay him fifty bucks to cover the past rent just to get into the place. There was also some women's clothing in the mess—whose they were, I never knew."

"The picture, is it of your brother?" Tommy asked.

"It's of Joe and Toby and two women. The girls look and dress identical-like; blondes, cute, tall, and one is pregnant. I still have it. Do you want to see it?"

I looked at Tommy; maybe we'd found a nugget in the bottom of our pan. "Absolutely," I said.

Bob went to the door, and just as soon as he opened it, three brown packages exploded out and ran directly to us. The Chihuahuas jumped up and down on their hind feet like wind-up toys. We couldn't help but laugh.

"Okay, boys, down. Be nice to our guests," Bob said as he returned, holding a small picture frame. "It's done okay over the years and hasn't faded much. It is my only picture of my brother; I made a copy for Mom. That's still with my aunt." He handed the frame to me.

The black-and-white photo was of four people, all in their early twenties. Boy-girl, boy-girl, all standing. The girls in bold-patterned summer dresses, the boys in slacks and tee shirts. One of the girls was pregnant, and she didn't try to hide it. The other girl had her arm draped over a guy's shoulder with a crew cut. He had a cigarette in his mouth.

"The fellow with the crew cut is my brother; the other guy

is Toby Wozniacki. As I said, I never met the girls. The one on the left is pregnant—Joe told me Toby knocked up some girl and seriously considered marrying her. Joe never said what happened between them."

"Did you ever hear their names?" I asked.

"I'm sure he told me, but I've forgotten."

"May I take the photo from the frame?" I asked. "Sometimes there's a note."

"Sure, go ahead—I never took it out of the frame."

I carefully adjusted the clips that held the photo and removed it. On the back, in pencil, was written: "Toby, Sheila, Joe, and Gloria—Summer 1962." There was also a folded piece of paper.

"May I?"

"Didn't know it was there, so sure. This is interesting."

I unfolded the paper. It was a simple but heartfelt letter.

> *Dear Toby,*
> *I love you with all my heart, and so does the little bundle. We can't wait to spend the rest of our lives together.*
> *Love forever,*
> *Sheila*

"This was from Sheila to Toby; do you know why it's here?" Tommy asked.

"Mr. Ellis, I didn't know it was there to begin with. Maybe the picture belonged to Toby; I wouldn't know. All I wanted was the photo of Joe."

"So, Toby and Sheila were together, and maybe he was the father?" Tommy said.

"Same answer, I wouldn't know. Joe and I never talked about the girls," Bob said. "The other name on the back is Gloria—still doesn't ring a bell. Sorry."

"May I take photos of the picture and the letter?" I asked.

"Of course. What are you going to do about all this?"

"Try to confirm who those people are. If one is your brother, I will let you know. One more request, if I may. Can I get a DNA sample? We can confirm Joe's identification through your DNA."

"Like they do on those TV shows? Guess it can't hurt. What can the government do to an old shit like me—take everything I don't have?"

CHAPTER 23

Late October 2024

There were four of us for breakfast at Bell's the following Wednesday.

"How's Garry doing?" Karen asked. "I talked briefly with Angela. She said he was okay. I need the truth from you guys."

"He is good, Karen, all things considered," Larry said. "Minor heart attack, minimal damage, no surgery needed. But he'll live on blood thinners his whole life. Angela has him in lockdown. Our visits are limited to ten minutes and just one-on-one."

I looked around. "Seems busy, even for a Wednesday."

"We are doing okay, can't complain—not that anyone would listen. It is summer, and a lot of people are on vacation," Karen said. "Prices for everything are up again. I've two staff out, so I work a few more hours. My cook is threatening to quit again. I just don't get it."

"Even here on the Southside, it's hard to fill all the jobs available," Mike said. "Especially jobs like these."

"Don't get me started," Karen said. "I compete with welfare and, looking at you guys, Social Security. Who wants to work for what I can pay? Any you guys want to make a few extra dollars? I'll throw in breakfast or lunch." She laughed.

"We are of the leisure set now, Karen. We did our time."

"And now you are busting your butts chasing down those stiffs in the freezer."

"Is that some kind of refrigerator humor?" Tommy asked.

"I mean it. What are you guys doing? It all seems like a waste of time. And from what you tell me, all this happened more than half a century ago—I ask you, who cares?"

"Karen, what you have here are five guys trying to put right a mystery that concerns Allen Fisher, our friend, and yours too," I said. "There's a disturbance in the balance of things, the force, if you will. Allen was troubled, and we see now what might have caused it. Maybe, just maybe, we can find the answers to what happened."

"I know about his sister and brother. They've been here a couple of times, once with Allen, maybe two years ago. It was loud. I gave Allen the eye, and he quieted them down. Then they left in a huff—not seen the two of 'em since."

"I thought that Allen never saw his siblings," Mike said, turning to me.

"That's what I thought," I said. "He never said anything to me."

"Then the day this all started, they show up at the house," Tommy said, "then you get whacked on the head."

"There's no connection," I said.

"You sure? Who else could it have been? Kids, ghosts?"

"After all that went on in that house," Larry said, "I'd go with ghosts. There's at least six I can think of."

"Seven, if you include Allen," Tommy said.

Karen looked at Larry, then Tommy. "Don't go and start all that ghost talk; they know when you are talking about them. They do not like to be reminded by the living that they are dead."

All of us looked at Karen. She gave us each a look, crossed herself, and asked, "The usuals?"

After taking over all the electronic research from Garry (Angela took his computer, iPad, and phone and locked them in a closet—then she handed him the TV remote), Mike found the name of an insurance company connected to some of the artwork. I called Janet LeBlanc, and she confirmed that it was the same insurance company her grandparents dealt with on settlements for the stolen art. Janet had said she was so far removed from all the insurance stuff after the murders she didn't realize what ensued until she was in college. Then her grandmother told her about the settlements and that they helped cover their college tuition and costs. The insurance company was in Omaha, Nebraska. It was the same name that Mike uncovered.

"I called the headquarters, and after being shunted through five desks," Mike said, "I got Gwen Turner, an insurance investigator. I left a short but compelling message. She called back, and I explained what was happening. I believe she fell off her chair while we talked."

"She didn't," Larry said.

"It sounded like it," Mike continued. "She said, 'Holy shit,' and 'You have got to be kidding me,' over and over. She said she was flying into Midway and would be here tomorrow morning. She asked to see the artwork and our attorney."

"Attorney? We don't have no stinking attorney," Tommy said with a laugh. "What does she think is going on here?"

"I haven't a clue. I gave her Audrey's police station address. Turner expects to be here at noon. I told Audrey. She laughed."

"She would," Larry said. "She's getting a kick out of the trouble we are causing. This investigator, what is she going to do? What can she do?"

"I haven't a clue. Garry is in Angela jail; I can't talk to him or his clubby insurance president. I'm at a loss. I have the photos we took. The originals are locked in the security vault, safe and sound. Could she get a court order that forces us to give her the art?"

I looked around the table; none of us had a clue. Karen brought breakfast. We ate in silence.

We needed legal advice—free legal advice. What we were dealing with needed the kind of counsel that a five-hundred-dollar-an-hour attorney gives. And none of us had a spare twenty bucks, let alone a few thousand, to spend on this little adventure. My gasoline bill was already over a hundred dollars. I thought that Karen, Penny, and Angela were right.

* * *

Larry, Mike, and I were at the Lincolnville police station, waiting in one of the interview rooms. We dragged in extra chairs from the lobby. Tommy had a doctor's appointment; he would join us if he could get away.

"We should have picked up a pizza," Mike said. "I'm hungry and feel this little meeting will not be short."

Audrey walked in. Following her was a young, pretty woman in a gray business pantsuit. Over her shoulder was a very expensive briefcase. The strap had snagged on her shoulder-length blonde hair. We all stood. The look on her face was priceless.

"Ms. Turner, these are my investigators," Audrey said. She introduced us, and we each shook her hand. I am unsure what she thought, but her look was classic befuddlement with a little "what the hell" thrown in.

She looked at the three of us, then Audrey. "Are these gentlemen professionals?" she asked.

"Larry is a retired chief of police, Mike is a retired businessman, and Craig is an architect."

"Was. I'm retired," I said. "The others in our group have

medical issues to deal with this morning."

Turner looked at us, expecting that we all probably had medical issues. "So, you decided to take on this case once you found all the art in that house?"

Larry smiled, then said, "Ms. Turner, it was Detective King, with her captain's approval, who offered us the opportunity to find answers to questions regarding the disposition of our friend's personal property."

"And this property included stolen artwork worth millions of dollars?"

"At the time, we did not know," I said, adding my two cents. "Later, we discovered the problems with the artwork and the other things found in the house."

"Like what?" she asked.

"Four dismembered bodies, wrapped in cellophane, and stuck in a freezer in the basement, a sixty-year-old Studebaker with bloodstains in the trunk, and—"

Gwen Turner turned white (actually whiter), wobbled, and just before she collapsed, Larry grabbed her by the waist and lowered her to a chair. She put her hands to the side of her face and slowly inhaled.

I looked at the boys, then Audrey, who rolled her eyes to the ceiling. Behind the detective, a shadow washed the wired translucent glass window in the door; a knock followed. Audrey opened the door. A tall bald Black man with a thick beard stood there. He wore an expensive suit, a brilliant white shirt, and a very expensive bow tie. I swear he screamed lawyer; I also knew who he was.

After our Wednesday morning breakfast, I called Janet LeBlanc, brought her up to date, and told her about the insurance company and our upcoming appointment.

"So, they are sending in an investigator, which is unsurprising. You guys have now found yourselves in the big leagues."

She laughed. "Murder and mayhem are one thing; artwork worth millions is something completely different. The artwork can be leveraged and, by that, I mean become even more valuable. I think they believe they have a chance at the prize."

"The prize?"

"I didn't tell you when you and Mr. Martini were here. The artwork belonged to my grandparents, my mother's parents, who raised us after their deaths. She felt the artwork, two Renoirs, two Pissarros, and a very nice original Picasso oil from his blue period, were better displayed at my mother's house. They bought the paintings when they were in France before World War I. They were the era's versions of well-heeled hippies. Grandmother's father was a senior banker involved in the exploding automobile industry. They were wealthy, and their daughter converted some of that money into artwork, especially the Impressionists. There were smaller pieces spread around the house. The killers only took those five."

"And settlements were made?" I asked.

"Yes, they paid one hundred thousand dollars, which was quite a lot in 1964."

"And they are worth now?"

"I'd guess a thousand times that, conservatively."

I nearly dropped the phone. "One hundred million dollars?"

"Yes, at the right auction or through a qualified broker. They are quite popular now, especially in China and the Middle East. Now you understand the importance of an attorney. Those pieces rightfully belong to my brother and me. The insurance company will try to prove that they own the pieces. With that much to win, you need the best. I will make a call, and I suggest you do not let the investigator know where the artworks are stored, at least for now. The attorney will work with you. I will cover the costs. He will represent all the works as a whole since the ownership and provenances of the other pieces still need to be clarified."

"First, thank you, Janet. Second, have him call me. And, third, what the hell did we get ourselves into?"

Her laugh said it all.

"Mr. Hugh Stone, I presume?" I said, standing and putting my hand out to the man.

"Mr. Martin, yes, Hugh Stone. Thank you for inviting me to this meeting. After the call from Ms. LeBlanc, I couldn't wait to meet with you and your team."

"Detective King, this is Hugh Stone. He is with Stone, Malling, and Hammer, a law firm in Chicago," I said. "Janet LeBlanc, the owner of the artwork in question, has retained him."

"Not all the artwork," Gwen Turner said. She stood and looked at Stone. "How are you, Hugh? It has been a couple of years."

"I'm great, Gwen. Got married, have a year-old son," the attorney said.

"Congratulations. And wasn't it those pieces of art acquired by the Milwaukee Museum of Art? Yes, I remember it well. It did work out for all the parties."

"Depending on your point of view," Stone said.

"No harm, no foul."

"You know that it was bullshit; now we have another one. Why are you here, Gwen?"

I enjoy a good discussion between professionals, and this one would be a doozy—but not right now.

"Okay, here's the deal," Audrey said, admiring the tall man beside her. "All the artwork and other assets are evidence of what most probably is a series of connected murders. Under my direction, these men are investigating the crime. Until now, they have done an outstanding job. Your only concern is the artwork, Ms. Turner, because your company paid out settlements for their theft years ago. Those pieces will remain in my custody until a time the city attorney believes they are no longer material. Only then can they be released to their rightful owners."

"I need to verify the paintings and confirm they are the pieces we settled on."

"For now, you will work from photos. I will determine when they can be physically inspected. I have seen the artwork and was there when the photos were taken. Be assured they are in a very secure location."

"You said they were part of a larger murder investigation?" Hugh Stone said. "Can you explain?"

For the next hour, we told Stone and Turner the who, what, why, and where of the investigation of the Ronald Fisher home. The two professionals sat stunned by what we'd discovered and connected. Having Dexter Millhouse there to help fill in the blanks would have been even more helpful. I'm sure there were still specifics about the murders that would come to him.

"Chief Martini," Stone said. "You said there were other pieces of art?"

"Yes, there's an inventory sheet. In addition to the Paine paintings, we found twelve additional paintings, two small bronze sculptures of dancers, and some etchings and prints. There was also jewelry, watches, cash, and gold."

Stone turned to Turner. "Are some of these pieces on your settlement list?"

Without looking, Gwen Turner said, "Yes. The notes in the file suggest that back in the early 1960s, between 1961 and 1963, there were at least a half dozen burglaries of homes that my company ended up settling thefts of artwork and jewelry. These were in Kenosha, Wisconsin; South Bend, Indiana; and

Grosse Pointe and Dearborn, Michigan. We settled on ten specific listed pieces in addition to the Paines'. Our payouts were almost $500,000."

"Ouch. Were all the victims involved in the automobile industry?" I asked.

"Yes, all were senior executives. All different manufacturers—Nash Rambler, Studebaker, Ford, and General Motors."

"It is safe to say that the thief or thieves were targeting successful automotive businessmen, had access to their homes, and knew their schedules?" Larry offered.

"Most likely. The notes in the file say they tried to connect the dots but couldn't. There are so many people connected to the automobile industry, hundreds of suppliers, dozens of dealers, and the investigation was across at least three states. It was beyond our scope. The costs were too high. We are not a law enforcement body; we have our interests at stake. The murders of the Paines, while incredibly sad, were not our concern. They were those of the South Bend Police. The other robberies were simple burglaries. No one was hurt; the police didn't take the time to connect the dots."

"Was there a suspect?" Stone asked.

"For the murders?" Turner asked.

"No, for the thefts. Did you develop a suspect list?"

"Yes, the lead investigator for my company compiled a list of twenty suspects. His boss said to hold onto the list and see if it can be connected after the next theft happens. After the South Bend murders and thefts, there were no more that we could attribute to this same MO. They just stopped."

"That was in the summer of 1963?" Larry asked.

"Yes." She turned to Larry. "And you believe that Ronald Fisher was the thief and murderer?"

"Yes, or the mastermind. Mike found an article in the Kenosha newspaper about the robbery of a Rambler executive during the winter of 1962. Just before Christmas, money, jewelry, and artwork were stolen. There was nothing specific as to artists or value. It had snowed, and the thieves left footprints in the snow. The impression was that these were amateurs. Three sets of men's footprints led to the street. The report suggests that they escaped in a car. No victims' names were given or released. We have not followed up on this."

"They were the Latimers, Howard and Lynn. One van Gogh and two Matisse oils," Turner said, still not looking in her files. "They were important pieces and promised to the Milwaukee Museum of Art at some time in the future—I assume for tax and estate reasons. Howard Latimer was about to retire. He saw the writing on the wall, so to speak, about the Nash Rambler Company and was preparing for the future. The settlement was for $275,000. Internally we believed it was a scam—Latimer needed the money, and a theft of the art would put cash in their pocket. The paintings, especially the van Gogh, are worth as much as the Paines'. I'll save you the trouble on the other two. We paid out close to half a million. We are into this for almost a million dollars, which was in 1960 dollars. We want to get our money back."

CHAPTER 24

Late October 2024

"It is always about money," said Barbara as I brought her up to speed on our investigation. "Money, money, money. Not the pain that my grandfather caused, not the damage to families, and the generations that followed—just the brutal truth of what greed can cause."

"The paintings were never yours, no matter what Allen's will read," I said.

"I know, and besides, all of it is tainted. The artwork, money, and gold remind me of the Nazi hoards found after World War II. Who did that all belong to? Who could claim it? It is blood money. Our father and mother, regardless of his parents, and for all my father's emotional problems, taught us well and gave us a moral compass that we still follow. But these others, the insurance people, the lawyers, the son of one in the freezer, are all driven by money. Craig, I'm sick of it."

"I understand. There will be discussions about the car."

"The car? That Studebaker? Why?"

"It is technically owned by the estate of Walter Paine, by his surviving children."

"She's the attorney in Michigan, paying for the attorney on the artwork. That doesn't involve my brother or me," Barbara said.

"I agree, but I also want to protect you from any implications or incriminations."

"About what?"

"That you may have known about what was in the house."

"Christ, you have got to be kidding. We knew nothing. When our grandparents died, I was seventeen, and Steve was thirteen. We lived with my mother in Oak Park. I was still in high school. I remember going to the funeral, and it was cold and wet. I barely knew them. My friends had their me-mas, grannies, gramps, and grandparents. We had Ron and Lois—cold fish comes to my mind."

"I remember them," I said, concurring. "Many of the parents on Marigold Court were friendly to them, but I can't remember a party or holiday they came to. Allen always did; often, he was the life of the party, but his siblings, your aunt and uncle, did not at all."

"Steve and I make sure our kids stay away from them. Thank goodness they didn't come to Dad's funeral."

"I told you they showed up when the word about the bodies went public. Nasty people." I did not tell Barbara about my bushwhacking; it would unnecessarily upset her. "I'm afraid they will not go away."

"You said something about the car. Isn't it evidence?"

"Yes, but both police departments, Lincolnville's and South Bend's, do not want it or need it. It will be turned over to Janet LeBlanc, and she can do whatever she wants. No rush on the disposition; besides, it has four flat tires, and no one has tried to start it in Lord knows how long."

"What do you fellows think we should do with the house? I can't see anyone wanting to buy the place after seven bodies were found there."

"Seven?"

"Remember, you found Dad there on the floor. He was the

third—until the freezer."

She didn't need to remind me about that awful day. No one had seen Allen for a few days. Garry went over to check on him. Allen's locked truck was in the driveway. He had a house key and let himself in. It was immediately apparent that something funky was going on. He walked through and found Allen on the floor of the living room. He was naked and face down. It appeared he'd just walked out of the shower; a towel lay on the floor, and his face clenched in a grimace. His eyes were mercifully closed. He was a ghastly gray color with splotched skin. The ME, Dick Saperstein, said it appeared to have been a powerful and fatal stroke about four days earlier. He also hit his head as he fell—there was a scrape on his forehead—but it wasn't the cause of his death; that was the massive stroke. All of us were upset at ourselves for not noticing Allen's absence sooner, not that it would have made a difference. I was the one who called Barbara, and she called Steve. They lost Bess, their mother, from ovarian cancer five years ago. When Garry found Allen and then called us, it was the first time we'd been in the house since Allen called me about discovering his dead parents. The house has spooked me since my family moved to the court. Now, like a premonition, the bodies, murders, suicides, and deaths have only multiplied the awfulness of the place.

"We will figure out the house," I said. "The housing market in Lincolnville is bad. Even empty lots are not selling. The existing houses are too small, and now most are over sixty years old. It will take some creative thinking."

"It's the taxes and ongoing insurance. Those are the killers. Steve says it would be better as an empty lot."

"As I said, there is no rush. First, let's get this all sorted out."

* * *

I wasn't sure what "sorted out" meant, nor did any of the gang. I sat with Garry for an hour in his study. Angela had a hair appointment. I slipped in just after she left.

"She will be gone for three hours; you can set your watch. So, what's the latest?" asked Garry.

I told him about the insurance investigator and the attorney paid for by Janet LeBlanc, and the approaching legal issues. Their confrontation got Mike and Tommy diving into the other paintings. The other names, provided by Gwen Turner, from Wisconsin and Michigan added fuel to their investigation. I assured Garry that he would be the first to know what they found—certainly before Gwen Turner or Hugh Stone. I told him about Barbara's concern for the house and the car and what she said about the cash and the gold coins.

"I figured that's what she'd say," Garry said. "She and her brother are the only bright lights to come out of the Fisher family. I'm arguing that Bess's DNA was the stronger in the family."

"Can't argue. Bess escaped with the kids when she could. Allen was a mess when it happened, and his folks were again living in the house. I can only imagine what they put Allen through. Then Lois got sick."

"Pancreatic cancer, right?"

"Yes, brutal, painful. Ron couldn't deal with it any longer; that was the story."

"Or excuse as we now know."

"Yes," I said. "What we've found has put another spin on what happened. Was Ron driven to murder and suicide by what was in the house? The things he stole and killed he kept in the house—why? I don't get it."

"Have the fellas found any other deaths connected to the

robberies?"

"No. There were break-ins and burglaries, follow-up news-paper articles, evidence photos, and what Turner gave us as support. We are working on family names, those that are connected to the original thefts. But no other killings—so far."

"Was this a one-off? Something happened that night to set off Ron," Garry added.

"Or Ron was there with these four, and something went very wrong."

"Yes, very possible. I've had too much time to sit and think—I'm going stir crazy."

"What do you think?" I asked. Garry had always been the most analytical, the spreadsheet king.

"Did we find everything in the house?" Garry asked. "Are there other hiding places? I am surprised that Allen left no notes for his kids or us. There was his will, but it was dated two years ago. He'd been sick a long time and knew things weren't going well. And considering the house was a puzzle box, maybe there's more."

"Larry and I had the same thought. Allen was smart. We know that. And with what was in the house, I don't know why he didn't say something to us. We would have been there for him."

"I'm beginning to understand now why his parents' deaths knocked him down. This secret was huge, like all their sins were now on his back."

"You believe he knew about everything in the house?" I asked.

"I don't know, but how could he not? The evidence was overwhelming, the money, the coins, the carpets—he had to have known."

"Was he involved?"

"When all this happened, he was fifteen—hell, *we* were fifteen. No, he wasn't involved, I'm sure of it. But he had to have learned at some point."

"The brutal deaths of his parents, his PTSD. For months afterward, he just shut down. You remember."

"I do, and Angela reminded me of all of it. Allen is not her favorite subject right now; she intimates it caused this round of my heart issues."

"And not the good life you lead?"

"You tell her that; I'll stand to the side. Craig, I carry what I brought. That finger can only point to me; Allen had nothing to do with it."

My pocket buzzed. The screen read, "Det King."

"Hi, Audrey, what's up? I'm here with Garry." I clicked on the speaker.

"Trouble. Our little bit of hide-and-seek has just gotten serious," Audrey said. "Gwen Turner just served me with a subpoena. They want access to everything we have in the vault. She claims that it belongs to the insurance company. She provided a list. They may try to serve you guys too."

Garry looked at me and smiled. "Pass me my pills?"

CHAPTER 25

November 2024

Hugh Stone told us, during a conference call, that he could delay the inevitable release of the artwork a week as he went through procedures. He'd also set up a meeting with the judge to discuss the particulars of the subpoena. Gwen Turner focused on the artwork from the thefts her company was involved with. Everything else was irrelevant. The thought that more than a half million in cash and gold was irrelevant to her boggled our minds. We also wondered if other insurance companies would start sniffing around once this became public. It would be open season.

I called Janet and thanked her for stepping up with Hugh Stone.

"I need to protect these paintings," Janet said. "They were collected by my grandparents more than a hundred years ago. It would be nice to keep them in the family—assuming we can afford to—the biggest cost is insurance. I've known Hugh Stone since I guest lectured at Loyola; he was a bright, inquisitive, creative student. He'll be good—any questions, ask him."

"We will," I said. "The car, the Studebaker?"

"I don't want it. It has no sentimental or even financial value to my family. Maybe a collector out there likes cars with a macabre provenance."

"It's more like something from a Stephen King novel."

"Yeah, I get that. I'll leave it to you and Larry to resolve its disposition. Have you found other victims?"

"The insurance investigator gave us names and settlements they made. We are chasing down what we can, calling police departments. The names we have are dead ends, so far."

"I would prefer that you don't involve Hugh in any of those other thefts. I would like him focused on my family."

"I understand."

"Thank you, Craig. And please make sure the others also understand my family's appreciation for what you fellas are doing. It is a thankless business."

"I will let them know." I clicked OFF.

* * *

What are we doing? I thought. *What have we gotten ourselves into?* Once lawyers get involved, no one gets out alive. Barbara was right about the money, and in this case, big money. Ronald Fisher, the assumed thief and murderer, had an excellent eye for the pieces he stole. The collection was nearly priceless or worth a hundred million dollars—maybe more.

We held an emergency meeting in the back of Bell's. Garry was available by phone if we needed him. He told Angela he was taking a nap.

"Well, this is a fine kettle of fish," Tommy said.

"We do one good deed and wham, we get whacked upside the head," Mike added.

"Teresa is fuming," Larry said. "She mentioned our liability, my age, cost, my age."

"You said that," I said.

"She said it three times, thank you very much. Each time I felt older."

"Penny isn't thrilled with me either. Wives."

"And what are we going to do? There is no off-ramp on this highway," Tommy said. "We could slam on the brakes, stop, and get off. Call it a day. Let the lawyers and insurance companies pick up the pieces. Let Audrey figure something out."

"You know we can't do that," I said.

"I know, but I sure as hell want to," Tommy added. "Craig, you're good with plans. What do you think we should do? This needs to be wrapped up."

"Yes, and summer is gone," said Mike. "The kids are planning a big Thanksgiving weekend at Geneva on the lake; it's at Jack's place. Everyone is on board. Lucy has passed on the planning to LeAnn and the boys' wives. For once, we show up and enjoy ourselves. And I want to go knowing this is all done, finished."

"Lucky you, I can't guarantee it."

"Yes, you can, Craig. We need to set a drop-dead date."

"Inappropriate choice of words, Mike," Larry said.

"I mean it," Mike continued. "This could go on and on if we don't put an end to it. So?"

Karen walked over and refilled our coffee cups, took our orders, and left. She wanted to stay and find out what was happening but walked away.

"Here's my take, and I agree that our part needs to be over. Our initial scope of work, as requested by Barbara, was to clean out Allen's house. It morphed into a bizarre Agatha Christie murder mystery. I want out, we all want out, but it must be on our terms, right? That is how it has been for the Marigold Gang for sixty-five years; we never back down. We are here for our buddy and each other. Barbara wanted the house cleared. Garry and I talked, and we need to do one more sweep through the house. Get the car towed and dumped—or sold. Janet wants nothing to do with it. As far as I can tell, it's worthless—it goes. The artwork—leave all that to the lawyers and insurance company. All the crimes are sixty years old. There's nothing to prosecute. Even the South Bend Police agree to that—sadly, the Paines will have to accept delayed justice, such as it is. We do that, and it's done, finished." I looked at Mike. "Finished! That work?"

"Yes," Larry said. "That's a plan I can live with."

CHAPTER 26

Summer 1966

The members of the Marigold Gang graduated from their respective high schools the first weekend of June. Craig Martin, Thomas Ellis, and Lawrence Martini finished in the top 10 percent of their St. Francis High School class. Garry Hughes, Michael Jasicki, and Allen Fisher did well, with Garry being the class valedictorian at Lincolnville High School. The ensuing years would do their best to pull the gang apart; it would create distractions (like marriage, kids, and a war), all to separate the inseparable. Thirty-five years would pass before we were reunited and reformed the Marigold Gang. However, that summer of 1966 was magic. Maybe it was our age, maybe the growing fear of Vietnam, maybe it was one last hurrah before true adulthood. Years later, we talked about it but could not decide. For each, it was different.

Sitting in my backyard that evening, a week after graduation, we were eighteen, shiny, bright, and bored. Looking back, they agreed they were also naïve, anxious, and yet, unbroken. Life soon would change all that.

"The dance starts at eight," Tommy said. "It takes twenty minutes to get to the VFW hall in Frankfort. I can't take my car; we don't have enough room."

"No matter what it costs, a Volkswagen is shit," Allen said.

"I got a deal. I wasn't planning on becoming a taxi driver for you guys," he answered.

The others looked at Garry.

"Not a chance. Dad lent me the Galaxie," said Garry. "I told him I was just coming over to Craig's. If he finds out I put an extra fifty miles on his baby, I am so screwed. So, no way."

Allen, Mike, Larry, and I still lived on Marigold Court. Tommy's family moved to Olympia Fields four years earlier, and Garry's folks moved to a four-bedroom ranch house in a new subdivision in the Heights.

"Mom and Dad are out tonight," Larry said. "First night out in weeks—they are celebrating the new store in Tinley. So, no car. How about you, Craig?"

"Dad had things to finish at the plant; Mom drove over to see him and took Chuck with her. Connie's not back from college. I got nothing, and I'm stuck here with you guys. Dad says if I put the time in at the plant, I can get a car before college."

"You need one at IIT?" Larry said.

"No, not really, but hell, a car is a car, right? It's freedom."

No one could argue with that summation of the greatest need of a teenager's life in 1966. They looked at Allen.

"Mom is in Wisconsin at her sister's with Brenda and Denny—thank God for that. She left right after graduation. She took the station wagon. Dad is in Michigan at Ford—he took his new Grand Prix, dark blue."

"Business must be good, a new car every other year," Larry said.

"I guess so," Allen said uncomfortably. He sat at the end of the picnic table, smoking a Chesterfield. "He said he'd be back Saturday."

"That's three days from now," Mike said. "We need wheels. Being stuck here is not right—we are the Marigold Gang, for Christ's sake."

"That and a quarter will get you a cup of coffee," I said.

"Maybe, but there's a dance tonight with girls," Tommy said. "We have to find a car in the next hour. Anyone on the court have one they might rent, Craig?"

"Not a chance. Give me a butt," I said. Allen slid the pack across the table.

"I could get in trouble for this," Allen said, taking the pack back. "I know where we can get a car."

"You do? Where?" Larry asked.

"My garage. Dad brought home a Studebaker Lark a few years back—been in the garage the whole time."

"You screwing with us? There's a Studebaker in your garage? Bullshit," Mike said.

"That's why they park on the driveway. There's no room in the garage. Father never drives it."

"No kidding. You say there's a Studebaker? I've never seen it," I said.

"The old man told me that it was special. I don't see anything special. I even tried to start it once when they were out of the house. It starts up nice. It's light blue. But if he catches me, he'll beat the shit out of me. I'll never get out of the house."

"Allen, when do you have to report?" Garry asked.

"July 5th, two weeks," Allen said. "Basic training at Fort Leonard in Missouri—maybe ten weeks. Then I don't know what."

"So, if your pop finds out, you will leave in two weeks. What's the problem?" Larry said.

"They could send you to Vietnam," Mike said. "That sucks."

"No worse than staying around here. Father's gotten a little crazy; don't know why."

"I've never seen that car," Larry said, repeating the conversation.

"It showed up maybe three years ago. I was up at Camp Betz with you guys. I come home, and there it is. It was the same time he fixed the rec room in the basement."

"And he did a great job. He never drives it?" Mike said. "We can find something else. Maybe Mrs. Ranieri will lend us her Chevy. Can we scratch together five bucks?"

"Look, guys, I'll get the Studebaker out. Swear that you will never say anything—we go to the dance, then home. That work?"

We all looked at each other and agreed.

Twenty minutes later, Allen was driving west on U.S. 30; the Frankfort VFW was just nine miles away. Larry and I sat in the front seat with Allen, and Tommy, Mike, and Garry sat in the back seat.

"What do we do if I find a girl?" Tommy said.

"You? A girl? Ask if she'll take you home in her car. That will leave us an open spot," Larry said.

"Works for me," Mike added.

Eighteen-year-old males are obsessed with three things: cars, beer, and babes. Anthropologists and sociologists have discovered this to be a universal truth—maybe it was chariots back in the day, but beer and babes have a long history. There may be slight variations depending on the seasons, and whether you are at a beach or in the mountains, it may be babes and beer. The order isn't the issue; it is the availability. And in summer, when hormones and desires peak, it is often easier to find the babes than the beer.

"There's that liquor store just past Matteson. Allen is the biggest and oldest looking. Maybe he can get us a six-pack or two," Garry said.

"If I get caught, even the Army can't protect me," Allen said. "I got the ride; you guys figure out the beer."

The first stop seemingly was a bust. When Larry walked

up to the counter and sat two Stroh's six-packs next to the register, the woman behind the counter looked at him, winked, smiled, and said, "Get the hell out of here, kid. I'm not losing my license over some punk-ass kid like you. Out, or I'm calling the cops."

Chagrined, Larry turned and walked toward the door.

"Stop right there, buster. These beers do not belong on the counter. Put them back."

Being a rebellious youth was new to Lawrence Martini. He respectfully returned to the counter, retrieved the beers, and put them back in the cooler.

"That will be four bucks," the woman said, tapping the counter.

"Four bucks? I didn't buy anything."

"Four bucks or I call the cops."

Larry had five one-dollar bills and eight quarters. The dance was three dollars. He would be broke if this extortionist asked for more.

"The four dollars on the counter," she said again, still tapping. "Then make sure you dump your trash in the can behind the store before you leave."

"I don't have any trash."

The woman scrunched her face up and then let out a long breath. She was maybe thirty, cute, with dark hair. She spoke with an accent—it was Mexican or Texan or something. "Everyone has trash, kid." She winked.

Larry's brain clicked; and told him he was an idiot. There was no disagreement from anyone in the store. He put the four dollars on the counter and walked to the Studebaker.

"Where's the beer? You had one job," Mike said.

"Screw you, Jasicki. I need to throw out the trash. Allen, drive behind the store; there's a barrel."

Allen did as told and drove behind the liquor store. Near

the back door was a black garbage barrel. On top were two Stroh's six-packs. Stuck between the bottles was a note.

Next time, leave your phone number, Juanita.

"I'll be damned. She's hitting on you. You get beer and maybe a date, nice service." I laughed.

* * *

We found a spot near the crowded parking lot, well away from the other cars. Allen was scared that if the car got dirty or dinged, his old man would find out and beat the crap out of him. As it was, he would spend the next day cleaning the car of every speck of Illinois dust.

We placed the beers in the trunk. We trusted no one.

"You see this? No spare tire. Did you know you have no spare tire?" Larry asked as he set the two six-packs on the newspapers spread over the trunk floor.

"One more thing I have to worry about, a flat tire."

"That's weird. The newspapers are from South Bend," Tommy said.

"That's where Studebakers are made," Allen said.

"And they provide local newspapers as trunk liners?" he asked.

Allen slammed the trunk closed.

The band that night was a Northside band called the Shadows of Knight, a rock band from around Mt. Prospect.

"They opened for the Byrds last summer when they came through Chicago," Tommy said. "WLS is still playing their song 'Gloria.' A girl I know says they were booked before they made it big with 'Gloria,' and their album came out. Probably cost a lot more tonight if they hadn't had them under contract."

Mike lit a cigarette and preceded the rest of us to the ticket table; three girls we didn't know were selling tickets.

"Six tickets, please," I said, stepping up beside Mike.

"That's thirty dollars," the blonde said. She looked at me and smiled as she pushed her hair away from her face. She wore her hair long and straight. That year at school, the look was puffed up and sprayed into tall piles. This look was different, very different. I liked it.

Behind me, Garry said, "Thirty dollars? We don't have thirty dollars."

"Look, guys, I don't make these prices up. That's what they are, five bucks each. I've got ten tickets left. That guy over there is with the fire department. There's a strict limit on how many can be inside. In fact, you will have to wait until six others come out before you can go in. Thirty bucks." She looked up at me again. Her smile was even warmer.

Allen pushed his way to the front. "I got this; you guys will owe me." He handed the blonde a fifty-dollar bill. We just looked at Allen as he waited for his change.

Larry leaned in. "Where did you get a fifty-dollar bill? Jesus."

"I did some work for my father. That's what he paid me with. No big deal."

To us, it was a big deal. Allen usually never had more than a buck in his pocket, and that was in dimes and quarters. We also never remembered when Allen's father involved himself in anything that Allen did, let alone some kind of work worth fifty dollars.

"What was the work?" Garry asked.

Allen spun around and glared at Garry. "None of your business, Gare. And never ask again."

We all stood there listening; even the girls at the table eavesdropped. Allen walked away. He held all six tickets and a handful of bills as his change. We had to follow; he had our tickets.

Five minutes later, four couples walked out of the hall together, all huggy and smoochy, as Tommy called it. We walked in—the packed hall filled with kids in their late teens and early twenties. The Shadows of Knight weren't starting for a half hour. A local six-piece band played; they had a black kid as a singer, three guitars, a drummer, and a tenor sax player. We all agreed that they weren't too bad. We found a group of girls and, trading off, danced a couple of songs. Allen stayed to himself along the concrete block wall, smoking.

When the Shadows of Knight started, most of the crowd moved to the low stage to watch. Most had never seen a real band that had their song played on the radio. To top it off, Art Roberts, the top DJ from WLS, took the stage and, after a few off-color jokes, which would never have made the radio waves, introduced the Shadows of Knight. They led off with "Gloria" and then into a standard set of covers of the most played songs on the radio. The girls were freaking out. We stood around, not sure what was happening.

"You smell that?" I said to Larry.

"Smell what?"

"That stink—what the hell is that?"

Allen leaned in, a smile on his face. "That's dope, Mary-jane. Pot, grass, weed, you dopes. You never smelled that?"

We looked at each other. Tommy added, "That stuff's illegal. Shit, you can go to prison. It can screw you up for life."

"It's harmless," Allen said. "I need to get out of here." He looked at his watch. "And I need to be home by eleven."

Two girls walked over to us. I recognized them from St. Francis. One was Penelope Parsons, and the other was Teresa Lombardi. They were both juniors.

"What the hell are you doing here, Martin?" Penelope asked. "I thought you never left Lincolnville."

"I get out, Penny. A guy has to experience life," I said.

"We are looking for whoever is smoking the dope. We want to get a couple of sticks for the ride home."

I could see that the guys were taken aback.

"It's illegal," Larry said.

"Always the good boy," Teresa said, patting him on the cheek. "And I love you for it, but we will score some weed. You can tag along or stay here. Adios, cowboys." The girls walked away. I watched Penny sniff the air and then point across the crowded room. Then they pushed their way through the crowd.

"You know that Penny has a thing for you, Martin. I can tell," Larry said.

"And Terry said she loves you. What's your point?" I said.

"In this world today, we could do worse."

"What do you mean by that?"

"Time is running out; time to make a move. The future is calling."

"You sound like a couple of dime-store philosophers," Mike said. "I need a beer, and we must get Fisher home before he turns into a pumpkin."

"He's our ride. We go where he goes," Tommy said.

"No difference. You staying or coming?" Tommy said to Larry and me.

We looked at each other, then across the room. The girls were talking to a tall, thin, bearded guy with long stringy black hair. The fellow was furtively looking around the room.

"We're going," Mike said as they turned to follow Allen. Larry and I followed in their wake. Allen unlocked the trunk in the parking lot, and we finished off one of the six-packs. In the night air, the beers were still cold.

"You should marry that girl, Craig. You could do a lot worse," Allen said.

"Marriage, that's a long, long way away. Not even on my radar."

"I bet it's on hers," Tommy said. "Didi knows all the rumors—Craig, you are on the top of Penelope Parsons's list. I've heard talk in school."

"If you know so much, where is Didi?" Mike asked. "You are screwing around with us—is she at home pining away for you as you go to dances?"

"She's in Peoria at her aunt's. She'll be there for a few weeks. We have the rest of the summer."

"I wonder what she's doing tonight? What do you think, Craig?" Larry said.

"I think she's at a dance trying to score some LSD or weed 'cause she is so lonesome without her man beside her," I said.

"Screw you guys."

Allen offered Tommy a cigarette. He lit it, then took a long slug of beer.

"Put 'em down, quick," Allen said, looking out to the street. A black-and-white police car slowly drove down the county road. The driver's white face shone in the parking lot's lights. He passed without stopping.

"We are out of here," Allen said. "We can finish the rest at home."

CHAPTER 27

November 2024

I couldn't disagree that we had to wrap up our investigation quickly. First, to appease our wives and reach an acceptable accommodation when it came to Allen; second, to complete the work at hand—clearing the house and disposing of the car; third, the disposition of the artwork and money; and fourth, for me personally, the proverbial millstone around my neck. Penny brought it home: "There is nothing here for you and the guys. Allen, for all his troubles, is gone. What you are doing is more for yourselves and his memory. What crime there was has run its course; sometimes, it is impossible to find justice. Let those who have money in the deal finish it. Be done with this."

She was always the wiser half of our partnership. We've been married eleven months short of fifty years, and I was husband number two for her. For some reason, I stuck. Her first marriage ended in a swamp along the Mekong River near Saigon in 1970. Rick was a guy she met in college. He dropped out, enlisted in the Marines, and was shot by a Cong sniper standing on the deck of a Navy PBR. He's buried at Camp Butler National Cemetery near Springfield. Rick grew up in Champaign, and his last name was Pennworth. She was Penny Pennworth for less than a year. She wore that Penny alliteration with a smile till it ended with a single bullet through Rick's chest. Penny and I reconnected during the summer of 1973 during the Fourth of July event in Lincolnville; soon after, we started dating seriously and married in May 1975. Best decision I have ever made. In time we became business partners after we opened our architectural studio. No kids, no debt, no worries, I guess. The rest, as they say, is history.

Larry married Teresa Lombardi in 1975, the girl from the dance. The first for both, and it stuck for them too. After high school, he went to Northwestern on a full-ride football scholarship. His future, that senior year in 1970, looked good. The pros were sniffing around. His knee gave out in a game against Michigan State as he blocked for an end around. Two years later, after surgery and rehab, he decided to become a Chicago cop. That's when he reconnected with Terry. She'd remained a close friend of Penny Parsons Pennworth, the future Penny Martin. They have two children, Julius and Anna, and three grandkids. Larry stuck with the Chicago PD until 2005, when he took his thirty-year pension. After Chicago, he was offered and appointed the Lincolnville police chief. He led the department for twelve years and fully retired at sixty-five.

Mike Jasicki was drafted and, like Allen Fisher, eventually ended up in Vietnam. He was there during the worst of it, 1968 and 1969. He was sent home with a nasty leg wound, and in the spring of 1970, he married Lucy Silverstein, a nurse he'd met during rehab. She helped him work through his PTSD issues and, like his father, alcoholism. He leads everyone with nine grandkids.

I told you about Tommy, our comic book collector, and his second chance with Heather after he lost Ellen. I worry less about Tommy than any of the boys. And Garry and Angela came in second to my worries until his recent heart attack. Now he has us and a gaggle of doctors and nurses watching him—and Angela.

I'm just a mother hen; what can I say? My take is that this investigation will go on in some form until I put it to rest. As I discussed with the gang, that time is soon. One more sweep of the house, removal of the Studebaker, find a real estate broker who doesn't know the house's history, and hope we don't end up on the news again.

We set the final walk-through for Friday morning, the week before Thanksgiving. Garry even received permission from Angela as long as he did not lift, push, or even fast walk. She dropped him off at ten and told him she would return at three. On the driveway, we discussed the possibility of hidden compartments in the floor and walls. I had the power left on in case someone was interested in the property.

We started at ten thirty in the basement. This time we all searched everything and everywhere. Frankly, it was silly. Five old men with flashlights stumbling around an empty house listening for squeaky floorboards and studying mysterious ghost shapes on the plaster walls. We even checked for hidden compartments behind the bathroom medicine cabinet. We spent as little time in the freezer room (as we called it) as possible. It still freaked us out—except for dust, it was empty now (the police removed the freezers weeks earlier). After the bedrooms (we paid particular attention to the floors), we did a cavity search of the kitchen cabinets and looked behind the oven and refrigerator (all Kenmore products—Ron seemed stuck on the brand). The living room still had Proverbs 11:21 spray-painted on the wall. *The only two living descendants*, outside Allen's kids, who had a dog in this hunt were Allen's sister and brother. Would one of them have clubbed me? I was sure of it.

One of my theories was out the window if these two weren't involved. That theory was that one or both knew what was in the house and had bided their time until they could be confident to take it all. They hadn't been able to do this earlier because Allen controlled what remained in the house. After his death, all bets and cautions were off. The gang and I talked about these two, and they all agreed. However, having everything in the security locker lowered the pressure. It was also the reason for this last strip search, as Larry called it. "We must eliminate all possibilities that may remain in the house." No argument from any of us.

The last stop was the garage. Tommy had boxed up the hand and electrical tools; a guy who does the flea markets was happy to get the free stuff. Allen's Harley was sitting in Larry's garage. He would have it appraised and pass on the information to Barbara. All that was left was the Studebaker.

"It's a nice car," Larry said matter-of-factly. "Not a show-stopper like a vintage Mustang or Camaro, but nice."

"Those cars came a couple of years later," Tommy said. "Remember when my father bought me that Mustang for college?"

"You always were a lucky dog," I said. "Yes, a bright blue Mustang. Sweet."

"Isn't this the car that Allen drove us to that dance in Franklin?" Mike said.

It came back—that one evening and the dance we'd all forgotten.

"I remember being stuck in the back seat. Damn, if I knew it had been used to carry bodies across state lines just a few years earlier, well, shit. It spooks me now, sixty years later."

"Me too," I echoed. We spent a few minutes walking around the carcass. It had a layer of dust you could carve your name into. Random fingerprints covered the side panels and around the door handles.

"This may be a stupid idea, but will it start?" Larry asked.

We all looked at him, and smiles grew.

"Only one way to find out," Tommy said.

"It's a good bet the battery has been dead a half-century. I've got long cables in the truck. It's in the driveway. Let's give it a go."

Mike rolled up the garage door. When we first got into the house, we had to pry out the lag bolts that Ron Fisher used to nail the door shut. As it swung up and open, the door complained like a dozen Irish banshees. Like snow, dust drifted down onto the roof of the Studebaker.

"The tires are flat," I said. "If we can get this started, should we try and back it out?"

"One thing at a time, Craig. I give it a 10 percent chance of starting," Larry added as he walked to his F-150 facing us on the driveway. Five minutes later, the hood of the Studebaker was open, the battery exposed, and Larry was ready to hook up the cables.

"The key?" Larry said.

"Garry, on the wall, there are two keys on nails, the one with the octagon-shaped top," I said. We had hung the keys back on the nails after we did the first inspection weeks earlier.

Garry pulled the key and tossed it to me. "Who wants the honors?" I asked, holding it up.

"Just a second, one more search through the inside," Garry said. "We must be thorough."

"We did that," I said. Since no one volunteered, I climbed into the driver's seat and carefully rolled down the window.

"What can it hurt? Did you do the glove box?" Garry said as he opened the front passenger's door. There was no answer. "Remarkably, the interior is almost brand new, with some dust, but it's not too bad for sixty years old." The Lark's massive glove box, labeled with the word Vanity, covered a substantial amount of the dashboard. When Garry dropped it open, I looked over from the driver's seat. It was like a TV tray with locations for drinks and a shelf wide enough for a picnic.

"Are those compartments?" I asked.

"Looks like it," Garry said as he carefully lifted a hinged cover on the right side. Inside was empty, probably good for maps, pencils, and stuff. The owner's guide for the Lark sat comfortably in one. Modern carmakers should consider this idea an alternative to their poor excuses for glove boxes (who wears gloves anyway?). It would be the perfect shelf for a bag of McDonald's fries and a shake. Garry then opened the compartment on the left side, a mirror popped open.

"I got a book," Garry announced.

"A book?"

"Yes, in the glove box."

He carefully removed it.

I leaned over. "What is it?"

Garry had started flipping through the pages. "It's a journal. Dates go way back to the 1960s, short entries. Is this Ron's?"

"The handwriting is Allen's. I recognize it," I said. "One more bit of evidence."

"You ready to try and start this sucker?" Larry called out.

I went back to the work at hand. "The odometer is one of those mechanical rotary types. It has only 648 miles on it," I yelled.

"That should kick up its auction value," Mike said. He stood next to the front bumper, facing the engine. He was visible through the gap of the open hood. The old battery and the newly attached cables were on the right side of the engine compartment.

"You ready, Larry?" I yelled.

"Do we have gas?" Garry asked as he climbed out, the journal in his hand.

"Don't know until we have electricity." I turned the ignition. There was squealing and a loud *clack-clack-clack*, a long clattering, leading to a very annoying grinding sound, then, to everyone's surprise, the engine caught and fired. A black cloud of soot and exhaust fumes washed over the car's rear, out the garage door, obscuring Larry's truck. "The tank's half full," I yelled, and all the dials on the dash lit up. It was like Frankenstein coming to life. The car shook and rocked, then coughed and rattled. I was stunned. I looked at the guys. They were as astonished as I was. The car settled down a bit into idle; I got out.

"It's a good bet it needs a serious lube job, oil change, battery, new tires, a lot of care—but it runs. Good job, Craig," Larry said, walking back into the garage. He held the cables in his hands. "The battery is dead, but for the moment, she runs."

Mike still stood at the front of the car. "Amazing, sounds good. Maybe we should shut it off. The oil may be shit, and it could seize the whole thing up."

I walked to the front and stood next to Mike. "Just a second more; I like the sound."

Smoke started pouring out from under the air filter. Then a pressurized stream of liquid jetted out from the same area, another aimed in the opposite direction. The pungent smell of gasoline filled the air, then another stream appeared, this time shooting to the left and over the interior quarter panel, then to the concrete floor.

"Turn it off," Garry yelled.

The engine compartment exploded into flames before I could pull the key. Mike staggered back; luckily, he was far enough away and avoided the spray of pressurized gasoline. Tommy stood even farther back. The two ran past me, along the car, to the outside. Flames and gasoline shot in a dozen different directions. I found the key through the smoke, turned it off, and pulled it. The engine stopped with a hard jerk, but not the fire. I followed Mike and Tommy; Garry had fled down the opposite side of the car. The fuel lines, now compromised, poured gasoline onto the fire. The flames had spread across the floor and reached the full plastic trash bags under the workbenches. These were going to be the last things we tossed. They were now burning, and so was the wood shelving above them.

Larry was on his phone calling 9-1-1. He gave the address and said it was a house and structure fire.

"Anyone have a fire extinguisher?" Mike asked.

Larry went to his truck and returned a moment later. The fire extinguisher was all of ten inches tall.

"I think we need a bigger extinguisher," Tommy said.

The garage was now fully engulfed. Fire trucks wailed in the distance. From across the street, Delmar Johnson ran toward us.

"Holy shit, what happened?" he asked.

"Ah, we got a little too crazy," I said. "Tried to start the Studebaker."

"Obviously. Did it run?"

"Yes, then it exploded," Garry said.

Larry quickly backed his truck away from the conflagration and parked beside our cars across the street. The tinder-dry garage was now entirely involved as the fire trucks arrived. By the time the hoses had been pulled and connected to the hydrant, the house was now burning. The flames had penetrated the exposed ceiling beams and roof. And it didn't help that a breeze had pushed the flames through the open interior doors and flooded the house with fire.

Once up and running, the fire department put the fire out in twenty minutes. However, the roof had collapsed by then, and the main floor had fallen into the basement. The garage and everything in it was a total loss. Where the garage once stood, the steel frame of the Studebaker was all that remained.

The exterior walls on the farthest end from the garage were all that remained of the house.

The five of us stood on the sidewalk, stunned and amazed.

During the next hour, we told the fire chief what had happened. He was not pleased. He repeatedly mentioned the words *stunt*, *stupid*, *irresponsible*, and *old enough to know better*, all in different arrangements. We couldn't disagree.

When Detective Audrey King arrived, I wasn't sure what would happen. Would arson charges be filed? Would we be spending the weekend in the hoosegow?

Her first words were, "Your wives are all going to kill you."

We could not disagree.

"I want to meet all of you at the station on Monday morning, ten o'clock. There are new developments, and since you guys are my prime investigators, you should be there to hear about the evidence we uncovered, some of it with your help."

"New evidence—what new evidence?" Larry asked.

"Monday, ten o'clock. Now all of you go home before something else happens."

THE CRIME
Part 1

Summer 1963

It was late afternoon, and Ronald Fisher stood on the patio of Water Paine's home and looked deep into the surrounding woods that enclosed the modern Prairie-style house designed by Frank Llyod Wright. Birds chirped and flitted from tree to tree. Fisher, dressed in a dark gray suit, white shirt, dark maroon tie, and black Florsheims, held in his right hand a Manhattan in a crystal tumbler and in his left a Chesterfield cigarette. He saw himself as sophisticated and educated. He was a war hero and was awarded medals for freeing Western Europe from the Nazis; now, he was playing his part in the most extraordinary capitalistic production machine the world had ever seen. He was the leading sales representative for Halsted Chrome, Inc., an automotive parts manufacturer headquartered in Harvey, Illinois. He inhaled his cigarette, and the aromas of June flowers surrounding the patio. Dinner was scheduled for eight o'clock to accommodate the other Studebaker managers and their spouses from the plant. It was good to be rich, he thought.

"Ron, thank you for accepting our dinner invitation. Clare was pleased to meet you finally," Walter Paine said, walking up to Fisher. "I've talked about you incessantly for the past year. And, of course, my company and I thank you for the fine craftsmanship and work Halsted Chrome has been doing for us. I don't think we've rejected one part."

"We try, Mr. Paine. Our goal is 100 percent customer satisfaction," Fisher said. He took another sip of his drink.

"Please, Ron. Here, call me Walt. Big things are happening here at Studebaker, a new line of cars for the growing American family, as well as our leadership in design. I can guarantee a long list of new parts and trims."

"Thank you, Walt. We look forward to bidding on the contracts. We have always enjoyed working with Studebaker."

Walter Paine took a drag from his cigarette and leaned into Fisher. "Do you know how our competitors are doing?" he asked with a smile.

"Only what I see on the stock exchange. And besides, I never talk about my clients. You, above all, can understand that. I heard that your new Avanti set speed records."

"One hundred seventy miles per hour from a production car blows away the Corvette. Our challenge is production. New techniques, fiberglass, and engine modifications—all while trying to run an automobile company for the average American."

"I am positive you and your people will make it work. Brilliant design, by the way."

"And with partners such as Halsted Chrome, I know we will. Let me show you around the house. It was designed by Frank Lloyd Wright just before he died."

A beautiful woman crossed the room that faced the patio. Walt and Ron met her halfway.

"It is a pleasure to meet you, Mrs. Paine," Ron said. "Your house is beautiful; it has a certain style about it. Do I see some Frank Lloyd Wright in the design?" He knowingly looked at Walt and nodded.

"You found us out, Ron." She did not ask him to call her Clare. "I was an architecture student at Michigan when Walter and I dated. I attended Wright's lectures and even visited many of his houses. When we were fortunate enough to afford this home, I insisted that we ask Mr. Wright."

"Didn't he pass away a few years ago?"

"Yes, but his studio is still open. We found a design we liked, and they modified it to fit the property. A true Usonian Prairie Style design, though a bit larger for our family of five."

The three continued through the house; Mrs. Paine pointed out the built-in cabinetry, the furniture, and the artwork.

"Fascinating. And the artworks . . . Renoir, Picasso; and the sketches—Mary Cassatt?"

"Walter, I like this man. Well dressed, educated, and smart. I suggest you keep him and his company busy. You know the Impressionists?"

"Yes, I spent some time in Paris after the war. Then the GI Bill and University of Illinois."

"Married?"

"Yes, my wife's name is Lois. Sixteen years, three children. She is vacationing in Wisconsin this month."

They continued through the house and returned to the patio, joining three others. Looking down the length of the one-story house, Ron spied three faces looking out one of the bedroom windows.

"We have an audience, Mrs. Paine," he said.

"Our children, Mr. Fisher. Janet, the girl on the right, is fourteen and about to start high school. Mark is eleven, intelligent, and plays the piano well. Our youngest, Louis, is seven. Walt believes Louis will become a star at Notre Dame in twelve years—he's our athlete."

"High expectations."

"Our families, Walter's and mine, have always expected the most from ourselves. We here in South Bend are the bedrock of the Midwest. We see an incredible future ahead of us, especially for our children. We are taking them up to my parents' house on Torch Lake this Friday afternoon for the first half of summer vacation. I'll be with them, hoping for some relaxation before the craziness of the fall when they introduce the new models. Walt will stay with us for a few days, then bounce back and forth. It is my family's estate; I do love it there. You mentioned children, Mr. Fisher."

"Yes, three. They are about the same ages as your children. Two boys and a girl."

"And they are with their mother?" Clare asked.

"Allen, the oldest, is at Boy Scout camp. He's one of the counselors. Brenda and Dennis are with their mother. She is staying the month at her mother's near Milwaukee. I'll see them in a week or two. I have appointments here in Indiana and Michigan left in my rounds. Most of the plants are resetting their dies and retooling."

"Walt tells me that you work for the other manufacturers."

"Our company has contracts with all the big automakers. We must stay in the game."

"Game?"

"Mrs. Paine, business is like a game. There are rules, expectations, players, and progress and growth from one year to the next. Those that can play the game well must be vigilant. The consumer makes the rules. A well-known economist once said that the market is supreme. You can never fool the marketplace, no matter how much you spend on advertising."

Walter Paine walked over from a conversation and kissed his wife on the cheek. "Well done, the party is a success."

"Walter, Mr. Fisher was giving me a lecture on Austrian economics." She smiled and looked at Ron. "Mr. Fisher, I am not one of those usual corporate wives, I assure you. Walt, Mr. Fisher is well versed in business; I think he and his company are keepers." She smiled again, turned, and joined another conversation.

"You passed the Clare test, Ron. My wife is very particular about her friends and more particular about her enemies. She comes from an old Detroit automobile family. Ford connections—her grandfather was one of Henry's top managers. Her parents are professors at the University of Michigan, lawyers, and economists. I was lucky. I fell for her. She tolerates me. Refresh your drink at the bar; we have a half hour until dinner."

Before dinner, Ron had other conversations but spent most of the time assessing the artwork on the walls. Yes, they were Renoirs, two Pissarros, and, in contrast, a fine Picasso oil of a boy from his blue period. There were other pieces, a couple of Cassatt drawings—some were valuable, but the Renoirs and Pissarros are what caught his fancy.

At dinner, he sat next to a young woman, who, though quite pretty, was dull. She talked incessantly about her children and her prize poodles. At times, Ron wasn't sure which. She used the same qualifiers equally for both. Dinner was an excellent chicken cordon bleu served with a French Chablis. Dessert was a lemon fruit tart. Ron was impressed. It was one of the best meals he'd had in years.

Earlier in the day, he had completed a deal for Halsted Chrome's most substantive contract with Studebaker. It was for twenty thousand sets of chrome trim for the new Lark. These included the new front grille, edge trims, headlight surrounds, and trunk and taillight trims. The contract included extensions for up to one hundred thousand sets. If his company didn't screw up (a big if), his commission would be an annuity for the next few years. He was also made aware of the future growth expectations for the new Avanti, Gran Turismo Hawk, and the expanded line of the Lark. What Ron appreciated more was the Paines' collection of artwork.

"I have a surprise for you all," Walter said from his spot at the head of the table. "Take your after-dinner drinks and follow me out to the garage."

Everyone dutifully trailed their host through the house; Ron mingled in the middle, smiling and chatting with the poodle lady. Reaching the garage, with grand ceremony, Walter clicked on the lights and illuminated a spectacularly polished deep-red Studebaker Avanti, the company's dramatic entrée into the high-end world of exotic, high-powered, elegantly designed examples of American automotive creativity. Chevrolet had its Corvette, Ford its Thunderbird, and England its Jaguar XKE. Buick's Riviera and Chrysler's Imperial were close and coming up from behind. There were worthies from Germany and Italy, but they hardly dented the U.S. market. Americans wanted speed and style, and Studebaker was offering the Avanti.

These guests were experts in the world of cars. The men and two of the women poked around and proclaimed it out of this world—they all, of course, worked for Studebaker. Mrs. Dull said she hoped there was room for her doggies.

* * *

Ronald Fisher began formulating a plan during his drive back to his motel. He knew and appreciated the fact that he was a thief. He considered himself to be very good at this sideline profession. He kept to those that could afford the losses—most had insurance, and the pain would be more emotional than financial. By his count, he had liberated close to a dozen quality artworks, boxes of silver (not silver plate) flatware, numerous valuable (and portable) sculptures, and, when found, gold and cash. He was quick, agile, and entirely unexpected. His job as a sales rep allowed him into his customers' houses, and all were proud to show him around. He'd keep his ear open to listen for an opportunity, and when one presented itself, he took advantage of it. When he returned, he even commiserated with his clients, and they privately told him about their misfortune.

He parked at the front of his motel on the south side of South Bend and walked across the street to Billy's bar, a dive he'd often frequented on his Studebaker trips. He'd been planning this theft for a year, and tonight was his second time in the house. The previous visit was a barbeque to celebrate the Paines moving into their new home. That afternoon there were at least fifty people. Tonight's dinner was more intimate and revealing.

"Jim Beam, on the rocks," Fisher said as he settled onto a barstool. He sat near the door. He would have one drink, then go back to the motel. There was a lot of work to do before Friday night when the Paine family would be on their way to Michigan.

Engrossed in his thinking, he was startled by the two young women sitting on each side of him. It was unsettling, more because he failed to notice them until their arrival. Looking left then right, he was amazed—they were identical blondes, maybe twenty at best, with gray-green eyes, a little too much makeup, and dressed in short shorts and chest-hugging tee shirts. The bartender was talking to two fellows at the far end of the bar, two couples were shooting pool, and two women sat in one of the booths. The Roy Orbison song "The Great Pretender" played on the jukebox.

"You are required to buy each of us a drink," the tease on the right said.

"And why is that?" Fisher answered.

"No one drinks alone at Billy's. It is a local ordinance or something. So, you owe Gloria and me a drink."

"And you are?"

"Sheila Lingermann, and this is my sister, Gloria."

"I thought she was your doppelganger."

"What the hell does that mean?" Gloria said as she waved toward the bartender.

"I can tell you are sisters because you look alike."

"We are identical twins, two for the price of one," Sheila said. Fisher wasn't sure if it was an explanation or a proposition.

"I hadn't noticed, and is this a proposition?" Fisher answered.

"What do you take us for?" Gloria said coyly. "Two gin rickeys, Sam."

Sam began constructing the gin and lime juice concoction.

"I hadn't agreed to buy you two the drinks," Fisher said.

"Oh, never mind. Sam will put it on your bill," Gloria said. "Now, what's a guy like you, all nicely dressed, doing in a juke joint like this?"

Fisher had not believed for a moment that the girls were out of place. They looked to be from central casting. *We need twin hookers for this scene in this seedy country bar. What do you have?* That was Fisher's first thought. Being generally amoral, Fisher considered the possibilities. He clinked his glass against the greenish tumblers of the girls. He had two days to kill before the Paines would be in Michigan; he did not want to drive the two hours back to Lincolnville and then turn around. The girls were cute in a wholesome Indiana farmgirl sort of way. He ordered another bourbon and waited as the girls finished their gins.

"Sorry, ladies, long day tomorrow. I'm back to my room." He left a twenty on the bar. "Have another round on me."

"You sure you don't want to party some?" Sheila said, placing her hand on his arm. "Me and Gloria, we're just trying to make ends meet. Mama's sick. And no one knows where our pa disappeared to. So, if you're looking for some company, we sure might make it worth your time."

"You girls finish your drinks and meet me outside. I'm staying just across the street. We can talk there about what kind of party you want."

The girls giggled and looked nervously at each other. Fisher saw the practiced exchange for what it was. He went on guard.

Part 2

Ronald Fisher, with an attractive blonde under each arm, stood next to his car. Both girls, all handsy, were making removing his room key from his trousers pocket difficult.

"Give me a second. Hold on," he protested.

Looking up, the incandescent lights of the parking lot reflected off the stainless-steel hunting knife held not two feet from his nose. The hand clutching the knife had dirty fingernails, and at the end of the arm, a swarthy Slavic-looking fellow with a round face in need of a shave. The man, three inches shorter than himself, sported a crew cut and wore a black tee shirt. Directly behind him stood another guy. This fellow was rail thin, with black hair, deep-set dark eyes, orange tee shirt. Both, while grinning, glared at Fisher.

"Your goddamned wallet," the swarthy fellow demanded.

"A lot of work to shake down a guy," Fisher said, glancing at Gloria, or the girl he thought was Gloria. "I'd have gladly tipped you extra, ladies."

"They ain't ladies; they're our girls," the skinny guy said. "Wallet, asshole."

"You don't know me well enough to call me an asshole. If I may, I'll get my wallet, and you four can get out of here. Is that okay?"

Swarthy was jumpy. He rocked back and forth on his heels;

the other kid was either drunk or high. It made no difference to Fisher; four years in the infantry had taught him one thing—always take the advantage.

"May I—my wallet?" Fisher asked as he slowly and carefully reached into his suit coat jacket. One moment his right hand was moving to his left inside; the next, he held a Colt Army service revolver that knocked Swarthy's knife away. He then pointed the muzzle at the spot between the man's eyes. Both girls screamed. Skinny had signs he would pee in his pants.

"Christ, you don't have to do this, man. We were having a little fun," Swarthy continued. "All's cool, just don't."

"Drop the knife, asshole." Ron smiled. "What's your name? I want to know whose brains I'm going to blow away."

The kid stared at Fisher, probably never more afraid than right now. He'd been a bully his whole life. Now was the time for the world to get even.

"Name, asshole," he repeated.

"Toby, Toby Wozniacki."

"You?"

"Joe Slauger."

Fisher used the gun as a pointer. "All four of you, to my room, it's number 12. We need to talk." Fisher picked up the knife from the asphalt when they were ten feet in front of him.

"Come on, mister, we was just screwing around, just let us go," Gloria said. "Nobody got to get hurt."

"Whether I hurt you or not is up to you." He passed the room key to Sheila. "Open the door. You two follow the girls, walk to the wall in the back, and stand there facing the wall."

They did as told. Fisher shut the door behind him. "Now, turn around. You girls sit on the floor, there and there. You two, on your knees between them, fingers interlocked behind your head." The four hesitated. "Jesus Christ, do I have to repeat myself?!"

Thirty seconds later, the four sat and kneeled on the motel room floor. Fisher pulled out the desk chair, spun it around, and sat. The Colt expertly held in his right hand.

"Now, let me see if I have your names right," Ron said.

He looked at each and repeated their names, Gloria, Toby, Joe, and Sheila. "Here's the deal, you are all a bunch of amateurs and could easily be dead. I fought in the war, and I've killed many men. You four would be a statistical blip."

"A what?" Gloria asked.

"Something that would not be noticed."

"Our ma would notice."

"Then you should not play with adults," Fisher said as he lit a cigarette. "However, I'm going to give you a chance to redeem yourselves and make some money at the same time. Sound interesting?"

The three looked at Toby, who, for the moment, was the apparent leader of this peculiar quartet. "What's the gig? How much is in it for us?" Toby blurted.

"Maybe a few thousand, hard to tell. It is a simple burglary. All you have to do is break into a house, collect some things I want, and leave. I'll give you each five hundred dollars for that work. If you pull this off, I may have other work for you. However, if you screw it up"—he looked at the four—"let's just say, don't screw it up."

"When's the job?" That question came from Gloria. Fisher now understood who the brains were and who was the brawn.

"The job is Friday night, one in the morning. The location is about five miles from here. I will give you an address, and all four of you will meet me there. This deal is off if one of you doesn't show. I will give you the address of the house. I will also give you precise instructions, and you will do as I tell you. Do you have a car?"

"Toby does, a Plymouth," Gloria said. Fisher could see she

was the most interested in the gig, as Toby called it.

"Good, the house is outside of town." Fisher leaned over to the desk and wrote on a notepad. "This is the address of a warehouse near here on Sample Street. Be there at eleven o'clock Friday night. I will give you the information then. All of you will be there. If anyone drops out, the deal is off."

"How the hell can we trust you? This could all be a setup," Gloria said.

"It could be. However, if I were a cop and this was a bust or a trap, I'd have your asses in jail right now," Fisher said. "Trust is earned, Gloria. I'm taking a gamble here; I need this work done, and I don't know your skills. Think of this as a test, a trial by fire. I may have other work if you pull this off without screwing it up."

"How do we know you won't screw us over?" Gloria said. "This has to be a big deal, enough to ask the four of us to work for you. Shit, we just tried to jam you up."

"True, but there's something about you that I can work with—besides, that's my problem—are you interested? Two grand cash for an hour's work. You won't get that at the Studebaker plant. What do they pay, three bucks an hour?"

"I worked there last summer," Joe said. "I got $1.75 an hour and had to join the union. Messed up my back and got no help."

"See, kid? What I'm asking is worth a couple of months' wages for each of you. Are you in?"

"We don't have to hurt anyone, do we?" Sheila asked. "I will not hurt anyone."

"No, the people will be gone. Yes or no. If yes, I will see you Friday night at eleven at this address." He held up the slip of paper. "In or out?"

The four looked at each other, then Gloria said, "We are in. Can I ask something?"

"Sure."

"Since we are broke, and you are our meal ticket tonight, can we have an advance?"

Fisher moved the pistol to his left hand, removed his wallet, and took out a fifty-dollar bill. "This is an advance; I'll take it out of Toby's five hundred." Fisher smiled.

* * *

Fisher used the old warehouse off and on during the past two years for the temporary storage of parts brought over from the Harvey plant. Studebaker people would move the parts, when needed, to their plant. The warehouse lease was to a sham company he'd set up in Racine, Wisconsin. He also prepaid the owner six months' rent in cash. There was no direct paper trail to him or Halsted Chrome. Only the shipping department knew about the warehouse, and they believed Halsted Chrome leased it.

Friday night, at five minutes to eleven, there was a sharp knock on the warehouse's steel door. Holding a pistol at his side, he opened the door. The four stood outside in the dark, wearing black jeans, black tee shirts, sneakers, and jackets.

Gloria pushed her way in past Fisher, and the others followed. He looked outside and saw what appeared to be a dark green or black Plymouth. Rust had already begun to eat away at the edges of the doors. He turned back to the four.

"Follow me." Once inside the warehouse, Fisher crossed the concrete floor to an office with dirty windows. The light from inside was all that illuminated the large room. His dark blue Pontiac Grand Prix was parked in the back of the warehouse. Inside the office sat a folding table and six chairs, a desk on the far side against the wall, and a filing cabinet. A 1961 Studebaker calendar hung on the wall over the desk; there was no phone. "Sit."

The four took chairs at one end of the table, and Fisher took the opposite end.

"Nice car," Joe said.

"Thanks."

"You know, you never told us your name," Sheila said.

"That's because my name is irrelevant. If you must call me anything, call me Mister. That's all. Did I ask your last names? Did I ask for identifications, a driver's license? Honestly, I don't care. I need you for this job, simple, that's it. When you are finished, you will get your money. Simple Simon."

"Well, we're here. Where's the house?"

Fisher went to the desk, picked up a manila envelope, opened the clasp, and removed five pieces of paper. "Excuse me for being rude, but I didn't ask an important question the other evening. Can you read?"

The four looked at each other. "Yes, Mister, we can read," Gloria said. "We may be idiots and down on our luck, but we can read."

"Good, no insult implied, just asking. Here is the map to the house. The instructions are specific on where to park and how and where to enter the house. Once inside, there are eight pieces of art on the walls, at least two boxes of silverware, and other knickknacks that I want you to steal. Their locations are described on the paper. Please carefully place them in the trunk of your car, then return them here. You should be back by one o'clock. I will be waiting and will open the roll-up door when you arrive. You will then be paid, and we are done. It will take you no more than fifteen minutes to reach the house. It is 8.75 miles from here. You will be in the house no more than fifteen minutes, ten minutes to load, and fifteen to return—at most one hour."

"That doesn't sound hard. The four of us will split up the

work."

"There will be three of you. One of you will remain here as my guest."

"Hell no. That's not going to happen," Gloria answered. "Not a chance."

"Yes, Gloria. That is what will happen. You decide which of you will stay here. You have two minutes. You are leaving in fifteen."

Fisher exited the office, lit a cigarette, and waited while the four picked the hostage. The squabbling was heated; at two minutes, he walked back in. "Who's the winner?"

"Sheila; she has a kid. Best if she stays in case something goes wrong," Toby said.

"You have a kid?"

"Yes, Mister. I have a boy not yet a year old. He's Toby's and mine."

Since Fisher was as sentimental as a snake, he just smiled. "Time to go. The clock starts now. You have one hour."

The three hurried out of the warehouse, slamming the door behind them. Fisher turned to Sheila.

"I'm going to tie you up. I need to do some things."

After he secured her arms and feet to a chair, he tried to gag her.

"Damn it, Mister. You got to do that? I got bad lungs, asthma, hard to breathe."

"Okay, Sheila, I won't gag you. If you scream, you saw where we are, no one will hear you. And if you do scream and it brings down the cops, I will shoot your sister and the others—and then you—then your kid will have no parents. So, keep quiet. I will be back soon."

Sheila, wide-eyed and terrified, glared at Fisher. She nodded her head.

Fisher hit the button for the roll-up door and then went

to his car. Two minutes later, after closing the door behind him, he took a shortcut across South Bend to the Walter Paine home. The map he gave Gloria took a circuitous route west of South Bend before ending up at the long driveway to the house. When the Plymouth's headlights washed up the driveway, Fisher had already parked and was hiking through the thick woods in the gray light of the nearly full moon. Standing in the shadows, he watched the car pull up behind another auto in the driveway. It was the Paines' Studebaker Lark. The three climbed out and walked around the car. Then Toby pointed to the back of the house. Fisher knew he must abort the mission and wait a day or two. Obviously, the Paines had not left for Michigan. He could wait a day or two. Still in the shadows, Fisher followed them to the back of the house and was about to say something when Joe swung a tire iron into the glass of the rear door. *Well, this is now shit*, he thought as the glass shattered.

Toby put his hand through the shattered door, unlocked the latch, and jerked the door open. The three strolled in. The interior was dark. Like searchlights, three flashlights lit the room and washed over the walls. Fisher moved along the side of the house to a window. There, he watched the three begin to remove the artwork and lean them against a couch. Then the interior lights flared on. He stepped back, and from inside came a guttural yell followed immediately by a sharp pistol shot. A man in white pajamas fell to the carpet, then another scream, and a woman in pink pajamas ran into the room. Instantly another gunshot, and Fisher watched Clare Paine tumble across the floor and fall onto her husband.

"No, no, no," Fisher said. He wanted to scream. He reached for his pistol and swore. It was on the floor of the Pontiac; he'd forgotten it. Looking back into the house, he saw that Joe held a pistol, probably Walter Paine's, and that Gloria was now laughing and was moving the paintings and other items he'd hired them to collect to the front door. Joe and Toby left the room, then a muffled scream, another gunshot—goddamn them, the children. More gunshots, then more laughter.

Fisher slipped around the house to the front. The front door was open, and Gloria and Joe were loading the paintings and boxes inside the Studebaker Lark. What the hell? Joe then climbed into the Studebaker; Gloria joined him. Toby came out the front door, walked to the Plymouth, climbed in, and followed Joe down the driveway to the road. The front door was left wide open.

Fisher ran through the woods to his car, his heart pounding. He pulled onto the narrow gravel road and came to a gas station five minutes later. It was near the warehouse. The whole thing had gone wrong. Maybe someone was alive. He went to the pay phone, and with a gloved finger, he dialed the operator for the police.

"How can I help you?" came the nasal voice of the operator.

"Police, this is an emergency, hurry." Thirty seconds passed.

"Sergeant Deets, what can I help you with?"

"I was driving by a house on Oak Road and heard gunshots. I know gunshots."

"The address?"

"I remember 948 on the mailbox, that's all. I raced to find a phone."

"Your name?"

Fisher hung up and ran to his car. Two minutes later, he was sitting in front of the warehouse, smoking a cigarette, when the Studebaker pulled in. Toby followed in the Plymouth.

"What the hell? Why do you have that car?" Fisher yelled at Gloria through the open window.

"It's a nice car. I wanted it," Gloria said. "You get your silly paintings; I get the car. We give it a spray job; Joe is really good at that. Then me and Sis have a car. Where is my sister?"

Joe sat next to her, looking pissed. A cigarette hung from his lips. Toby parked behind them, then joined them.

"Move the paintings, which I assume you have, inside," Fisher ordered.

"Joe, inside," Gloria said. "He gets his shit, and we get paid. Then we are gone. Now, where is my sister?"

"Patience," Fisher answered. He unlocked the door and went inside. A moment later, the roll-up door opened. The only hint of light came from the office in the back until the Studebaker's headlights washed the warehouse's interior. Joe and Gloria exited the car and headed toward the office. Toby followed. Fisher was about ten feet behind them. The roll-up door slowly and noisily lowered behind them. Joe parked the Studebaker about five feet from the back wall. Gloria quickly crossed over to the office to release her sister.

Now standing at the Lark, Toby turned in the wash of the headlights as Joe closed the driver's door.

"Where the hell is your car, Mister?" Toby said. Then Fisher saw the gun in Toby's hand. Fisher's Colt was already raised and pointed at the man.

"You didn't have to kill them. That was not part of the deal," Fisher said, watching Joe stand straight at the Lark's door. He had a chrome revolver stuck in his belt.

"How do you know what happened? There were no witnesses, Mister. Anyway, the guy had a gun. Joe's got it. I had to do it. Ain't gonna die by the hand of some rich prick. So, no problem."

"Big problem. Steal a few pieces of art and some silver; they have insurance. Kill a family, and they will hunt you to the ends of the earth."

"So, what you gonna do, old man?" Toby said.

Fisher fired once and hit Toby in the face. Joe reached for Paine's revolver and caught a .45 round in the chest, blowing out his heart. From the office, one of the girls, it was impossible to tell which, was running toward the door. With an experienced hand, he fired. The girl tumbled across the dusty concrete. The other girl, screaming like a demon, ran straight at Fisher. The knife she held flashed in the headlights. Gloria was dead before she was halfway across the warehouse.

* * *

Three hours later, Ronald Fisher, driving the Lark, pulled into the garage of his house on Marigold Court. The two-hour drive from South Bend allowed him to devise a plan to make all this disappear. The killers were dead. If their bodies were never found, it would be impossible to connect him to them. The drive was sheer terror. With the four bodies jammed in the trunk of the Lark and a million dollars' worth of paintings in the back seat, he would have difficulty explaining any of it to a state trooper. He drove carefully, conservatively, and was grateful that the early Saturday morning traffic on the state highway was light. He did not take the newly opened toll road.

It was four in the morning when he closed the garage door. He was exhausted and hungry. He fried some eggs and made a sandwich. He drank a beer with breakfast and called the Chicago Heights bus station at five o'clock. The bus to Cleveland, by way of South Bend and Toledo, left at 8:35. He would sleep on the bus. The man told him it was a two-and-a-half-hour leg with two intermediate stops. He reserved a seat, took a shower, and changed his clothes. He called a cab at 7:45. He carried one small overnight bag to lessen any suspicion, not that he expected any. And no guns; those were all left in the Studebaker. Everything in the Studebaker was left until he would return later that same afternoon.

The trip across a third of Indiana took the promised two and one-half hours; the stops were in Gary and Michigan City. At eleven, he arrived at the South Bend bus station, where two uniformed officers stopped him.

"What's up? Lots of police around," Fisher asked. He'd seen the two police cars parked in front of the station as the bus rolled in.

"Murder, a family. Nasty stuff," one of the cops said.

"Damn, I've just come in on the bus from Milwaukee. Murder?"

"Yes, a man and woman. He works for Studebaker. Full-court press, as we say. Three kids were also found. Lucky—one shot in the back. The others had hidden themselves. What a thing; nasty business."

Fisher, for whatever reason, and one he didn't understand himself, was relieved about the children. He left the station and enjoyed the warm June morning as he walked to his Grand Prix parked on the street behind the warehouse. Two hours later, he rolled onto the driveway of his house in Lincolnville.

Part 3

Allen Fisher parked his Harley-Davidson Softail near the rear door to the garage, being sure to keep it out of sight from the street. There was no need to tempt someone driving by to think they might have a chance at stealing it. During the winter, he parked it in the garage behind the old Studebaker, the car he never talked about with his father. Besides his bike, his fifteen-year-old Ford pickup was the only operable vehicle at the house. And since his folks, Ron and Lois, never left the house, he was their only lifeline to the outside world.

During the past year, everything had all begun to collapse around him. His mother's cancer and growing dementia had reduced her to a shell of a woman; she looked twenty years older than her sixty-nine years. She seldom left her bedroom where she ate her meals, and he was responsible for her hygiene. His father was an empty shit of a man. Days would go by when Ron wouldn't even come up from the basement except to eat, and Allen had to deal with his mother alone.

His father had reduced him to the role of servant. He'd fill the refrigerator and shelves, collect their prescriptions, cash their Social Security checks, and do his best to keep them alive with his bus-driving paycheck from the school district. Days would pass when he wouldn't see his father. He could hear him in the basement—the TV and a ballgame—but he never went into the basement. His existence had been reduced to cooking, cleaning, and serving his mother.

That morning had been hell. His father confronted him in the kitchen and demanded why breakfast wasn't ready.

"You worthless shit," Ron yelled. "You only have one thing to do each morning—get breakfast for me and your ma. That's it. Get it done, and then you can go out and play. For Christ's sake, that's all we ask. I gave you this roof over your head; you can't do one simple thing. You ungrateful shit."

All Allen could do was glare at his father and slowly inhale and exhale. The man's brain was so rotted by whatever was eating it he had forgotten that he'd made them breakfast and spoon-fed his mother oatmeal that morning.

Other than his friends in the gang, he had no one else. Bess, his ex-wife, lived in Tinley Park and had managed to keep their two kids away from his parents. He'd talk to her a few times each year to find out how fifteen-year-old Barbara was doing in high school and how Steve, now eleven, was handling growing up. When she started in on their need for a father, he would hang up. The only satisfaction he got in life was knowing they were all well.

He walked through the garage and into the kitchen. As usual, the only sounds were the whir of the compressor in the refrigerator and the ticking of the wall clock. Seeing the time, he knew his mother would be sleeping and his father would be in the basement. It was still baseball season.

As he stood in the kitchen staring into the refrigerator, hoping to make a sandwich, the muffled sound of a gunshot from somewhere in the house instinctively dropped him to one knee. A year in Vietnam did that; a gunshot was a gunshot. He waited; nothing more. He then warily walked the hallway past his bedroom, then his father's room, and his mother's. He found his father standing over his mother, a Colt pistol still in his right hand, a pillow in the other. On the bed lay Lois Fisher, her yellow nightgown now a mess of gore and blood. Ron continued to stare at the body. He looked distracted, almost uninterested.

"What the hell have you done, old man?" Allen yelled.

Ron Fisher raised the pistol toward Allen, but before he could fire, Allen, almost a hundred pounds heavier, slammed his body into the man knocking him across the floor and into the dresser. The gun banged across the wooden floor and slammed against the far wall. The man fought back, and Allen was shocked by his father's strength. The man wrapped his arm around Allen's neck and squeezed. Allen twisted away and slammed his father against the floor again. He would not stay down.

"Why? She was almost gone. Why?" Allen screamed at his father. He held the man to the floor, his arm against his neck.

"Her pain. I didn't want to see her pain. She pleaded with me to stop it. It was the pain."

"The pain? Her pain—likely, it was your pain. Maybe she couldn't live with your lies and what you turned her life into. The two of you buried here in this mausoleum surrounded by death. Maybe you wanted out."

"What the hell do you know? You've always been weak—my own flesh and blood, pathetic. I can't believe it: worthless shits, all of you. Hell, you can't even keep your wife in line. Now she's screwing some other guy, and your kids probably don't even know you. I did what I could for all of you, but you turned your backs on me. Well, to hell with all of you. At least I will leave nothing behind." Ron pushed Allen away and slowly tried to regain his feet. Allen slammed him again into the wall, knocking him to the floor and close to the gun. He found it before Allen.

Allen ran to his room and pulled his pistol from the dresser's lower drawer, the same type of weapon his father held.

"I need to finish this, Son. This must end today," Ron yelled from down the hall.

"Who are they? Who are those people in the basement?"

"They are not your concern; they ignored my orders. I could not leave them to talk. Besides, they are nobodies, and they murdered two people. They disobeyed."

"What the hell are you talking about? I know about the money, the paintings. I've found them all—and you won't spend any money on helping Mother—you are a monster."

"It's mine, all of it. I earned it. It was owed to me."

"Good God, who are they? Why?"

"Let's get this over with, Son. This must end; you have always been against me."

"What are you talking about?"

Ronald Fisher slammed open the door to his son's room, raised his pistol, and aimed. For Allen, the shock of seeing his father about to kill him lasted only a second before he fired his pistol. Ronald staggered, then collapsed to the floor.

Allen, paralyzed, stood in the middle of his room, looking at the man on the floor. He lost count of how many times he'd imagined this. Gathering himself, he lowered himself to the edge of his bed and stared at the man he'd lived with for forty-four years. A man he never once loved. Feared, pitied, even loathed, yes, all of those—but not love like that he'd seen among his friends—nothing. Ronald Fisher only produced an emptiness. The man sucked the life from everything he touched, especially his wife and kids. Allen fought it but knew he would become like his mother, an empty husk, a shell. He went to his mother's room and stood for a moment looking at her, hoping for a reaction, something to show him he was human. There was nothing, no gratification, no respite. However, at that moment, Allen knew that his mother finally found the peace she deserved.

During the next two hours, Allen staged the house for the inevitable official investigation. He would create a charade. He carefully moved his father to the bedroom and placed the body beside Lois's. He left the man's vacant eyes staring at the ceiling. Using his father's weapon, he fired another round through the existing wound, ensuring the bullet would be found in the mattress or the floor underneath the bed. He spent an hour removing the blood from the floor near his bedroom door. He removed his clothes, showered, and redressed. Later he would destroy the clothes he wore during the killing. He knew enough from TV shows to know that Ron had gunpowder residual all over him from shooting his mother. He placed the gun where it might have landed after firing a suicidal shot. Allen straightened the room and then went to the garage. There he opened the trunk of the Studebaker and hid the pistol in the space between the panels in the trunk. He then opened the passenger's-side door, removed his journal, made a few notes, and returned it to the hiding place in the glove compartment.

Allen felt as if he were wading through a thick fog. Fear and anxiety washed over him; his PTSD was returning, enveloping him. From the top drawer of his dresser, he downed two Prozac, a new drug that helped calm his nerves. It also helped to thicken the fog for just enough time to prepare him for what was to come. He made himself a sandwich and drank a beer. He then inspected the house and his handiwork. The mess of his parents' hoarding would make investigation difficult. He would claim ignorance when they found what was hidden in the basement. It would be easy. He would blame it all on Ron. He then called Craig Martin.

CHAPTER 28

Monday Morning, November 2024

The Marigold Gang sat on one side of the steel table in one of the interview rooms of the Lincolnville police station. Angela permitted Garry to attend, and it was my job to ensure he didn't exert himself. I studied the other guys. Larry was comfortable. He sat, arms crossed, with a bemused look. Mike and Tommy scrutinized their phones like they had important business (it looked remarkably like *Wordle* to me). The day was hot, and I wore my best Hawaiian shirt that matched Thomas Magnum's famous floral. As old guys, we deserve some slack.

The door opened, and Dick Saperstein strolled in, a bundle of papers under his arm. Behind him marched Detective Audrey King. Behind her, another young woman walked in. I didn't recognize her.

"Good morning, guys," Audrey began. "You know Dick, of course."

We all said hello.

"This is Cook County Assistant State's Attorney Nancy Spelling. She has been my sounding board during this investigation. She has also been as curious about all this as I am."

"Gentlemen," Spelling said, acknowledging us.

Like a class in school, we all said, "Good morning, Ms. Spelling."

Audrey pursed her lips and was about to scold us when Nancy said, "You guys have done some incredible work, thank you. I also want you to know that we have been in touch with the police in South Bend, and they are also thankful for helping solve this crime. Detective King, I'll sit back while you tell them what you've found."

We all looked at Audrey, wondering what she had kept from us.

"There are many ways we can go about this, so let's look at it chronologically," Audrey began. "To answer the original mystery, we have unconditionally identified the four bodies in the freezer. Dick, please do the honors."

Dick Saperstein began, "Relying on the evidence collected, the old and new fingerprints, the DNA extracted from the remains, and the DNA samples you collected, the female bodies are Sheila Lingermann and her identical twin sister, Gloria Lingermann. Based on the autopsies, one of the twins had given birth within the last year of her life. As such, we identified that body as Sheila's. The DNA confirmation from the sample provided by Henrik Lingermann directly connects, through the paternal line, to one of the other male bodies. From the information provided to Audrey and a lucky match to the fingerprints provided by the South Bend Police, I have identified that body as Tobias Wozniacki. And lastly, the DNA sample Robert Sauger provided confirms a filial match to the last body. I have identified that body as Joseph Sauger. So, the mystery of who the bodies are is solved."

"Thank you, Dick," Audrey said.

"I am going to ask someone connected to this if he would be willing to cover the funeral expenses," I said. "There are no guarantees, but I think he might."

"Thank you, that will take one more item off my list," Audrey added. "I have reported all of this to Chief Bellows in South Bend. She will pass on the information to Detective Brandt. And she will also let Dexter Millhouse know the results of these tests."

"Larry and I will give him a call, as well," I said. "He will have questions. We should be able to answer most about the one case that got away." We all looked at each other, thinking we were finished. I slid my chair back.

"You guys think this is over? On the contrary, I have just begun," Audrey said. "The DNA found on the newspapers in the trunk of the Studebaker proved to be from three of the bodies. The DNA is from one of the girls, Tobias, and Joseph. This confirms that the car, stolen from the Paines' residence the night of their murders, was the car that transported the bodies to the house on Marigold Court. The house that you guys burned down last Friday. By the way, I am not pressing arson charges. The fire chief agreed it was an unfortunate, preventable accident."

"Gee, thanks, Audrey," Larry said.

She smiled at her old boss. "The curious thing is that the Colt automatic you found in the trunk was not the gun used in the killings of the four people in the freezer. The ballistics of the two slugs Dick pulled from the bodies did not match that gun. As you provided me with information, I began to make some guesses. I went to the evidence stored from the Fisher murder-suicide. There was a similar weapon in the box. It was a Colt 1911 automatic WWII issue—the weapon Ronald Fisher used to kill Lois Fisher with one shot through her heart. Back then, the detectives, and you, Craig and Garry, were at the house that same day and believed what they saw: two bodies lying in a bed, both dead from single gunshots, the weapon on the floor near the body of Ronald Fisher. According to the police reports, Allen was distraught—you guys cared for him. I had the bullets in the evidence box tested, something surprisingly not done then. And there were two bullets and fragments in the evidence and a note that pieces were removed from the wood floor under the bed. I had the bullets and fragments tested—the bullet found in Lois Fisher and the pieces of a bullet found in Ronald Fisher were not fired from the same gun."

"What the hell," I said. "Of course they were."

"No, the bullet that killed Ronald Fisher was fired from another pistol, also a Colt 1911 model but from the Vietnam era. It is the pistol found in the trunk of the Studebaker—the ballistics match. After checking with the South Bend Police and passing on the information we found, Dick determined the gun used in killing the four people in the freezer was the same one used to kill Mrs. Fisher. The bullets did not match the bullets that killed the Paines. They were .38s."

The five of us sat there, brains spinning. Finally, Larry said, "That means Allen Fisher, using an Army pistol he brought home from Vietnam, the one found in the trunk, killed his father, hid the weapon in the trunk afterward, then called Craig. He arranged the scene to look as though it was a murder-suicide. The .45 found at the scene was assumed to be Ronald's old service weapon—and now, sixty years later, is linked to the killings in South Bend and the four bodies in the freezer. Well, shit."

"I can't believe it," Garry said. "Allen killed his parents? It all makes sense."

"No, I believe Allen killed only his father," Saperstein said. "It appears from looking again at the evidence, and with fresh eyes, Ronald Fisher did shoot his ill wife. She was dying of pancreatic cancer, a mercy killing. Then Allen found out, or was there, and killed his father, and arranged the scene."

Tommy added, "That means Allen knew where the Studebaker came from—the Indiana plates, the money under his bed—even though it looks like he never used any of it. Garry, you said, 'It all makes sense.' What did you mean?"

Garry pulled from a leather shoulder bag the book he discovered in the glove box of the Studebaker. "Craig, you were right. The writing is Allen's. I checked it against some letters of his I have. He haphazardly kept this journal over the last fifty or so years. I read it over the weekend. All I can say is our friend was severely damaged by the Vietnam War, broken, and not put back together well. It is a litany of chaotic thoughts, disconnected emotions, and distorted realities."

I looked at the book. Garry had stuck Post-it tabs in places. "What did you find?" I asked.

"There're no confessions, but based on what Detective King and Dick said, there are ramblings around those days in 1991 when his parents died, incoherent and nonsensical." He opened the journal.

It is done. The monster is dead. I have killed evil and set free the souls.

"This was from around that date?" I asked.

"Yes, we were there, Craig. I remember every moment." Garry continued, "He writes, *So much is lost, her gentle soul did not deserve this madness.* After their deaths, Allen was out of it. He spent a few weeks in the hospital; we were concerned he would harm himself."

"Yes," I said. "But killing his father? He had to know what was in the house—in the basement."

"So maybe he saw his father kill his mother, and then Allen killed him?" Mike speculated.

"It is possible, in fact probable," Saperstein said.

"God damn, what a tortured soul," I said.

"He kept it all inside. Did we fail him?" Larry said.

We looked at each other. There was no answer.

"Why didn't Ron Fisher drive the bodies to the nearest river and push the car in?" Mike asked. "Between here and South

Bend, there has to be a dozen places—the St. Joseph River in South Bend, even the Calumet River."

"We know that Allen was a hoarder," Dick Saperstein said. "I'm guessing that his father was too. That's why the paintings, and the money, were never sold or spent. What he stole, he had to keep. He was the mastermind behind at least four other robberies, most likely even more. He could not let any of this go. He had to maintain control, and as long as the bodies were in his control, like the artwork, he would never be discovered. What Ronald Fisher couldn't figure on was that he was going progressively crazy, paranoid, even schizophrenic in the classical sense."

"And it's still not over," Audrey said, pulling out more papers. "Your work had us dig into everything. That's why we looked closer at Allen Fisher. We checked the Studebaker gun for DNA. Enough was found in the checkered grip to confirm he had handled it. Dick also rechecked his cursory medical report on Allen Fisher's death. He confirmed that he died from the results of a stroke. I asked him to relook at the bump on his head. We believe it occurred as he fell from the stroke—hit his head on the metal bedstead. Then he stumbled into the living room where you found him, Mr. Hughes. "

"Yes, naked, face down, alone," Garry said.

"I don't see that now," Saperstein said. "It appears he was struck on the back of his head as he left the shower, hit with something like a metal rod or a metal cane. The stroke occurred after he fell, leaving him to die."

"Someone killed him?" I asked. "When we found him, it was hard to tell anything."

"I looked again at the X-rays. A full autopsy was not performed. I wish I had done one, but there were other priorities then. We could exhume the body but need his children's permission."

"He was cremated," I said.

"That answers that," Audrey continued. "On Saturday, I asked Dennis and Brenda Fisher to come to my office to discuss the house fire. I was playing a hunch, and my hunches are good—look at what I got with you guys. Nancy Spelling joined me in the interviews."

"And what did those two say?" Larry asked a question we all had.

"They immediately denied setting fire to the house—they didn't know about you arsonists. They were defensive and didn't want to discuss anything in the house. When I pressed Dennis about what he knew about the artwork and money, he quoted the Bible: *Assuredly, the evil man will not go unpunished, but the descendants of the righteous will be delivered.*"

"You are kidding," Garry said. "Proverbs 11:21, written on the wall of the house. You are saying that Dennis and Brenda clobbered Allen over the head, causing the stroke, leaving him to die."

"When I asked Nancy Spelling to join me on Saturday, I told her I needed to be sure of the legal ground I was walking on."

We all looked at the assistant district attorney. She hadn't said a word up to this point. I looked at Audrey and said, "How much did these two know?"

"It seems, after pressing them separately," Nancy said, "that they knew about everything in the house: the artwork, the money, even the bodies. It was why Brenda left fifty years ago. She couldn't live with her abusive father and knowing what was in the house. She told Dennis. He left a few years later. They tried to get their mother to leave, but she wouldn't. She said that Allen would protect her. When their parents died, they demanded that Allen share all the money. They didn't care about the artwork; my guess is they couldn't tell the paintings from a Dr. Suess cartoon. It was the money. Allen wouldn't hear of it. It had to stay where it was, all of it. That's what their father wanted—and, according to Mr. Saperstein, it fits with the hoarder persona."

"Lord, this craziness runs through the whole family," I said. "Are you going to arrest them?"

"Right now, there's just circumstantial evidence," Audrey said. "We got a search warrant, and I was just texted that they found nothing this morning at their house in Tinley Park. They maintain that everything in the Marigold house is theirs. When I told them about the house burning down, I thought they would have a stroke."

I rubbed the back of my head, wondering if what hit Allen may have also whacked me.

Audrey smiled. "Yes, I thought of that, too, Craig. It seems that Dennis has both a fondness for scripture and canes."

"Doesn't make my head feel better," I said.

"Understood."

"Is there any more concerning the artwork?" Garry said. "Mike and I put a lot of time into that, and it feels as though it was all jerked out from under us."

"Understandable," Audrey said. "Hugh Stone told me he is setting up a conference between the parties. They have found two other families with claims to the artwork. One also claims that the gold is theirs. Once this went public, I've been getting at least five calls a day. Do any of you guys want to volunteer to man the phones?"

CHAPTER 29

Three weeks and Thanksgiving, have passed since our Monday morning meeting with Detective Audrey King, Ms. Spelling, and ME Dick Saperstein. At this week's Wednesday breakfast at Bell's, I sat at the head, and the guys flanked the table. A lot had happened since that meeting.

"Did you finally get ahold of Janet LeBlanc?" Garry asked.

"Yes. She apologized for not responding to my calls or texts," I said. "She and her husband were at their lodge in the Upper Peninsula. There's no cell coverage, only an old landline, which she had not given me the number."

"I fondly remember those days," Mike said. "Today, it would drive the grandkids crazy. To think I could take a vacation and not diddle with my phone, check emails, or in any other way be distracted from the serious business of doing absolutely nothing would be welcome."

"She has turned everything over to her attorney, Hugh Stone," I said. "He will contact you, Tommy, through Audrey, about the artwork and their release from the storage locker. There have been numerous meetings, lots of claims."

"He sent an email. I will respond later today," Tommy said. "Gwen Turner has also been bugging me. She wants the other pieces."

"I will talk with Barbara and Steve; I have a Zoom call

scheduled for later in the week. They are stunned by what Audrey told them about their father and grandparents. It has been one bizarre revelation after another. They are ready, I believe, to release the paintings to the insurance company—at least the ones the company can verify some connection to. That will leave five that are unaccounted for. She said they will deal with those in time—assuming the police don't get involved."

"The money?" Larry asked.

"Now that it appears to be a link to a crime," I began, "the murder of four people—the bodies in the basement—and the deaths of the Fishers, the county sees a possible windfall and is seeking to seize the gold and the cash through civil forfeiture. Audrey can't do anything about it, and I'm not sure she wants to get involved. It's blood money, according to Barbara. She wants nothing to do with it. Chief Bellows in South Bend says they don't have the time or budget to deal with it. They feel comfortable with the resolution as summed up and forwarded by Audrey."

"And now new vultures are circling," Garry said. "I understand that Allen's siblings have backed off."

"Audrey says they disappeared. Their car is gone; they left their rental house, took their clothes, and left no forwarding address. Two old people on the lamb—kind of funny."

"Was she going to charge them with Allen's death?" Mike asked.

"She said there wasn't enough evidence. Allen's death was declared natural, so they would have to change the cause of death and reopen an investigation. And as you remember, he was cremated. Then they would have to prove one of them was involved. Now that they've bugged out, she isn't sure it is worth the dollars to chase them down."

"Maybe we could find them," Tommy said. "Is there a reward? I want to recover some of my expenses."

In unison, we all turned to Tommy and said, "NO."

"The house?" Garry asked.

"Barbara said there is some insurance money to cover clearing the site and making it safe. They have listed it with a broker, but no takers. There are a hundred other empty lots in town, and this one is no better."

"With its sordid history, I'm not sure you want to put that in the sales brochure," Larry added.

* * *

We reassembled at Garry's country club two evenings later in one of the larger rooms. The wives joined us for this memorial dinner for Allen Fisher. We also included Detective Audrey King and Karen Quist from Bell's. We would all kick in to cover the bill.

After dinner, we gathered in the backroom bar of the lounge, drinks in hand. The expansive picture window looked out onto the eighteenth green, enveloped by the early evening light. The last two golfers of the day were walking up to the green. Audrey was the first to speak.

"First of all, I want to thank myself for putting you gentlemen on the scent," she started with a smile. "I am not sure there is a better group of unpaid investigators in the whole state that could have done as good a job. Kudus to all of you."

"Is this when we submit our invoices?" Tommy said—a chuckle from the audience.

"Ahhh, no, Mr. Ellis. No invoices, just thanks." She turned to the ladies that had separated themselves from the gang members. "I also want to thank the wives for putting up with all this. Now you understand why the police and detective businesses have such a high divorce rate." No chuckles on that one.

"I want to thank you, fellows, for what you accomplished. There are families out there that now know the truth about their loved ones. Some may not like it. Nevertheless, answers to tough questions were found. Closure was made. Sometimes that's all we can do."

Glasses were raised and clinked. Larry walked up next to Audrey.

"I want to thank Audrey for her leadership and support personally," Larry said. "I am glad that the Lincolnville Police Department has such people in its ranks. The village should be proud."

"Hear, hear," we answered.

"Craig, you wanted to add something?"

"Quiet, everyone; Craig has a plan," Garry said. A couple of the gang joined in, "Craig has a plan."

I looked around at these friends of more than half a century. Stalwart, caring, and loyal comrades, there was not much more to add to the bond that we'd created. Memories flooded over me.

"I have one memory of Allen that I would like to share. I don't believe anyone in the Marigold Gang has heard this one. It is special to me, and I don't think Allen would mind. You all know that the six of us spent much of our high school summers together, and the most special times were our trips up into Canada and the Boundary Waters areas. We forged many of our greatest memories then."

"Floating Dead Moose River," Mike said and raised his glass.

"Dead Moose River?" his wife asked.

"I'll tell you later," Mike answered to laughs.

"Yes, the river, the jobbies, walleye on sticks drenched in butter, the sudden storms . . ."

"The peach brandy and cigars," Tommy said.

"You were all seventeen," Penny interrupted.

"And I remember a young lady looking for a doobie around that time," I added.

"To be young again," Larry said; murmurs of agreement followed.

"On our last trip, we camped on that island for three days. It was our base camp. In the center of the island, high above the surrounding lake, towered a granite nob scraped clean by some past glacier. There was a rough slope to its back side where we could climb to the top. Up there, the breeze blew away the mosquitoes and provided some relief. One night, I couldn't sleep. The mosquitoes were doing their thing, and I thought of the nob. The full moon's light filled the lake basin and illuminated the surrounding granite walls. I climbed to the top. Allen was there, smoking a cigar."

"You were such bad boys," Audrey said.

I smiled; the growing memory was intoxicating. "He offered me a cigar and padded the rock next to him. I sat.

"'Do you know that we all live lives of quiet desperation?' he said as he blew a gray cloud into the stars. 'Henry David Thoreau said that. Depressing fellow if you ask me. But he was probably right. Most of us will stumble over the trash thrown in our paths, hoping not to fall. Look at us; we haven't even been with a woman, virgins all. Yet, with bravado, we make claims and brag.'

"He was right, you know," I said. "I asked him, 'How can you be depressed with all this grandeur? Good God, Al, look at that sky; a billion stars wrap our world, the Milky Way, that moon, an infinity overhead.' The smoke from our cigars drifted into the night.

"Allen looked up, and I thought I heard a smile in his voice. 'Craig, yes, it is grand and wonderful, yet I feel so small, a pinprick in the fabric of this universe. Every day is a battle with the demon and his succubus.'

"'What the hell are you talking about?' I said.

"'For a few weeks every year, I can escape them, be with

you and the gang, free my soul for a few days—then I must return. I thank you for this but don't tell the others. This is just between us.'

"Allen and I were close for reasons I didn't understand. Closer than he was with most of you. There was always a pall around Allen. We all saw it. And after Vietnam, most of us weren't sure he would make it. His PTSD was insidious and cruel. Luckily there were new drugs that helped."

"These demons, what were they?" Angela asked; she was holding Garry's hand. He looked tense. I knew he knew who they were.

"His parents, Ronald and Lois—the demon and the succubus. That night Allen and I sat there for hours; we talked about the future—a future he wasn't sure he would be alive to enjoy. He told me that after high school, he would join the Army. It would be another way for him to escape them. He also told me to marry that Penelope Parsons girl. She was my other half, and she would complete me. 'You both need each other,' he said."

"You are making that up," Penny said. There was laughter.

"No, he did tell me that. It took me a few years to work up the courage, but here we are fifty years later." I threw her a wink and a kiss. "Allen then stood and took in a great breath. At that moment, he was a giant on top of the world. Then he gave out a wolf's howl that lasted a full minute. It echoed from the walls of the lake basin, back and forth. Then returning calls, unsettling answers to Allen's challenge, came from the far side of the lake."

"I remember that night," Larry said. "I lay in the tent and heard the cries; they went on for an hour. Still have chills when I think of it. It was Allen—he started that?"

"Yes, he started it. I sat there enthralled with this primal conversation. It was as if he was talking with them in some primal voice that they all understood. Then he stopped and, in the darkness, said, 'Time to get some sleep, Martin. Busy life ahead of us.' I followed his shadow down from the nob to our camp. He was right; all we had then was ahead of us."

The End

ACKNOWLEDGEMENTS

The inspiration for The Marigold Gang came from a restaurant we frequent in my town. Almost every Wednesday (and I'm sure other mornings as well), a bunch of fellows gather for breakfast. Sometimes, they are a bible group, sometimes retirees with a shared past, and sometimes, they have been buddies for a half-century. Every village and city in America has them. For some of us, the idea of this type of friendship and fellowship is wistful. Don't we all wish we had this kind of support group? Such was the motivation for the story.

The town of Lincolnville is very similar to the village I lived in in the early 1950s and near to until I went off to college. That village is Park Forest, Illinois. It's the village I wrote about in my first non-fiction work, *America's Original G.I. Town, Park Forest, Illinois*. There are many stories from that post-World War II community, so many they could fill many more novels.

Much of the backstory events about the Boy Scouts and the Explorer posts are as accurate as I can remember them. I was an avid and loyal Boy Scout and worked hard for my Eagle badge. Those who trash the Boy Scouts, and there's much reason these days to do that, forget the millions of young men, and now women, who benefited greatly from the world of scouting. It is truly an outstanding institution; hopefully, it will weather the storm and return stronger.

The Marigold Gang is the first of my more than two dozen novels to include my wife on the cover. Truthfully, she is in every book I've written. We've spent countless hours at that same diner (see above) discussing plotlines, stories, characters, marketing, and the direction of my work. After fifty years, she is truly a partner who works tirelessly with me in this vineyard.

The six primary characters in this book are fictional but are, like most characters, combinations of people I've known and grew up with. Even I can't put a finger on any one specific character who is a match to anyone I know. However, Craig Martin was an architect; I was a landscape architect for fifty years. He grew up in Lincolnville, and I grew up near Park Forest. Make of it what you will.

I never owned a Studebaker. I was a Ford guy with dalliances with GM, Mercedes, and BMW. The Studebaker story is a fascinating one. I recommend it to you.

A sad note here. When I finished the manuscript, I was looking for readers for feedback. One gentleman, in particular, I turned to was a writer friend, Les Edgerton. During our correspondence, he told me he grew up in South Bend and had connections to the Studebaker company during his youth. Since much of this story takes place fictitiously in South Bend, Indiana, he was excited to give it a read and comment. I then was informed that he died the following week from COVID. Les was one of a kind. He was generous with writers, an excellent writer in his own right, and a great guy who loved his San Francisco Giants baseball and Notre Dame football. I will miss him.

The most significant part of writing fiction is creating from nothing, something. The characters, the world they live in, and the problems to be solved are those that you place before them. There are style points for the language skills, creativity, and structure (I leave that to the critics) – but it is mostly getting your characters to solve the problems you put in their way. How much fun is that?

A Note from the Author

Gregory C. Randall was born in Traverse City, Michigan. He grew int he Southside suburbs of Chicago. Greg has never forgotten his Midwestern roots. Mr. Randall makes his home in Northern California with his wife and co-author for this book.

Mr. Randall is the author of fiction and nonfiction works available through the usual outlets.

For more information about the other books that Mr. Randall has written and planned sequels, please visit and connect with Greg online:

www.gregorycrandall.info

See his occasional blog:

http://www.writing4death.blogspot.com

Other books by Mr. Randall:
Fiction
The Cherry Pickers
White Rabbit
Sector 73

The Sharon O'Mara Chronicles
Land Swap For Death
Containers For Death
Toulouse For Death
12th Man For Death
Diamonds For Death
Limerick For Death

The Alex Polonia Thrillers
Venice Black
Saigon Red
St. Petersburg White

The Tony Alfano Thrillers
Chicago Swing
Chicago Jazz
Chicago Fix
Chicago Boogie Woogoe
Chicago Back Beat

The Max Adler World War II Thrillers
This Face of Evil
Pawns in an Ancient Game

The Deputy Sheriff Jordan Tynes Modern Westerns
One Yellow Dog
The Killings in Paradise Valley
Blood in the Yellowstone

Nonfiction
America's Original GI Town, Park Forest, Illinois

Additional copies can be purchased through Amazon.